TO BE TRIED

BY: MACAIRE O'GRADY

To Daddy for being my Blackhawk One
And for always reminding me
Of what is most important

PROLOGUE

"I heard she took out the Council Head in a single blow."

While most of the heads seated around the bonfire were facing the speaker of this statement with expressions of awe and admiration, one of his packmates chose to scan to surrounding area frantically.

"Keep your voice down, Chris," she warned wisely.

However, he was not to be deterred, especially now that he had caught the attention of the others. "I heard that after she left headquarters, she let her vampire Turn her, and now she's some kind of crazy hybrid thing!"

Marcella was torn between rolling her eyes and punching her very obnoxious and misled packmate. Luckily, the decision was taken out of her hands when Dylan, who was seated directly next to Chris and, therefore, was directly subject to all the stupidity, punched his shoulder and set him sprawling over the log that they were sitting on.

"Hey! What was that for?" Chris struggled to get back to an upright position, and Marcella took this opportunity to graciously help him with a fist in the front of his shirt.

"Have you ever actually stopped for a moment and used that organ between your ears," she hissed. "You don't know who's in these woods, Chris. At least keep your voice down."

With a pout of dismay, Chris casually massaged the spot on his chest where Marcella had gripped him during her reprimand. "I'm just passing along what I heard. What's wrong with that?"

"Oh yeah? Where did you hear that? Your beauty parlor?"

The rest of the group found themselves laughing at Chris's expense, which he did not appreciate one little bit.

"Ha ha. Funny guys." The twinkle of mischief had returned to Chris's eye, and Marcella very nearly groaned out loud. "Think about it, though! What if she was a hybrid now? Think of how crazy that would be!"

"There's never been anything like it. She would be undefeatable." Almost everyone jumped at the sound of Madea's quiet voice.

This time, Marcella really did groan. "Oh, not you too, Madea!"

Another tiny voice popped up. "I heard that she was actually descended from werewolves, and that's how she Changed so easily."

Even Marcella was surprised to hear this. "What? That's impossible..."

"Aren't her parents dead?"

"Nobody knows a damn thing about her family," Marcella interjected firmly. *She's made sure of that.*

"You know, I heard she goes around lookin' for unsuspecting, little puppies in the woods."

"I heard she likes to feed them to her pet vampire."

As Chris looked around for who was sprouting this newfound gossip, the empty space in front of him suddenly wasn't so empty. Without pause, the new figure leaned down and very quietly whispered, "Boo."

Girly shrieks and other very unmanly sounds erupted from the entire campsite.

Except, at least, for the quiet chortling and very unladylike cackling that echoed around the clearing.

CHAPTER ONE

Hands on my hips, I leaned down to Chris's level once again. "You little shit," I said pleasantly. "You should know better than to try and bait me when your pack is looking for *me* in the woods. And *you*!" I pointed an accusing finger at Marcella, who was currently sprouting gray hair faster than Grandmother. "You'll be very lucky if I don't tell your older brother how easily I snuck up on you. Austin will hang your hide, and I might just help him."

Marcella hung her head ashamedly. "Sorry," she mumbled.

Knowing she had thoroughly learned her lesson, I strolled over and ruffled her hair affectionately. "Just be sure to take care of yourself, squirt," I told her, softening my tone. "I may be very good at tip toeing, but so are other things out here. This isn't your safe, little campus."

A determined expression overcame Marcella's face as she nodded solemnly. I could feel the tips of my lips twitching in a smile.

"But if you're here," Chris started cautiously. "Where is-"

"Her vampire?" A companionable arm was casually slung over Chris's shoulder. "Right here."

"WHY DO YOU GUYS KEEP *DOING* THAT?"

"Keeping you on your toes, little one." Daimon stretched as lazily as a cat before joining me in front of the fire.

Feeling a gaze on the side of my face, I slid my eyes over to meet a pair of assessing ones. Raising an eyebrow, I worked to prompt the question she obviously wanted to ask. "Something on my face, trainee?"

"How did you know we were looking for you," she questioned.

"Very good observation." I looked at the rest of the curious glances, and pointed a thumb over my shoulder at her. "She passes with flying colors."

"We received a missive some time ago," Daimon answered patiently. "We were traveling close by."

"In other words, you guys are now officially serving escort duty." I looked around their campsite with a contemplative eye. "You've been resting enough. Time to get your butts in gear. We leave in 15."

Our arrival to headquarters was made in good time, and we were greeted immediately by the local psychic.

"You are late, little wolf."

"You're sense of time is skewed, Grandmother."

With a small sound of amusement rumbling in the back of her throat, Grandmother stretched out her arms and received me with a warm bear hug. She smelled like smoke and herbs and *home*, and I hadn't realized until this moment just how much I had missed her. Tears prickled at the back of my throat as I dug my face into her shoulder and held onto her for all I was worth.

Seeming to sense my rising emotion, she tutted softly. "None of that now, little wolf. There are many things that must be done. You will have to work to make me cry later."

Pulling away from her slightly, I nodded. A small smile immediately crossed my face. God, I had missed her so much.

Her gaze, however, was not for me. Small, black eyes narrowed on a spot over my shoulder as her mouth twisted in distaste. "You are still stringing this one along?"

"Quite successfully," Daimon interjected before I could scold her. "How are you fairing, Chief?"

"Well enough to beat you with my staff, should the occasion arise."

"Less than five minutes I'm here, and you two are already giving me a migraine." I rubbed my temples delicately.

4

Heedless of my words, she looked beyond Daimon and lifted a curious eyebrow. "You are attempting to kill my trainees, little wolf?"

"What?" Turning around I saw that Marcella's pack had been reduced to gasping for air and lying on the grass. "Oh, for crying out loud. We didn't even run that hard."

"Don't listen to her, Chief," came a plea from Chris. "She's a slave driver!"

"You deserved it," I retorted. Turning back to Grandmother, who was looking on amusedly, I questioned, "Why on earth are you sending trainees off campus to retrieve me anyway? Did they piss you off or something?"

"I'm afraid you only have yourself to blame for that, little wolf. The world is a much safer place now that werewolves and vampires aren't constantly attempting to exterminate one another. I must come up with new ways to challenge my trainees."

Ah, that would be my fault, then.

I always found myself reeling in shock when I realized The Worst Night of My Life occurred less than a year ago. The pain that came with the murder of Kate, my best friend, my alpha, and my sister in all but blood, was still so fresh.

The nightmares that starred the Council Head I personally deposed were always there waiting for me when I fell asleep every night.

It had to be done, I kept telling myself.

The Council was responsible for numerous horrors. They indiscriminately massacred every vampire coven they came across, committed acts of violence for their own selfish gain, and even the people they ruled over lived in fear of them.

Being forced to remember the acts of that night brought me to end of my pleasantries.

"So, Great Leader of the Wolves, care to explain why I've been pulled back from my vacation time?"

A decidedly unnerving weight settled in the pit of my stomach when Grandmother's face immediately sobered and her eyes became cold.

"I had a very good reason to bring you back, and you as well, boy." Her gazed traveled back and forth between us. "Your search is at its end. Your vampire has been spotted in the area."

Oh good, another one of nightmares had come out to play. "My vampire" was a term given loosely to the other individual responsible for the death of Kate. I had only been granted the privilege of meeting him once before, in a duel that would decide if I had the skills to be of use in the Council's army of werewolves. He had turned up the creep factor and almost killed me in that match.

The same kind of weapon that had been used illegally against me in that fight ended Kate's life. This vampire was the only living creature who could answer all of the questions I had about the Council's motives and Kate's assassination.

In other words, I would not rest until he was brought to justice.

I felt Daimon stiffen next to me in the same instant I did. "He's here? By headquarters?"

Gravely, Grandmother nodded her confirmation. "He has been hovering around the area for close to two weeks now. We were unsure of his identity at first, but now we are certain that this is the one you have been searching for."

All of a sudden, she stopped abruptly and her head whipped around to face the woods that bordered the campus, as if something had called out to her from the trees and shadows. She tilted her head and closed her eyes, obviously listening for something despite the sudden silence around her. I casually sharpened my hearing to check the surrounding area, but heard nothing of interest.

Without warning, Grandmother turned on her heel and began to walk into the main building of headquarters. "Come with me, little wolf. We have much to discuss, and there are little ears everywhere."

I looked to see if Daimon had caught on to whatever had arrested Grandmother's attention, but, knowing what I was getting at, he eloquently shrugged his shoulders and crossed his eyes in a very un-Daimon-ish manner. I couldn't restrain a snort of laughter.

"Less flirting, more walking," Grandmother snapped, continuing up the stone steps.

Daimon was wearing an impish smirk when I faced him. "Are you trying to get me into trouble?"

"Always," he responded smoothly with a gentle hand at the small of my back, guiding me in the direction of the stairs.

The inside of the building was a surprise to me, seeing as it had been in a state of ruin when I'd left it. This was where the most significant fights had occurred that terrible night, but, in the time I'd been gone, it had already been restored to its former glory. Somehow, the space seemed brighter than before, and the people running around in it seemed livelier. Without really meaning to, my eyes slid over to the rebuilt main desk in the lobby, only to be disappointed when I didn't see Aunt Rose sitting in her usual throne.

"Don't worry, little wolf. You will see your family soon enough."

Can that woman really still read my mind?

As we walked through the hallways, I noted that people seemed more casual with Grandmother than they had been with the Council. There was no more bowing and scraping. Instead, there were friendly waves and warm greetings. The whole atmosphere felt lighter. Somehow, this place felt right this way.

"How have you been holding up around here," I asked her seriously. "Have you had any problems since I left?"

"Naturally, there have been some who were...less than content with the way things played out," she noted wryly, "but, shockingly, they have been few and far between. Dissention towards the Council ran deeper than we expected. Since then, those who have been foolish enough to revert back to the old ways have been dealt with kindly." She looked up at me with serious eyes. "I will not be met with the same fear that greeted that regime, little wolf."

"They obviously don't know you well enough," I assured her.

"Well," Daimon quipped, "I still happen to be *quite* afraid of the Chief."

"As you should be," she muttered.

Before I could reprimand her, I noted the worry that pinched the corner of her eyes, and the lips I normally saw quirked in a small smile were turned down at the corners in an unhappy grimace. "There's something else, isn't there?"

She sighed deeply. "Yes, but I don't know what to make of it."

I placed a comforting hand on her shoulder. "Want an outsider's opinion?"

She scoffed. "You are hardly an outsider, little wolf, but I shall tell you anyway. There have been…disappearances. Each full moon cycle, since the overcoming of the Council, we've had at least one wolf go missing, sometimes even more. There is no rhyme or reason to it. They've been old, young, and everything in between, trainees and graduates alike." She looked like she wanted to say more, but, frustratingly, she seemed to bite her own tongue and continue on, "That is an issue we must resolve later, we are almost where we need to be."

For the first time, I noticed that we were not heading towards the main audience chamber or one of the war rooms like the one I had worked in in the final days of the Council, but rather the infirmary.

"Grandmother, why are you taking us to the infirmary? I thought you were going to tell us about the vampire?"

She didn't pause in her steps, but I noticed that they faltered slightly, as if she was so lost in her thoughts she forgot where to put her feet. Had she not resumed her normal rhythm within seconds, I would have reached out to help her.

"There are some things I simply cannot explain to you," she responded. There a steel edge to her tone that suggested something deeper than her words. Had I said something to upset her? "I will do my best for now, and then put you in more capable hands."

I must have seemed worried because the hand Daimon had placed at the small of my back moved up and down slightly in a soothing motion. It was a small comfort.

"So start explaining, Grandmother. Like, why did it take so long to identify him? And why is he targeting the campus?"

"All we knew at first was that there was an unidentified intruder at the outskirts of our territory. I would send patrols out only to chase smoke. No one could find him unless he wanted them to, and no one would see him unless it was his intention. He had us wrapped around his little finger."

I knew for a fact that there were very few vampires who had the ability to outsmart an entire pack of werewolves, especially ones with the honed and elite tracking skills that patrollers were supposed to have.

"What changed?" Daimon's voice was smooth and unruffled. He had probably dealt with his fair share of rogue vampires running around and causing problems over the years. "You've confirmed his identity. Surely he's tired of running around and has stated his intentions towards your territory."

"It's not so simple," she snapped without traces of her usual bite. "You are mistaken if you think that this vampire has had anything to tell us."

I resisted the urge to rub my temples again. "You've just led us in a complete circle, Grandmother. How do you know who it is if he hasn't even told you anything yet?"

Grandmother paused at the door to the infirmary, resting her hand against it. "All of the information and tidbits that we have received aren't meant to make sense. He is purposefully keeping us as in the dark as possible. However, despite all of his cryptic vampire nonsense he has been unendingly clear in his intentions."

I loved Grandmother to death, but there were times, much like this, where I wished she would skip the dramatics and get right to the point. "And what would that be? Whatever he wants to do here?"

She stiffened as if I had hit her back. "You are mistaken, little wolf. The intentions that this vampire has have nothing to do with our territory." Looking back at Daimon and I, she opened the door to the infirmary with a single shove of her hand. "But they have everything to do with *you*, little wolf."

The infirmary was as bleak and depressing as I remember it being. Its sterile atmosphere spoke of tension and the white walls made the place seem more like an inescapable cage than anything else. I was too stunned to note anything else about it other than the fact that there was a single pack in the room, seated around a patient whose complexion was paler than the walls.

I tried to smother the fear and surprise on my face as I took note of the tired, baggy eyes of the pack members as they turned their serious faces towards us. The hand at my back had become a solid wall that remained frozen for a few moments before firmly moving to my hip and anchoring me to Daimon's side, as if he had seen the vampire in front of us.

Grandmother strolled up to the bedside of the patient, a young boy who looked like he hadn't even made it out of training yet. His face was shadowed by memories of whatever had landed him here. When Grandmother stood next to him, he turned his head to face her, looking but not really seeing her. It was the look of someone who had just experienced something that would whisper in his ear and haunt his dreams for some time to come.

I knew the feeling.

"How are you feeling today, young Malachi?" His face remained blank and unseeing. She sighed. "You have a message to deliver, do you not?"

For a moment, his eyes gleamed with understanding. While she tried to get through to him, I gently pried myself away from Daimon's grip to stand with one of his grim-faced packmates. She tilted her head towards me and her expression became sad.

"Thank goodness you're here," she whispered.

I nodded, taking her hands in mine. "I'm sorry it couldn't have been sooner. Care to fill me in?"

Sadness gave way to anger once more. "We were sent out on a practice patrol, as a part of our training, and warned about the vampire in the area. We were out in pairs with older wolves, just to be safe, but somehow Malachi was separated from his. We found him nearly catatonic. He didn't respond to anything we were saying. He just kept repeating: 'I have a message for her.'" Her mouth tightened. "It was days before we figured out 'her' meant you."

"The message is for me?" Disbelief colored my tone to hide my fear. I had this scary feeling that I wouldn't like what that message would entail. "What is it?"

But she shook her head. "He won't tell anyone else. The message is for you and you alone."

I felt the grimace form on my face. "I was afraid you'd say that." I turned back towards the bed to see that Malachi's wide eyes were locked on me. It was slightly unnerving. Hooking one of my feet in the leg of a nearby stool, I dragged it over and sat.

Grandmother inclined her head slightly, and I moved to replace her presence by his bedside. The entire time I was moving, Malachi's gaze never left me. It was slightly unnerving. Hooking one of my feet in the leg of a nearby stool, I dragged it over and sat.

I had a feeling I would need to be sitting for this.

Knowing that I had had some part in causing this boy's distress, a heavy feeling that weighed suspiciously like guilt settled over me. Automatically, I reached out for the hand closest to me and held it tightly between mine.

"Hello Malachi," I greeted warmly. "Do you know who I am?"

The sound of his voice shocked the room's occupants; they jumped out of their skins when it's rough and gravely sound filled the room. "I have a message for you."

"That's why I'm here, kiddo." A slight squeeze to his hand garnered no reaction from him. "Tell me what he said. What message does he have for me?"

Haunted eyes pierced mine, and for a moment I could swear that I saw *him* through this boy's gaze. The vampire I was hunting. "You never seem to disappoint me, human. Is there no end to your surprises?"

I swear to God there were chills running up and down my spine, but in that next moment, the one side of Malachi's mouth tipped up into a smirk that was more than enough to make my heart stop. It was *his* face lying in front of me.

"Prepare yourself, my dear, you're next."

I ripped my hand from his grip with more force than I intended and shot to my feet. I couldn't even look at him. Air was struggling to get into my lungs in its usual manner, making me light-headed.

The hand that settled on my back startled me so much that I reacted in the way I'd been taught. My fist was stopped by an unrelenting force, though, and I was pulled into the circle of a warm embrace that I would have recognized anywhere.

"I'm sorry," I whispered disbelievingly. Had I actually just attacked him? "I'm so sorry."

"Hush," he chided softly. "You are not yourself. Take a moment to push him from your mind again."

I only noticed that I was shaking when I brought my hands up to my mouth in horror and felt the tremor in my fingertips.

"I'm not the only one who needs to get him out of my head." I looked over my shoulder to see Malachi watching me with wide, horrified eyes.

"Maria," he breathed. "I'm sorry. I didn't..."

The sight of his distress was enough to help me push aside my own. Turning to face him fully, I smiled weakly. "You delivered your message, Malachi. You did what had to be done. Thank you."

A rough hand brushed lightly over the one hanging at my side. "Come, little wolf. I fear there is much we still have to discuss."

My nod was mechanical, but the way I leaned back towards Daimon was all human.

I was going to need all the support I could get.

12

Grandmother ushered us into one of the informal meeting rooms. The space was much warmer, much more inviting, than the great formal room the Council preferred to use.

Don't think about that right now, I chided myself. *Now is definitely not the time.*

With Daimon as a solid presence behind me and Grandmother taking her seat in front of me, I should have felt at ease, but there was this feeling under my skin, an uncomfortable tingling that I only got when everything was about to go down the tubes.

It certainly seemed that way.

"All right, Grandmother." I had to start talking or else these thought processes were going to start getting out of hand. "What can you tell us about Mr. Lunatic?"

"Mr. Lunatic?" Daimon echoed curiously.

I gave him my best side-eye. "If you saw my Trial match against him, you would be calling him the same thing."

"Really," Grandmother intervened, "because I saw that match and I'm quite inclined to call him something else." Resting her ancient staff against her knees, she looked up at me. "Your vampire's real name is Nikolai."

Surprisingly, as soon as the words left her lips, Daimon jerked in surprise behind me. The small movement might as well have been a sledgehammer to my memories because it was only then that I remembered Nikolai's (Lunatic still sounded way better) words from that day.

'So you are the one Daimon is searching so desperately for?'

Mental note: be sure to interrogate Daimon for any previously withheld information as soon as possible.

Returning my gaze to Grandmother, I knew from the look in her eye that she had seen the same thing I had. Her silent nod only confirmed that fact.

"Okay," I affirmed, "so we have a name and a face. Next, we need to find his favorite locals or distinct patterns of behavior. Got any of those for me?"

"In a normal situation, I would say no, but now that you're here..."

"I'm sure he'll be more than happy to show his face when the object of his affection goes out looking for him," Daimon interjected with more bite than I would expect from him. Huh.

"Oh, don't go getting all jealous now," I joked, bumping his shoulder with mine. "I'll be going out to haul his ass back to the Kennel. There's no competition."

My lightheartedness seemed to have a positive effect on him. A slight smirk tilted the corner of his lips as he slanted his gaze towards me. "Mind if I join you?"

"Actually," Grandmother cut in. "That has already been taken care of. I've arranged for a highly-skilled retrieval party to accompany you on a run."

She had that twinkle in her eye that always made me nervous. "And who would that be...?"

She opened her mouth, most likely to say something dry and sarcastic when, suddenly, the doors to the meeting room burst open and I was, quite literally, attacked from behind.

The sudden impact of three *very familiar* weights knocked me to the floor and took all the breath from my lungs.

"*RIA,*" They chorused in my ears.

"Guys, I missed you, and I love you, I really do, but I think you broke a rib." As much as I tried to reprimand them, the words came out between peals of laughter as I turned under them and reached out to hug all the random body parts I could reach.

A hand I recognized as Vince's reached out and patted my cheek. "A month out looking for...what was it? Psycho?"

"Lunatic," Austin quietly corrected.

"And he shows his sorry face here! Nice tracking skills, Ria."

"Vincent. If you spoil this heartfelt reunion by insulting my unparalleled skills I will throw you out this conveniently-located second story window behind me."

A dusky hand entered my field of vision, and I smiled appreciatively up at Carter as I took it and let him help me up.

I could count the number of times Carter has hugged me as exuberantly as the others with one hand and four fingers hacked off. Today, a ghost of a smile hovered around his normally-stoic lips, and he reached out to ruffle my hair. "Hey."

"Hey yourself. Is your sanity still hanging on?"

"By a single thread. Thank you for finally coming back."

"See? Even Silent-But-Deadly missed you."

Carter cut murderous eyes in Vince's direction and the suddenly-pale werewolf hid behind a much, much smaller Cindy. Sensing an oncoming battle, Grandmother saw fit to intercede on our reunion.

"Before young Carter is forced to violence, I think it would be best if the Elite did what it does best," she said wryly, laughter shining in her aged, black eyes.

Vincent pointed a thumb at Daimon. "Is the camp follower coming with us?"

"Austin," I begged. "If you would so kindly?"

"On it," he answered, putting Vince in the standard headlock.

"Sorry," I whispered loudly to Daimon. "He's house trained, but we still have yet to put him through obedience training."

"Ah." Daimon's eyes were alight with mirth.

"You are losing moonlight, children," Grandmother chided. "Go to work."

We all saluted her. "Yes ma'am."

Her smile turned sharp. "Bring me back a Lunatic."

CHAPTER TWO

"Isn't this great?" Vincent called out as we walked out of the main building together. "The whole fam damily is back together again! Just like old times!"

"Vince," Cindy said, shaking her head. "We're going out on a hunt; it's hardly like a reunion."

"And she's killed the moment."

"We'll have a proper reunion when we get back," I promised, throwing my arm over his shoulders. "Maybe a good few hours spent sitting on the roof of the school playing target practice with first years?"

"Or maybe," supplied Austin. "We can just reminisce over fond memories and laugh heartily as we drag this vampire through the woods?"

Cindy's giggle echoed in my ear in a way that made me smile. "I like that idea."

"You kids ready yet?" Carter was already waiting at the woods' edge, arms crossed over his chest. Anyone else would have assumed his question indicated impatience, but I saw the spark of amusement in his eyes and knew that he was playing along...in his own way.

"Yes, Mother."

Carter's eyes narrowed and Austin immediately intervened, "Vincent, another word and Carter will be throwing *you* off the roof at the first years."

Rather than push his luck, Vince settled with pouting childishly.

"Come on Vince," Cindy called sweetly. "You'll have more time to prod Carter when we bring back Ria's vampire."

Pointedly looking at me, I raised an eyebrow and answered, "Let's roll, kids."

Running through the woods with my packmates came more naturally to me than breathing. In the months I'd been gone, I'd nearly forgotten how it felt to be a part of a family that moved like one being, to feel as powerful as I did when I had them at my back supporting me.

Seeing the empty space to my left, however, poked at fresh wounds. It was where Kate should have been running next to me. I could almost see her if I tried hard enough, and knew at that moment that I would do anything to have her back in that spot.

It wasn't just Kate I missed, though. Without her here, that connection that we had shared between our minds was completely gone. The familiar weight of being linked thoroughly to my pack was just a memory.

I couldn't linger in those memories, though, because for the sake of the friend I was remembering, I had to find this vampire who had a hand in her death.

Looking over my shoulder, I nodded for Cindy to move in front of me. We would follow behind her infallible tracking skills.

But just as I finished the thought, Cindy came to a sudden halt in front of us, signaling that we do the same. We all Changed back the instant she did.

"Cindy, what gives? Did you lose the trail?"

"No, but," her voice trailed off distantly as she searched the woods. "This has never happened before…"

"Cindy," I said firmly, bringing her back. "The suspense is killing me."

"He's close, but I can't pinpoint him. It's like he's everywhere at once."

Austin visibly shivered. "Ria, could you have picked a creepier vampire?"

"I can tell you one thing, Austin. I sure as hell didn't pick him." Turning the situation over in my mind, I brought my attention back to Cindy. "Are there any distinct trails?"

Immediately, she indicated three separate directions. Great.

"All right, here's what we're going to do. Vince and Carter, you take west. Austin and Cindy, you get north. I'll take the east."

"Why would we let you go alone?" Carter asked. "You're the one he's after."

"That's precisely the reason I'm going alone, Tough Guy." Where Vincent trembled under the weight of Carter's glares, I simply returned them with a spine made of steel. "Look, I know he's just chomping at the bit for a chance to get me alone, and I have a feeling that we'll be at this all night otherwise. So, let's just be super proactive now."

"Ria gets all the fun."

"Vincent, another word and I'm cutting out your tongue."

With that being a quick conversation closer, the others scampered off as I told them to, and I turned toward the east with a quickening pulse.

There was a reason I chose this way.

Knowing I was within spitting distance of my prey gave me the energy to run faster towards where I knew he was leading me. Not ten minutes later, I stopped and Changed back, finding myself in a familiar place.

The place where Kate had died.

I didn't have to wait long for him to show himself.

A chill pervaded the air around me and would have caused me to shake in my boots had I not locked every muscle in my body. There would be no weakness in front of this Lunatic, not after what he had done to me.

"Hello, darling," I heard his purring voice, knew he was close, but he kept himself out of sight in the dense forest surrounding the clearing. "It's been far too long."

"Come out and greet an old friend then, Nikolai."

His lilting laugh made the hair on the back of my neck stand on end. "I have you all to myself, too. What a treat. We do have so much to discuss."

"Enlighten me, asshole."

Two seconds later, I was flat on my back with his *stupid, smiling* face hovering near mine and his hand at my throat. With his free hand, he held a finger to his lips, shushing me softly. "Please do watch your tongue, dear. This *is* a memorial."

Bringing my knees to my chest and kicking out, I pushed him off of me with enough force to throw him a good 50 feet. "Tell me, Nikolai, did you have any hand in this?" I may have had his knife, but I wanted proof. I needed to hear if it was true, if he would admit it himself. Was he a part of the plot that ended in Kate's death?

Setting himself aright, his eyes gleamed as brightly as the tip of the canine he let fall over his lip. "More than just a hand, much, much more. Maybe an arm or a foot," he smirked sharply, "or even a fang."

I could have killed him right then. I could have ripped his dead heart from his chest and danced on his grave. The only thing holding me back was the idea that he would share Kate's memorial.

I knew he saw the desire in my eyes, though, because he solidified his guilt by saying, "You should have known it was me the instant you saw the present I gave that young vampire, darling."

"Oh, I did. Believe me, I did." I could still vividly recall Kate's final murderer, his face twisted with unholy glee as he plunged the dagger – Nikolai's "present" – into her heart in front of me.

"And yet you leave my courting gifts behind, how fickle. Is it another man?"

The parallelism here was actually killing me. "I'm happily taken, but jealousy doesn't become you, Nikolai. You waste your presents on someone like me."

For the first time ever, I saw a stroke of anger in that expression of is. It only lasted for a split second, though. Devilish amusement soon overtook his face once more. "Maybe you'll find your next present in Daimon's heart."

Oh *hell* no.

Bursting into a wolf as I lunged at him, I seized his arm in the grip of my teeth and threw him against one of the larger trees. As he was getting up, I lifted my head and howled for my packmates to return for the retrieval. Together we would bring him back to face justice for his actions.

But not before I had the chance to appease some of my anger on his lawless hide.

After a thoroughly disgruntled pack arrived on the scene, Nikolai was surprisingly quick to hand himself over. We didn't take any chances, though. Vincent pulled Nikolai under a potent sleeping spell before throwing him over Austin's back, and I even ran behind Austin the entire trip home, not willing to let him and his cargo out of my sight until we reached the Kennel.

The Kennel was the name jokingly ascribed to what was, essentially, our prison. It was certainly the ugliest building on campus, in my humble opinion. It lacked any of the beautiful stonework seen on many of the other structures. Instead, it was a very utilitarian, concrete square, with a single entrance to make escaping all the more difficult. Even if someone managed to make it through the door, it was in a central location on campus, surrounded on all sides by werewolves and, thus, thoroughly protected.

I didn't come to this place often. Whenever we had previously done a retrieval mission, the criminal was usual left at the front gate to the command of the guards trained especially for Kennel work. Kennel dogs got testy when their domain was intruded upon by us "outsiders," but this situation was in no way normal.

Everyone knew that this was our hunt, that it was personal. No one dared to get in our way.

The very moment we entered the interrogation room, the only thing I wanted to do was throw Nikolai in the nearest chair, snare him in a good ole set of manacles, and slap him around until he squealed like a pig.

Clearly this desire was shared by more than just me because Austin really did throw him in the nearest chair, and sweet, little Cindy clamped the manacles on with enough force to bruise.

Maybe it was for this reason that Grandmother came in and took over.

Her voice, even with its usual drawling tone, possessed a hint of steel that none of us could disobey. "As much as I would like to see him dead, children, there are some very important things he has left to tell us. Vincent, if you would so kindly…"

Gripping the hair over Nikolai's forehead roughly, Vince forced his lolling head forward and whispered the counter-spell in a hiss of breath. For all his joking earlier, he was as serious as the rest of us.

Despite Grandmother's tempering words, I was immensely proud of how well I was handling myself. There was no blood spillage, all of his bones were still intact, and he was still in one piece. As his eyes blinked open, though, and his gaze ultimately settled on me, I knew my good behavior had a short expiration date.

"Ah, my favorite place in the word," he said lightly, glancing around the small interrogation cell like he was checking out the mini bar in a five star hotel room.

"I'm pleased you like it. You will be enjoying plenty of time here."

Looking back at me with an eager light in his eyes, Nikolai boldly ignored that hint of steel in Grandmother's voice. "When you are finished with me am I going to get to play with the children again? Or maybe you'll simply let me have the prize from my last match?"

Screw good behavior.

With the speed of a cobra, I watched my fist hit his face and his head snap back in a very satisfying manner.

And yet that infuriating little smirk still stretched across his face.

"Who's jealous now?"

I could have killed him. Just the idea of him inflicting that same kind of mental and physical damage on another trainee had me clenching my fist for another go.

Later, I would look back and be shocked by the sheer force behind my reaction, but there was something about Nikolai that brought out the worst in me. It wasn't from the trial match that we fought, or even the fact that he had had a hand in Kate's death; a deep part of me had hated him from the moment I set eyes on him and the first time he smirked at me.

This time, my lunge was halted midway as an arm reached across my stomach, holding me back with a firm, but gentle, hold. The only reason I was not startled out of my skin was because the touch was so familiar. Daimon, with his back facing a dangerous enemy, looked down at me in a way that reminded me of the day Kate had died, when he somehow managed to halt my transformation into a wendigo with nothing but an open expression and an outstretched hand.

"Don't let him win Maria," he whispered so that only I could hear him. "His greatest strength is controlling people with their anger. Don't let him see it."

The instant Daimon whispered the words into my ear, Nikolai's gaze snapped towards him in a way that suggested familiarity, a familiarity that was confirmed by what he said next.

"Ah, finally, a friendly face. Care to assist an old comrade, Daimon?"

Someone was going to get a serious talking-to later because I had this frightening feeling that Nikolai wasn't kidding around.

If Daimon's strained grimace was any indication, he did not appreciate Nikolai spilling the beans. "It appears that we find ourselves at odds at the moment, Nikolai."

"So quick to hostility," he laughed. "Are you so certain we are on opposing sides in this game?"

"I believe I gave you my full opinion of your games a long time ago. I wish for no part in your schemes."

Not deterred in the least, Nikolai's eyes narrowed to fit his amused smile before sidling over to land on me.

Aw, hell.

"But your lady is much too fun to leave alone, brother. Perhaps you will simply leave us to play?"

The sudden, chilled atmosphere warned Grandmother that the number of supposedly civil companions was dwindling.

"Enough of this," she commanded in a voice none of us could ignore, one of the benefits of her being her tribe's chief, I suppose. "Your words are running wild; make them useful or I will see to it that you will never speak again. And you," she said turning to the rest of us, "leave and let the Kennel dogs do their work. You are only encouraging him."

"Come on, Ria."

Cindy's soft touch was at my back and Austin's firm hand on my shoulder, while Vincent and Carter walked to the door, already obeying Grandmother's orders.

Daimon stood just behind me, walking in the shadow of my steps. The moment we strode through the door's threshold, we both turned around to see Kennel dogs closing in on Nikolai. Despite this, he looked supremely unconcerned, giving one final wink in our direction as the interrogation room door slid shut.

Sometime later, I sat on the opposite side of the one-way glass, eyes peeled on the most unsuccessful interrogation session ever. That is, until the frustrating view was suddenly obstructed by a steamy coffee cup.

"How are you holding up," Cindy asked me quietly.

"Better than if I was a Kennel dog."

The distasteful grimace that overshadowed her expression did not fit her usual demeanor. "He's being stubborn then?"

I snorted, gratefully accepting the proffered cup. "He's toying with them. They've got nothing. Absolutely nothing, and it doesn't look like they're making any progress either."

With a soft sigh, she gracefully lowered herself into the chair next to me and, without even thinking about it, reached out to hold my unoccupied hand.

"They'll find something. Kennel dogs are good at what they do, but you'll only stress yourself out sitting here. Why don't you get some rest?"

I could feel her gaze resting on the bags forming under my eyes. Self-conscious, I tried to keep them as wide and alert as I could. "Do you honestly think I'll get any sleep anyway? I'm right where I need to be."

"And avoiding Daimon has absolutely nothing to do with it."

I winced slightly before I could help myself. "That obvious?"

"I know you too well at this point," she bragged. "I saw your face." Even now, she looked sympathetic. "You've been through so much lately, and even though you've finally found him again, you haven't hide time to fix the gaps between you two."

Taking my attention off of Nikolai, I turned to meet her gaze. A few beats of silence passed in the air around us as we simply took a moment to read the thoughts hidden in each other's eyes.

"Is it hard for you?" I finally whispered.

Her soft eyes held indescribable sadness, a sadness I was all too familiar with. In response to my question, she looked away and took in deep breaths, collecting herself.

Before everything had gone down with the Council, back before we had even become a pack, or finished our training, Cindy's life was torn apart by the death of her beloved sister. The two were attached at the hip, and there was no one in the world that she adored more.

Cindy's sister had been stationed nearby campus with the rest of her pack. It was a conflict-free area, they should have been safe. However, one day, the entirety of her pack had been mowed down with ruthless efficiency, leaving none alive to tell the tale.

This happened several times throughout the years. Entire packs would be wiped out without any rhyme or reason to it. The Council had put the blame on the shoulders of a single coven, and sent us, the Elite pack, out to eliminate them once and for all.

That coven belonged to Daimon.

It was something we had never discussed before. He never mentioned it, and I had no clue how to even broach the topic. In my heart, I couldn't possibly believe that Daimon was capable of unjustified murder. I couldn't picture him eliminating an entire pack of werewolves for no apparent reason.

Regardless, the matter remained unresolved and the proverbial finger was still pointed at Daimon. I was supposed to be their new pack leader, and I couldn't even fix this.

The guilt was a constant shadow over my heart.

When she turned back to me and shared her gaze with me, I knew that, despite my own feelings on the matter, Cindy did not blame me at all for the way things had turned out. Cindy wasn't the sort of person who let hate fester in her heart. She would never demand vengeance from Daimon. Cindy's heart was too kind and her mind too wise to fall into that trap.

At least, more so than I had been a few months ago when I had almost traded my sanity for ill-begotten revenge.

Sighing deeply, she stood up and kissed my forehead, brushing hair away from my face. Her voice was as soft as her touch. "Someday, we will find the right words to say to one another. You and I have a relationship too strong to be threatened by even this."

A feeble smile was all I could manage as a response as she turned and left the room. It was truly one of the great mysteries of the world how I managed to find such loyal friends.

Bolstering my patience level, I lifted the warm coffee to my lips and took a generous swig of it as I returned my attention to the interrogation. It was a miracle I did too because, at that precise moment, I spotted something that sent a little warning signal off in the back of my mind and made that awful tickling feeling at the back of my neck return.

Nikolai sat lazily across his chair, arms folded behind his head, but, instead of looking at the Kennel dogs, or even at the plated glass towards me as he sometimes had, his attention was aimed at the clock on the wall.

Time was an interrogation tactic of its own. People rely on time to be a constant in their lives. Messing with that constant is sometimes enough to put someone over the edge.

In this space, the Kennel dogs controlled time. They could speed it up and make the person believe they'd been trapped in a room for hours, or they could slow it down and draw out each, aching minute.

At the very least, I'd always thought it was an intriguing technique, but it was usually less than useless when it came to powerful vampires like Nikolai. Their sense of time, after hundreds of years, was a little different than a more mortal prisoner. In that case, then, the clock should have been set at the normal time.

So, why was Nikolai's attention so peeled on it?

Before I could think any more on it, though, the door to the room I was in burst open, and a young recruit rushed inside.

"Maria?"

I was up and out of my chair before he could even blink. "What's up?"

Panting with extreme exertion, he had to force the words out between breaths. "There's been a break-in, the guards are compromised, and we need assistance."

Normally, that's all it would have taken for me to set off in whatever direction I was needed, but there was something keeping me planted right where I was, something that knew this was where I had to be. Instead of letting him lead me away, I turned my gaze back to Nikolai's face. "Have you already sent the Kennel dogs out?"

"Yes, all of the gate guards are on route."

"How long ago?"

He seemed genuinely confused by my questioning at this point, but, just as he spoke, I saw the corners of Nikolai's lips tip into his trademark smirk.

"Um… I don't, I don't know. Uh, about ten or so-"

But before he could even finish his sentence, the outer wall of the Kennel blew in knocking us both to the floor in the midst of the explosion.

CHAPTER THREE

I don't know if anyone here has been privy to the experience of having part of a building explode over you. If not, I'll try to guide you through it as best as I can.

I have no clue how long I was on the ground, but it wasn't until the pieces of the building had fully settled that I was even able to even open my eyes. The first thing I noticed was the dust that lingered in the air, stagnant, as if time had stopped around us. It took me a few moments to realize that I couldn't hear anything; my ears were ringing with the aftereffects of the explosion, but some instinctive part of me knew that I couldn't just stay where I was. I had to keep moving.

Bracing my arms under me, I attempted to push myself up and onto my feet, only to be impaired by a monumental weight above me. Ignoring the pain sparking in my shoulders, I turned my head only to find myself confronted with a large piece of concrete that was not only holding me down, but damn-near crushing the young messenger who was less than an arms-length away from me.

None of my thoughts were coming clearly or quickly, but I had the sense to look up and check to make sure the ceiling wasn't going to come down on us. The walls, on the other hand, were not in good shape. I couldn't see the source of the bomb from my vantage point, but I could tell it had done its job well.

That wasn't even the worst part.

As I turned back to assess the situation in front of me, I froze when I noted that the interrogation room had been burst open, and that the prisoner I had worked so hard to bring in to justice was now walking free.

In a cool and unruffled manner, Nikolai lightly dusted off his shirt with the back of his hand and recollected himself, stepping out of the space where the two Kennel interrogators lay either unconscious or dead, I couldn't tell yet.

It was then that he noticed me, awake, dazed, and struggling on the ground before him. Unable to resist a good taunting, he strode over to me with a pleasant smile on his face.

"Oh dear, you seem to have gotten yourself into quite a snare here." His voice, which would have sounded kind enough to anyone else, was chilling to me. "I would gladly help you, but I'm on a bit of a tight schedule."

"I noticed," I forced out through gritted teeth. "Got a date?"

"Ah, there's that jealousy slipping out again." Crouching just in front of me, Nikolai tipped up my chin with his fingers and scanned my face intently, in a way that made me want to squirm. Instead, I bared my teeth and gave him a look that could freeze hell over. Rather than eliciting the effect I wanted, Nikolai became pensive and only looked harder, as if searching for something.

"There is so much of her in your gaze, dear one. Is it fate, perhaps?" His words made my insides freeze, even if I didn't completely understand them, some part of me knew it couldn't mean anything good. Before I could even think of demanding he tell me more, his trademark smirk returned to his face and, maddeningly, he was back to his normal self. "Perhaps you like to play games too, hmm? I know! How about a game of tag? Would that entice you at all?"

"If you're looking to *entice me*, try putting a stake through your heart."

His laugh was loud and boisterous, but it did nothing to warm the chill brought on by his previous thoughts. What game was he playing now? Behind the pretext of tag, that is.

Knowing I had to move quickly if I wanted to catch him and save the trainee still trapped under the rubble, I tried again to push the constraining load off my back, only to cry out when my muscles screamed in agony.

Nikolai tutted softly at my failure and stood up from his perch. Turning to leave, he couldn't resist one last over-the-shoulder parting shot.

"I really expected more effort, Maria. Perhaps dear Kari was wrong to put such unwavering faith in someone such as you." The impact of his words very nearly knocked the wind from my lungs, but when he spoke again I was bolstered by the heat of my anger. "Shall I tell you what she said of you in her final moments?"

"ENOUGH."

Channeling the magic I thought I was too weak to summon, I heaved all of my strength into my arms and, with a yell ignited by fury and overwhelming sadness and guilt, I heaved the piece of wall over my head and threw it straight at Nikolai.

Even knowing that he would, without a doubt, dodge my impromptu missile, the sight of his amusement only succeeded in making me angrier than I had been before.

"That's more like it," he said appreciatively. "Now, don't make me wait too long. I'll pine."

And, with that, he was gone.

Torn between the tug of the string I knew he was leading me by and the duty I had to my fellow comrade, I dove to remove the remainder of the rubble from the messenger beside me. Surprisingly, he was already awake, mumbling something so unintelligible not even my advanced hearing could make it out.

I knelt by his side. "What did you say? Say it again. I'm here."

"Go get him."

I didn't need much more encouragement than that.

Shaking off the aches and tears that would probably have me bedridden as soon as the adrenaline wore off, I whispered a spell Vincent had taught me to numb the pain as I took off through the hole in the wall that Nikolai had just used, starting my hunt.

I wouldn't let him get away.

Throwing myself into what I did best was second nature. It was child's play, literally. He wasn't making the slightest effort to avoid me, but I knew that was probably his goal in the first place. He wanted something from me and was probably leading me straight into a trap, but, even then, I couldn't deter myself.

That being said, my determination was blindsided, figuratively and literally, by a huge force from my side. Taken by surprise, I was immediately thrown to the ground, jostling all of the injuries I had gotten from the explosion. Gritting my teeth, I maneuvered myself into a defensive crouch and looked up, ready to tussle with Nikolai's sharp words, but didn't quite get what I expected.

A different face looked down at me, not with a smile, but with a bitterly cold expression that made the blood freeze in my veins.

Not to sound conceited or anything, but I'm a pretty smart cookie. I was one of the top students in the Academy, and I can usually outsmart an enemy any day of the week. I didn't get caught off guard much, but, judging by the company I was suddenly keeping, I was in a lot of trouble.

Because, if Kate's brother was really here working with Kate's murderer, there was more going on here than I had previously thought.

"Well done, Rowan," Nikolai drawled as he strode up behind me. "The look on her face was, indeed, priceless."

But Rowan had nothing to say, as per usual. Instead, he stared me down as I shifted to work myself back to my feet.

"What in the seven hells do you think you're doing, Rowan?" My voice was low and calm, but I couldn't hide the undercurrent of anger that made the words simmer as they sat between us.

"What I must, human, my duty, something you will never understand," he responded in that tone that made me want to punch him square in his arrogant face.

"Why so surprised, Maria?" Nikolai's breath touched the back of my neck in a way that made me wheel around with a fist. Too slow, though, I was too *damn slow.*

Nikolai caught my fist in his own and twisted my arm around with so much force that I was sure he busted my shoulder. I stifled my cry of pain until it was only a gasp. He pulled me closer and lightly placed a hand on my jaw so that he could guide my head to meet his amused gaze.

"You see, Maria? I am more than capable of making friends wherever I go. You are just being far too stubborn," he scolded as I bared my teeth in a feral grimace. "Take Rowan for instance. Why, how could I have ever dreamed of escaping the Kennel *twice* if it weren't for his help? Friends are so useful in that way, you know. Although, yours do seem to be dwindling slightly…."

"Nikolai," Rowan interrupted firmly. "Enough of this. We have things to do. Save the gloating for later."

Nikolai simply directed a miffed look in Rowan's direction. "We really need to loosen you up a bit. Winning the game isn't satisfying unless you take the opportunity to enjoy it."

"You haven't won anything yet," I informed him sweetly.

"Hmm," he agreed, "but yet is just one play away, my dear."

That's when I felt the pinprick of a blade at my neck and noticed that Rowan wielded a very familiar knife. A knife that should have been safely locked up in my room.

During my final Trial match, I had been pitted against Nikolai and managed to hold my own for a little while. That is, until he had broken the rules and attacked me with a weapon he shouldn't have had.

The knife he had possessed was a weapon created by hunters to fight werewolves. It was lethal to our kind. The nick he had given me should have been the end of the match, as well as my life, but, somehow, I managed to survive.

I didn't know if I was willing to push my luck a second time around, though.

This was going to fun to try and get out of. If those knives even scratched me, I was down for the count.

Time to get creative. And cheat. A lot.

Throwing my head back, I gave Nikolai one solid head-butt before twisting my arm back around to kick him square in the chest. He fell back with the knife still in his grip. I knew I didn't have any time to wrestle for it, though. Turning back on my heel, I dodged a hit from Rowan, whom I was much more worried about facing.

"How does it feel, Rowan," I asked as I danced around him with the help of years of hard training and experience, "to be at the beck and call of the man who murdered your sister?"

His eyes narrowed, and I suddenly had the sinking feeling that taunting Rowan was a very, *very* bad idea.

Ducking down, I let Nikolai and Rowan clash blades, rolling away from their reach, but I was stopped by a boot on my sternum.

Silver eyes (*they look just like hers*, I thought, *why do they have to look so much like hers*) glittered dangerously as he glared down at me. Leaning down slowly, he responded to my taunt inches away from my face.

"We'll see how long that self-righteousness lasts, human." I felt the cold kiss of a blade against my cheek, but didn't dare look at it. "You won't last long in a game like this."

I forgot how overwhelmingly painful it was to be hit by one of these blades. I sometimes thought that my mind over-exaggerated the sensation in the one memory I had of it, but I was very wrong.

However, as blindingly excruciating as the scrape was, it wasn't anywhere near the size of the scar on my arm. Moving without thought, I gripped the ankle that held me pinned to the ground and twisted with all the strength I could muster, breaking the bone and throwing him off of me.

Staggering, I made my way to my feet, looking all around me for the goddamned vampire that brought me into this mess in the first place. My vision blurred slightly, and the universe tilted on end a few times.

"You really are quite impressive." I wheeled around when the voice came from behind me, only to fall on one knee at the sudden movement. "I had led myself to believe that it was simply adrenaline or the thrill of your Trial that allowed you to overcome the effects of the wound I inflicted." A firm hand gripped my hair and pulled my head up. "I, for one, will take care never to underestimate you part in this game."

In my mind, I noted that this was at least a little comforting. His words implied that he had no plans to kill me just yet. However, as relieving as that was, I had a terrible feeling that I had a larger role in this than I ever wanted to play.

"Just what is it you want, Nikolai? What are you really after?"

"You ask all the right questions, my dear, but it isn't time to give the game away. Not just yet."

With that said, he drew up my arm, the unscarred one, and laid the blade against the skin with the same precision and force that he had used on the other. As the beginnings of the burning pain took over my system, a newly-risen Rowan came behind me and struck the back of my head with enough force to make my vision go black.

As I slipped into unconsciousness, the only things my mind registered were the sounds of my comrades approaching (too late, of course) and the sight of the enemy slipping away unharmed once again.

For the second time in my life, I let my eyes fall shut without knowing if I would ever open them again.

Waking up after receiving one of those knife wounds was worse than waking up after being run over by a bulldozer driven by an elephant. Seriously. Maybe next time they could show a little mercy and just shoot me in the face. It might be less painful. Each ray of sunlight was like a needle to the retina.

As I rubbed my hands over my eyes, trying to wake myself up and orient them to daylight, I caught sight of something out of the corner of my eye. Was someone by my bedside?

As I turned to get a better look, I took a mental note that it was officially "Pull One Over On Ria" day.

Lo and behold, Kate was sitting next to me, curled up and sleeping in the chair by my bedside just like when I had woken up from my last Trial match. Only this time, she woke up without me flinging a pen at her.

Slowly opening her eyes, she immediately held my gaze and smiled softly. "You're okay."

I faltered finding something, *anything* to say to her. Seeing my muteness, she merely smiled softly and turned her face towards the growing light from the windows, as if seeing something of interest.

I looked too, only to be temporarily blinded. Confused by the spectacle, I returned my gaze to Kate as light engulfed the entirety of the space we inhabited. I could not hear her; I could only see her now-terrified expression and her lips moving as I clung hopelessly to the dream that was ripped from my grasp. Within seconds, I was vaulted into the conscious world again.

A much duller brightness greeted me there, as well as pain. Surging upward, I turned to the seat at my left, only to find it painfully empty. Groaning as the ache in my chest spiked, I laid down and willed myself to breathe past it.

Whether it was my heart or my injuries throbbing, I could not tell.

CHAPTER FOUR

The silence of the hospital wing was soon disrupted by the kid who had appointed himself my personal physician.

"Riddle me this. Why is it that whenever a situation of obvious peril emerges before you, you automatically launch yourself into it headfirst? And while we're pondering the great mysteries of the universe, why am I always the one that has to drag your sorry ass back from death's inviting doorstep?"

"Because," I reasoned with a small smirk, "if I didn't, you would simply have nothing of worth to complain about."

He didn't look very amused, but I saw the crinkle in the corner of his eye that meant he was holding back his laughter.

"I'm telling you, Ria, it was a miracle you survived that knife wound the first time. This time you should have been done for. Any normal wolf would be having a nice memorial service right about now."

"You people keep assuming I'm just a 'normal' wolf. That word doesn't exactly fit my repertoire," I teased, attempting to lighten the worry that still hung over him. "Now, stop trying to distract me, and tell me what Nikolai's real agenda coming here was."

Vincent sighed. "You are in no shape to be contemplating the thought processes of Lunatic."

"Vince. I'm tired. A wall exploded on top of me. The vampire I've busted my ass to capture waltzed away thanks to his lackey Wonder Boy, and they both managed to stab me with very painful and dangerous anti-werewolf weapons. If you're withholding information to spare me a bad day, it's a little late for that."

"Well, when you put it that way." Taking a seat in the chair Kate had occupied in Dreamland, he held his face in his hands for a moment, collecting himself.

"Come on, Vince," I said, knowing he needed a little more encouragement. "You know I trust you to tell me the stuff no one else will. It's been that way since day one."

"Oh, sure, butter me up before I delve into the workings of our resident sociopath." Resting his chin on his closed fist, he met my gaze again. "While you were watching over our, as of then, detainee, there was a break-in across the property in the residential quarters."

"They broke into someone's room? How petty."

His smirk was utterly ironic. "Guess whose?"

"You have got to be kidding me."

"And you thought your day couldn't get any worse." Reaching out, he checked my pulse and whispered something that dialed back the anxiety that was building rapidly.

"That's cheating."

"You need it. Anyway, you're gonna have to go in later and do a run-through, see what was taken." Leaning back, he rested his head against the back of his chair and closed his eyes. "It's weird, though, when we had one of Cindy's cousins in there, he couldn't find any traces of the vampire who broke in."

There appeared to be something caught in my throat. "That's because it wasn't a vampire," I whispered.

Not so restful anymore, Vince's head snapped in my direction, his eyes uncharacteristically sharp. "Werewolf?"

"You share your gossip, I'll share mine. See if you can think of anyone who fits this list of requirements: MIA, personal ties to Kate, intimate knowledge of our prison system, and quite the vendetta against everything I stand for."

Vincent was frozen in his chair. "There's no way..."

I shrugged my shoulders and winced when the nearly-forgotten pain flared up. "When he went missing that night, we all just assumed he dove off the deep end and was swallowed up in grief. None of us could have predicted he'd be a turncoat. At least, none of us wanted to, and that was our first mistake."

"So, we believed that someone could surprise us and prove he's the good man that everyone expected him to become. Is that so awful? Anyone who attempts to convince me otherwise can go-"

"Am I interrupting something?"

Both of our attentions quickly shifted to the newcomer whose innocent question provoked an air of silence that spoke of more serious questions to come.

I had no response, merely settling for a solemn expression to let him know exactly how I felt right now.

Clearing his throat, Vincent stood up from his chair. "Well, excuse me. Looks like you and your friend awkward tension need to have a little chit chat." Looking down at me, he became Dr. Vincent for another nanosecond. "Send someone for me if anything goes wrong, Ria, and don't even think you're getting out of this bed anytime soon."

"All right, so, end of the day?"

Shaking his head in the disbelief he saved for his most uncooperative patient, Vincent turned on his heal and left the room, not sparing Daimon a single glance. I resumed my staring contest.

He raised an eyebrow, not perturbed in the least. "Is this a bad time?"

"No, no, it happens to be a great time. Have a seat, you'll be talking for quite a while."

"Ah, explanations then."

"You got that right." I nodded my head towards the chair next to me. "Come on, Vincent kept it warm for you. Your story better be as interesting as his was."

Not nearly as chastised as I wanted him to be, Daimon did just as I asked and sat down beside me. "What is it you want to know?"

I had the sudden urge to growl, but settled for clenching my teeth so hard I had to force my answer out. "Everything I should have known before my various jaunts in the woods with Nikolai; a story that should have started the instant you recognized his name."

"There isn't much that gets past you, is there?"

Or Grandmother, or Cindy, or the rest of my pack, or the Kennel dogs. In fact, I'm pretty sure everyone had noticed by now. "I trust you, Daimon, but even that's a fragile thing. Don't make me doubt you."

Pausing for a moment, he looked me in the eye, examining my face before taking my hand in his. He lifted it up to his face and brushed his lips against my knuckles.

"I have lost you once. I will not lose you a second time, especially not by my own folly."

I squeezed his hand and smiled, a silent thank you. Taking a firmer hold of my hand in his own, he intertwined our fingers as he began his story.

"As you've undoubtedly guessed, I am a man born of neither this place, nor this time. The land I come from is so old my village is nothing but ruins, and so much time has passed, it makes my head ache just to ponder it."

"Your love of ambiguity is adding a nice poetic element to all of this, but it clears nothing up on my end," I informed him plainly. "Let me try a straightforward question: Where are you from?"

I could see in his eyes that he was in another place, another time. There were shadows lingering there that I knew were older than I was. "A place in what is now Eastern Europe, where myths and legends come alive, and where darkness can overcome daylight."

I shivered at the thought. I'd heard enough stories about the birthplace of modern vampire lore. "Creepy. Next question: How old are you?"

His face hardened into a grimace. "That is something rather personal to a vampire. I will tell you one day, but for now know that it is beyond a few centuries."

While a part of me couldn't help but be a little stung by his tight-lipped answer, any hurt was quickly overshadowed by the sheer length of time he had given me already. A few centuries was pretty hefty, but a few more?

He was right, my head ached just thinking about the amount of time he had seen.

"Okay, before I give myself a migraine, let's get to the interesting part: how do you know Nikolai?"

He sighed deeply, adjusting his hand so that he had a firmer grip on mine. "To fully understand our story, you must first know something; the time and place I come from is nothing like the one you live in now. Peace did not have the chance to lull us into a sense of safety in our daily lives. Back then, a man's life was shaped on the sharpness of his wit and his sword. To be powerful, to be a leader, depended on it. In my own village, small as it was, there was but one other my age whom I had to contend with."

"Nikolai," I whispered, already enraptured by his tale.

"Yes, from the time we were children, he declared himself my rival and fought with me constantly to prove his superiority, but, whether it was a battle of blades or words, he could not best me."

"Solidifying your ego from day one, I see," I noted drily.

"With good reason, my love, trust me. After some time, Nikolai became frustrated with his lack of success and turned to darker, forbidden ways to become the best. Back then, such methods were easily obtained, and it was not long before Nikolai encountered his solution in the form of a powerful *strigoi*, what you now know as an ancient vampire."

"A vampire can masquerade as a human for the initial period following their Turning." I knew all of this from my studies, knew the solution that Nikolai had found without needing to hear it. "Paired with the strength he would receive, it would be just enough to make his point and sooth his ego."

"Precisely," he responded, much in the way a proud teacher does when a student has drawn the right conclusion. "When he told the *strigoi* his story, he was intrigued. Having spent much time ensconced in his personal studies, he was bored enough to seek such a diversion. The next full moon, he began Nikolai's Turning process.

"However, Nikolai underestimated the depth of the vampire's ennui. He had no clue that the vampire would later sneak into our village and begin that same process with me."

It was a stab to my heart to hear the words. "You were Turned against your will?"

"In a sense, yes. When this strange man came to me in the middle of the night with promises of unmatched strength and immortality, I thought it all a dream. It was only when the pain started that I knew my error for what it was and knew what in reality I was to become."

For all werewolves study up on "the enemy" and all the histories we've obtained, not much is known about the intricacies of the Turning process. As horrifying as this was to hear, my inner academic was nearly mad with curiosity. "Is there any way to reverse the process? I know that once you are bitten the Maker returns one month later and makes you drink his blood, sealing the deal and all that, but what if you refuse?"

"There is no consequence if, one month past, you do not consume the Maker's blood. You will simply return to being human. However, what chance does a human have against a persistent ancient who wants to Turn him? And what human, after feeling the thrill of power that comes with being a vampire, would willingly give it away?"

"Point taken. So, you were Turned. What about Nikolai?"

"A month later, we both underwent the same conversion and he publicly confronted me, boasting of newfound strength. It was then I realized what had happened, why I was chosen to become what I am today." He paused in his story.

I knew from experience that this was usually the point such things got ugly. "So, what did you do?"

My suspicions were immediately confirmed. "You must know that back in that time, I was a different person, a different man, and my new instincts were driving me to such a rage as I'd never felt when I was human. I'm sure you know the feeling."

I nodded carefully knowing full well that Daimon had seen me at such a time.

"I responded to his provocations with such violence that Nikolai immediately knew I had been Turned with him. Like me, his anger was new and untamed, and our fight became a spectacle of such proportions that the villagers discovered us for what we were and were quick to drive us out.

"Conveniently enough, when we had nowhere else to go, our Maker showed himself and took us into his care."

"That's terrible," I said it like a curse.

"That is what I believed at first, but it quickly became a relationship that we both benefitted from. Our Maker was renowned for such knowledge that all of the ancients came to him for advice and information. The brute I had built up in my mind as the villain was in actuality an intelligent man, lonely amongst his books and looking for companions with whom he could fight eternity. In return for my company, he provided me with the knowledge and history that had not been available to me in my isolated, little village. He would send me out into diverse places of which I'd only dreamed of visiting to fetch ancient tomes, scrolls, and what have you. When I returned home, we would spend hours piecing together strands of fact from each story in order to discover a more complete truth."

Well, this was great and all, but he was leaving out the most important detail. "What were you studying exactly?"

"The origins and history of vampires, as well as that of other creatures...including werewolves. We studied characteristics, strengths, weaknesses, and such."

"I'm sure you guys were a hot commodity."

"Luckily, we ourselves were driven by our own curiosity. Others who came to us, however, were determined to gain such knowledge for less than polite reasons. Such people became our Maker's downfall."

"Let me guess. Nikolai."

He studied me so thoroughly that I found the urge to squirm under his gaze. "You've known him a mere blink of time compared to me, and yet I have this frightening feeling that you may understand him better than I do."

To hear him say such a thing chilled me to the bone. "Believe me, it's not something I'm proud of."

"That, at least, is comforting to hear," he said, relieved. "But you are right. I grew closer to our Maker until he became a mentor of sorts to me, but Nikolai never allowed him close. The influence he received was less than idyllic, leading him to become a darker being. It was the misguided influence of others that led Nikolai to eventually slay our Maker and flee our homeland."

I stared at him in openmouthed shock for a moment, not believing what I was hearing. "I may not know too much about vampire customs and laws, but even I know that killing your Maker is considered an unforgiveable crime. Super taboo."

The look he sent my way was full of irony. "After all you've seen of Nikolai, you think one small precedent is going to stop him?"

"No, I suppose not," I said distantly, not really keyed into the conversation at this point. I was almost drowning in this new story, letting all of the new information soak in. When it finally did, I reached to hold his hand within both of mine. "I'm sorry."

Now he was confused. "What could you possibly be sorry for?"

"Your Maker, I've heard what a strong bond that is, and you spoke so highly of him. You two must have been close." He didn't meet my gaze, but a squeeze of my hands let me know he acknowledged what I was saying. "I'm sorry you had to lose him like that."

When he faced me again, his expression was sad. "He was not the only Maker Nikolai slayed. Kate was your Maker, and he murdered her all the same. He has no regard for such relationships."

I nodded solemnly. "Do you have any idea what he may be up to now?"

To my great disappointment, he shook his head. "All I know is that he has unfinished business hundreds of years in the making. I've been following him around for the past two centuries trying to figure it out myself. I have not truly spoken with Nikolai in many years," he murmured.

"Great. If you can't figure it out in 200 years, what hope do we have wrapping this up by next week?"

He chuckled and stood, bending down to kiss my forehead. "Lay your worries to rest, you may pick them up again when you are healthy once more. For now, just focus on recovering."

I smiled softly. "I don't know if I've given you quite enough heart attacks this week."

"Hm," he brushed my hair from my face and looked me in the eye, "you are very lucky my heart does not beat, or I should have been dead twice over just from today's adventure."

I suddenly felt very tired. The fingertips I brushed against his cheek felt like lead weights. "Try not to worry too much," I whispered. "I'm a big girl. I can take care of myself."

He took those fingertips in his hand, letting his lips brush them lightly as he said, "Impossible."

Even now, his little words of love and devotion were enough to make my heart flutter. Happiness swelled inside of me as I slipped asleep with him beside me, almost making me forget the dark story he had just shared and all of the worries I had of what was to come in the future.

Chapter Five

Not so surprisingly, my recovery was much slower than last time. The knives sapped my energy to the point where I remained bedridden for a full week. I wasn't sure if this prolonged stay was due to the fact that this was my second time around or, rather, because I'd gotten a two-for-one special. I tried not to dwell on the thought very long. Something in my gut told me that this wasn't going to be the last time one of those damned knives got a taste of me.

By the end of the week, though, I was ready and rearing to get out of the hospital wing and back on my feet. Amidst the sounds of whiny trainees and geriatric nightmares, I kept myself sane thinking of all the ways I could torture/maim/kill Nikolai.

Note: sanity is a relative state of mind.

The morning I was due to be released, I sat up in my gurney for hours, ripping the sheets in my impatience, much to the displeasure of the nurses. However, before they could even think to reprimand me, I shot them my best bitch face and a growl that had them scuttling to the other patients in their care.

Needless to say, I am not a welcome sight at any of the infirmaries in our jurisdiction.

At the sound of approaching footsteps, I prepared myself for another scaring, only to find myself growling at Grandmother.

Never a good idea.

A single raised eyebrow had me sinking into my mattress.

"You've spent a lot of time in the infirmary as of late, little wolf," she started sweetly, taking her place at the foot of my bed. "You wouldn't happen to know why half of the nursing staff has suddenly requested an immediate transfer?"

I couldn't help but snicker.

She shook her head at me, as if beyond words. "You are incorrigible."

"Tell me something I don't know. Are you here to break me out?"

Smiling mysteriously, she threw me a pile of clothes, carefully watching as I rolled out of bed onto unsteady feet. "How do you feel?" she asked honestly.

"Fine, just fine." I may have answered that too quickly. She suddenly seemed unconvinced. I started dressing anyway. If she changed her mind and tried to keep me here, it would be easier to run away in my favorite pair of jeans than in a hospital gown. "I'm not made to be stuck inside and absolutely useless, Grandmother. Another day and my sanity might have just snapped."

"I do not doubt it." She still seemed unconvinced, though. "What will you do now?"

"Well," I started as I hopped and pulled the jeans up, snapping them shut and turning to make the bed out of pure spite. "I'm going to hit some archives and stalk Nikolai as thoroughly as I can before deciding my next move. Then, maybe I'll stop by Mrs. Johnson's class and take out a week of pent up anger on her more arrogant trainees."

"You are becoming more sadistic by the day, little wolf."

"It was her idea, actually," I countered, recalling the conversation with a shiver. "She likes the idea of bringing them up to speed on how well their training is actually progressing rather than where their delusions of heroism place them."

Grandmother chuckled. "I knew I liked that woman. Before you embark on that adventure, though, I wondered if you could do me a favor?"

My response was automatic. "Of course. Anything."

If I had been paying attention to the little smirk that came to her face at my answer, I might have run for the hills then.

"I have begun a new curriculum for this year's newest set of trainees. It would seem that in recent years we have become a little too out of touch with the world around us, an oversight of the Council's that I will not continue."

"Tell me about it, I'm pretty sure Aunt Rose is the only person on this campus who knows how to work the internet." At Grandmother's confused expression, I found myself confronted with the fact that she would probably consider it black magic and try to eradicate it from the world. "Never mind," I said quickly. "What was it you needed me to do?"

Turning on her heel, she gestured for me to follow her, and I immediately complied.

"As you spent most of your life as a human, you will have had the most experience out of anyone here as to the workings of the human world."

"What exactly are you proposing here, Grandmother? Field trips into the heart of human civilization? No offense, but, for the most part, these kids live in a world that is centuries behind the modern age, electric lights and plumbing aside, thank God. Most of them have never even used a computer! Your intentions are noble, but I just don't see anyone else having enough experience to teach these kids anything of use."

"I'm so glad you see it that way," she answered. My eyes automatically narrowed at her. She came to a stop in front of a closed door. "I've already presented this idea to your other previous instructors and our decision was unanimous."

Like she had with the infirmary, Grandmother pushed the door open in a single swing. Peering in, I saw, to my great horror, a classroom filled with wide-eyed trainees.

"Maria, I give you your first class of trainees. Trainees, this is Maria, she will be teaching you all about humans for the next year." A push with more force than I thought her capable of had me stumbling into the room. "Try not to make her angry; you will most likely be fighting her in the mornings as well."

And, with that, she slammed the door shut behind me.

"*Grandmother!*" I howled to the closed door, "When I agreed to do you a favor, I had no idea *babysitting* was on your mind!"

I could hear her chuckling on the other side of the wood.

Swearing under my breath, I turned my attention back to the other occupants of the room, only to find myself facing fifty or so pale and terrified trainees who looked like they were about to wet themselves.

Fantastic.

Keeping my face stoic, I cracked my neck on both sides and began sauntering up to the front of the room, resisting the urge to smirk when I heard several gulps as I passed.

My reputation tended to proceed me.

"Apparently," I dictated firmly, "you are all in sore enough need to learn about the human world that the other instructors and Grandm – the Chief – have seen fit to call upon me to teach you, as I happen to be the resident expert. Now, I've never taught a class of trainees before, nor did I ask for this job, but make no mistake, failure is not in my vocabulary."

Finally at the front of the lecture hall, I stared at the podium distastefully for a moment before violently kicking it over, making several of the trainees in the front row flinch. Taking a seat on my makeshift bench, I hitched up one of my legs to rest my elbow on as I stared down the room.

"You are expected to learn about the human world and all of its inner workings." The smile I let adorn my face was by no means friendly, nor did it seem to comfort any of them. "Fine, then that's what you're going to learn about. You are going to become experts on humanity, even if I have to personally ram the information through your ears and into your brain myself." Taking another moment to gaze around the room, I tilted my head to the side and innocently asked, "Any questions, comments, concerns?"

At the sound of a quiet thump towards my left, I turned to find myself confronted by familiar faces. Marcella's unofficial pack sat together towards the front. The thump I had heard was the sound of Chris, the smartass's, head hitting his desk.

I heard his muffled voice as clearly as everyone else in the room. "We are so screwed."

My smile spread, and I turned back to the others. "Let's begin, then, shall we?"

Less than ten minutes later, I was just beginning to understand the hopelessness of my situation.

"Are humans still too afraid to come out at night?"

"Do human teenagers go through training like we do?"

"How many human clans are there?"

This can't be happening right now.

The longer the questioning went on, the more determined they were to have their curiosity sated. The innocent Q&A had become a frantic peanut gallery. Everyone was so eager to have their questions answered first that the raised hands turned into everyone shouting at once.

"*All right that's enough,*" I yelled over the cacophony while jumping to my feet; they were all immediately rendered speechless. "Has anyone here actually interacted with a human before?"

"It's forbidden." I found myself recognizing the quiet, but firm, voice of Marcella's friend. I gave her one of *those* looks and she took that as an invitation to elaborate. "Werewolves are not permitted to interact with humans."

"That was the rule under the Council," Chris argued next to her. He was quickly silenced when she turned a glare on him that was disturbingly similar to Carter's.

They were answered by a voice on the other side of the room. "It's a universal rule. No werewolf is allowed to reveal themselves to any human. It's always been that way here."

"I didn't ask if you had gone and blabbed to anyone about your true colors." I informed them, bringing the attention back to me. "I'm asking if anyone here has just...I don't know, talked with one or something?"

My innocent question was met with a snort of derision by some kid in the front row. I was deciding whether or not to smash his face into the desk when he chose to add insult to injury.

"Why would we ever need to, or want to for that matter," he asked highhandedly. "Humans as a whole are beneath us, they always have been. Why on earth would we want to waste our time consorting with the likes of them?"

My eye was developing a tell-tale twitch I usually associated with Kate. I didn't sign up for another round of this kind of bigotry. I'd heard enough of it over the past few years, and the last place I wanted to hear it was in *my* Human Studies 101 classroom.

So, what could I do to handle it now?

I wanted to scream and shout obscenities in his smug face. I wanted to throttle him until his face turned blue. I wanted to hang him upside down from the ceiling by his toes and give him a *real* reason to dislike humans.

But, as I stared down the newest annoyance in my life, I couldn't help but notice something I'd missed at first glance. Sharply defined features, honey-golden locks of perfectly straight hair...

And bright, silver eyes.

With a start, I realized that he was an exact male replica of the menace of my training years: Desiree.

I didn't know she had a younger brother, I thought to myself, but that's what he had to be. There was no denying it.

It seemed, for a moment, like I was given a golden opportunity to re-inflict all of the psychological warfare and physical abuse that I had been forced to endure at Desiree's hands onto her personal mini-me.

And yet, I found myself thinking of a different pair of silver eyes. Ones that had been raised in the same family, ruled over by the same Council, and who, in the end, had found themselves to be the complete opposite of Desiree. If Kate could grow up in a human-hating household and turn out so great, what was to say this kid couldn't be re-educated?

"Beneath you, huh?" I graciously asked.

"That's right."

"And always have been? You almost make it sound like werewolves came first or something."

"Well, everybody knows they didn't," he hastily defended, though it didn't sound like he was giving up his argument just yet. "I'm just saying we were created to be superiors to humans."

Planting my hands on the desk in front of him, I leaned down to get right in his face. In my softest, most threatening tone, I asked him, "So, that's why the werewolf curse was created? To make a whole species superior to humans?"

Absolute, utter silence.

He paled so quickly I honestly thought he would faint right out of his chair. "Well…uh, it's – it's not…"

"Oh my, are we starting to second guess ourselves?"

At this point, I was pretty sure all of my students were so uncomfortable with the current conversation that they were barely breathing. It wasn't necessarily the atmosphere I wanted dominating my classroom, but I had to make a point now if I ever wanted to get anything done with these kids.

Before I could change their opinion of humans, I was going to have to downsize the opinion they had of themselves.

Pushing myself away from the desk, I turned my gaze to the open-mouthed faces in front of me.

"It would seem to me, children, that your fellow trainee requires a history lesson. Would anyone be so kind as to provide?" The silence prevailed. "No takers? No problem."

Searching for a moment, I found a bookshelf in the room filled to the brim with history books, including all of the textbooks my trainees found themselves carrying. They were the same ones I had carried around not so long ago. I reached for the one I had used and perused for my paranormal creatures class. Pulling it out, I skimmed through it in front of them.

"The world is full of all sorts of things that go bump in the night. You study them every single day, their characteristics, habits, powers, weaknesses, but why? We're strong enough, more than capable of protecting ourselves. So, why on earth do we even bother?"

"To–"

My head snapped around along with everyone else's at the sound of a voice other than mine. Wonder of wonders, Marcella had decided to speak out. Not that I doubted her courage one little bit (this *was* the girl who, as a toddler, had attacked Vince with a tree for stealing her doll), but with all eyes on her, she was hesitant to continue. However, my wink seemed to give her more than enough encouragement.

"We learn all of these things to hunt vampires. It's why the first werewolf was created."

"Aha! Therein lies the problem. Werewolves were, indeed, intended to fight vampires, but that's the sole reason why they were created," I nodded proudly at her before turning back to the Desiree clone. "Have you been through the ancient tomes of the archives?"

"Of course not," he answered haughtily. "Only scholars are permitted access to those."

I paused for a second before sending an evil smirk his way. "Oops."

Impossibly, everyone's eyes grew even wider.

"There are some great reads down there, a little long-winded and dusty, not for the faint of heart or the asthmatic, but interesting nonetheless. Now, for someone like me who doesn't read any tongues of old, it can be a tricky endeavor, but the hidden gems I've found down there have certainly made it worthwhile. I know!" I cried, snapping my fingers. "I'll tell you one of my favorites."

A hop, skip, and a jump later, I was sitting cross-legged on the large desk that the pompous child sat himself behind. They were more like tables than desks, really, sitting four to each one, and you better believe all four of these kids were halfway to falling out of their chairs when they found me suddenly seated in front of their faces.

"Once upon a time, far before any of us were ever born, back before the Council began their reign, and werewolves roamed freely throughout the New World. Before werewolves even *existed*, there were only humans, and these humans knew and feared the supernatural well. They were superstitious, cautious, and much easier prey in those times, for the creatures that hunted them were not, nor had they ever been, human, and they felt no qualms in diminishing them one countryside village at a time.

"As if that wasn't enough to fear, it was also around this time that a darker, far more perilous creature came into being. Born of human flesh and fed by the blood that flowed through their veins, this once-man was dangerous in that he could masquerade in the general populace. Faster, stronger, and immortal, this creature was soon regarded with such terror as no one had ever felt before and rendered the humans utterly helpless. Not only that, but this creature made others of its kind. Like a sickness, this species spread across the length and breadth of the land, a trail of death following in its wake.

"These vampires, as they soon came to be known by, were nearly invincible compared to normal mortals. They had fatal weaknesses, silver, stakes, and the like, and groups of humans banded together in order to fight against the spread of vampires, forming the first families of hunters, but it was still not enough to contend with the scourge.

"And in this chaotic and dangerous world, there lived a human man. This man possessed no special talents, he was not known for great wisdom, nor could he boast a fortune of gold or jewels. In fact, the only thing of great value this man could call his own was the woman he loved with all of his heart, and this man feared one thing over all others: the loss of his beloved. Knowing he had neither the knowledge nor the means to protect her from the vampires that seemed to surround them more every day, the man chose to try and fight supernatural with supernatural. He began, then, searching endlessly for a way to keep his love safe.

"After some time, he heard news of a witch living in a nearby wood, one that despised vampires. Taking a chance, he told his love that he was leaving on a hunting trip and would return soon enough. Bringing his faithful dog for protection, he set off for the rumored wood.

"As if she knew he was coming, the witch made herself known to him shortly after his journey began, demanding he state his purpose. Pleading with the witch, he told her his story and asked for the power to protect and safeguard the people closest to his heart. Finding his intentions noble, she saw in him an opportunity to drive back the vampires she so hated. With this in mind, she told him, 'I will give you the power you desire, but with this power you will not only be responsible for protecting your loved ones, but all the humans you can. You, like your dog, will be a hunter, a hunter of anything that poses a threat to the human race.'

"He accepted his new responsibility, and the witch drew from the power of the same full moon vampires used to create more of their kind and made him new. Half wolf, half man, he would have both the strength to protect his loved ones and the heart to keep that love strong.

"And that, boys and girls, is where werewolves come from."

"That can't be the end of the story," someone hastily said, caught up in the moment. "There had to be more written in the ancient tomes."

"It isn't," I countered, "and there was."

"Well, what happened next?" The obnoxious one wanted to know.

"Oh my," I feigned shock, holding a hand over my heart, "have I caught your interest?"

"Ria, please," Chris begged. "The suspense is killing us. At least say it ends well."

I couldn't help how my face fell at his words, but it was soon obvious to them that this story didn't have the happy ending they wanted.

"As a matter of fact," I told him, slipping off of the desk and towards my fallen podium, "it doesn't."

Lifting the podium off the ground, I rested my elbows on its surface for a moment, holding my head in my hands and collecting myself.

"The first part of the story, that which I've already told you, is what I believe to be the origins of the werewolf curse. The second part, what I've yet to share, is what I believe to be the origin of the animosity that exists between werewolves and humans, despite our promise to protect them.

"You see, the man who became a werewolf was so desperate to find a way to protect his love that he was not nearly discreet enough in his search. In those times, the use of witchcraft and sorcery was thought to be evil, and, knowing this was exactly what the man sought, the people of the village desired to drive him out before he could bring it into their lives. How better to drive him out than make sure he had no home to return to?

"So, banding together in a terrible and angry mob, they marched to his house, torches and makeshift weapons in hand, ready to dismantle it board by board, but when they demanded he show himself, they found he was not even home. His love, the one he took on the curse for, was the only one there. She tried to convince them that the man was good and had only left to go hunting with his dog. Not believing her, the villagers decided that it was better to act before he could return and wreak havoc upon them."

I found myself swallowing a hard lump in my throat, vaguely wondering why the story had such an effect on me. The first time I read it, I had very nearly cried too, and the pain of its ending had not faded in all these years since I had initially read it.

"They set the house on fire and barred the exit so the woman could not escape. She burned with it, and the villagers were completely assured that the man would never return to their home."

Stunned silence filled the room; my students seemed to be caught between the spell of the ancient story and disbelief.

"They killed her?" For the first time, Desiree's brother spoke with no derision or pride marring his tone. In fact, his voice was so quiet and hesitant it was nearly unrecognizable. "Just like that?"

I could only find the heart to nod.

"And you want us to learn about and respect humans? After telling us this story, telling us the depths of their cruelty?" I was shocked by the sheer amount of pain in his voice. Was he really so affected by the tale? "Why would we ever want to protect such beings?"

"Because she died," I answered easily enough.

His face was bewildered. "What-"

"And she didn't have to," I finished, looking him in the eye. "Hear me out…"

"Camden," he answered stiffly, not meeting my gaze.

"Camden, I never do or say anything pointlessly, it's a waste of time I don't have. Yes, this story shows the horror humans are capable of, especially when they fear and don't understand something, but the dark shadows of their nature are only seen when a light sits among them. Their initial plan was to kill the man, for when the woman said he had gone away from home they were sure it was in pursuit of dark magic. Fearing for his life, she offered up her own instead. If she died, the woman told them, he would have no desire to remain in a place that reminded him of her."

"She sacrificed herself for him," Marcella whispered.

Again, I nodded, and found myself addressing the entire class once more. "Human action is so foreign to you because of the sheer depth of emotion they carry. Day in and day out, their lives are governed by feelings you have been taught to suppress your entire lives. Their fear can lead to horror, their sadness to inescapable depression, but their love makes them capable of doing the impossible."

Casting a glance towards the front row, I found that Camden was once again looking up at me. There was no malice or anger on his face anymore, but there was still confusion, and, now, an openness that had been lacking before.

I sent him a bright smile and assured him, "That's the first thing I want you to learn about humans and the thing I want you to remember above all others: they're worth loving, and casting more hatred into the pot will only result in pain and sorrow."

He seemed to ponder this for a moment. His eyebrows coming together and his jaw set for a moment, as if he was debating something.

"What happened to him," he asked suddenly, "to the man who took on the curse?"

My smile became sad. "He went back to the village, and, when he learned what happened, he murdered all of the villagers. The witch learned of this, and truly cursed him. He was given immortality, just the same as his foes, so that he could wander the earth without her forever in retribution for his sin. The only time he could truly die was only after he made another like himself to take over his responsibility."

"So, that's why werewolves only age after they have children."

"Correct," I approved, "When that was done, he returned to the village he had destroyed and to the house where his life was ended and remained there until he died of sadness."

On that bombshell, the sound of the bell chiming declared my first class officially over.

"All right, here's what we're going to do: your homework for tonight is to come up with any *reasonable* questions about the human world. Tomorrow I'll just go around and answer whatever I can, and I'm sure we'll come up with something to talk about."

They still sat in their places, though some of them shifted nervously.

"Oh!" I realized. "Class dismissed."

Breathing a collective sigh of relief, they all stood from their chairs and filed out of the classroom, moving quickly so that they reached their next class on time. Once they had all vacated the room, I breathed a heavy sigh and moved to slump behind the big desk in the corner of my classroom.

What on earth had I been roped into?

I was perfectly content to wallow in my own frustration and confusion until the sound of the classroom door opening filled my ears.

"Sorry," I called out, not bothering to lift my head from the desk, "we're closed for today."

"But, but, Ms. Ria, we have so many questions about humans!"

Oh, God.

"Can humans fly?"

"Do they turn into wolves on the full moon, too?"

"Is it true they have a third arm growing out of their back?"

With a monumental effort, I found myself lifting my forehead the five inches it took to give my packmates, all seated in the front row of the class, a proper evil glare.

"You guys are such assholes."

"Yes, but we're *your* assholes," Cindy remarked cheerfully.

I remained unmoved. "Did you little shits know about this?"

Cindy, Austin, and Vince traded overdramatic aghast expressions amongst each other. I rolled my eyes and looked to Carter, who usually was on my side with these sorts of shenanigans, but even he had his half-smirk of amusement planted on his face.

Even Carter has betrayed me, I thought hopelessly.

"It'll be good for you," Cindy consoled, "and even better for us."

"It's high time everyone learned a thing or two about humans," Austin agreed, giving a sagely nod.

I knew Vince couldn't help himself when he added enthusiastically, "And now we have a real live ex-human to study!"

I ignored him valiantly. "I don't know a thing about teaching babies, though!"

"Nonsense," Vince waved me off, "you tell us what to do all the time."

"But what exactly am I supposed to teach them? They're missing centuries of human history and tradition. I don't even know where to start."

"Anything," Carter cut in before Vince could strike again. "Anything you can is better than the nothing they have now."

"But we're not going to worry about that now," Austin rallied the troops as he swung himself over the desk. "We took a group poll, and it was decided that you have forgotten what fun looks like."

I gave him a look of disbelief and pointed my thumb at Carter. "Have you ever met this guy? He wouldn't know fun if it bit him in the ass."

The air shifted behind me, and I couldn't help but gulp as I looked up to find Carter looming over me. I laughed nervously. "Kidding? You're practically a clown?"

He raised an eyebrow, and his half-smirk widened just a touch.

"We," Vincent announced, slamming his hands on the desk in front of me, "are the fun police, and you are officially under arrest."

"What are my charges," I demanded jokingly.

"For being an operating workaholic and contributing to the general peace," Cindy responded straight-faced. "You are sentenced immediately to-"

"*Day drinking,*" Vince announced solemnly. Turning on his heel, he made his way to the door, but not before snapping his fingers and calling, "Boys, bring her into custody."

And, with that, I was hauled out of my chair, to rest on Carter and Austin's shoulders like a log. I tried to reprimand them, but found I was laughing too hard to do so, and we hadn't even started the festivities yet.

That afternoon (and late into the night) was filled with nothing but smiles and laughter, and I completely forgot about sad legends and mounting responsibilities. I even forgot about Nikolai, for however brief a time it was.

I remembered how to have fun again, with the people I love more than life itself, and, when the night was late, I found myself relaxed enough to raise a toast to our fallen leader, one that everyone joined in on.

And, strangely enough, it was almost like she was there with us.

Chapter Six

Before I even opened my eyes, I knew I was in trouble.

First, I felt the softness of my pillow under my cheek and knew I was safe and sound in my bed, even if I couldn't really recall how I had gotten there.

Second, I remembered snippets from the night before: finishing my first lecture, going out with my pack, drinking, drinking, and more drinking.

Third, my very honed inner clock told me it was way too early to even consider being awake, especially after last night, but my instincts wouldn't just let me roll over and snooze after something had obviously woken me up.

Then, the pounding started.

It felt like someone was taking a hammer and chisel to my brain and a jackhammer to my skull. For a brief moment in my life, I considered decapitation a reasonable option.

Moaning in pain, I rolled over onto my stomach and held my pillow over my head in a short-lived attempt to smother myself.

That is, until I heard the chortling.

Cracking open one eye, I looked up to find Daimon standing at my bedside staring down at me. He had an amused twinkle in his eyes and a small smile that immediately told me I did some very embarrassing things last night.

"Good morning, darling," he sounded borderline delighted. My eye narrowed suspiciously at him.

"Morning?" I croaked. "What the hell are you doing up? More importantly, why am I awake?"

"Have you forgotten already?" He reminded me gently, "You have a class to teach, my love, and there was no way in the world I was going to miss this."

This was going to be the worst thing about teaching children for Grandmother. As a rule, werewolves need very little sleep; so, they're up and about pretty much all the time. Children and families usually function more during the day, and this goes for trainees as well. Then, as they go out into the world hunting dangerous things that only come out at night, they find their schedules accommodating that.

My class yesterday was the exception only because it had been purely experimental. Obviously, Grandmother had had to wait until I was cleared to leave the hospital, but, now, I was joining the standard schedule, which meant early mornings were now going to be the norm. At least I wasn't teaching the physical classes, which started at dawn.

My background being a lazy, human teenager deeply rebelled against the usual four hours of sleep the people of werewolf society believed in, even if my body could handle it with no trouble at all.

Removing the pillow from my head, I propped myself up on my elbow and tried to rub the sleep away from my eyes. As I found myself waking up steadily, I attempted to think back to last night and remember how I'd gotten back here, but, to my surprise I couldn't. Maybe Daimon knew?

"What time did I come back last night?" I asked him.

"More like this morning," he chuckled, as if amused by some private joke.

My heart sank. I knew well enough what it meant. "What did I do?"

The man had the audacity to grin like a Cheshire cat. "Where shall I start?"

"Shit." My face sank back into the pillow. My muffled voice was clear enough, though. "The beginning, then."

"Well, it was nearing sunrise, and I was growing worried. I was just about to retrieve you while I could, when you crashed into the window-"

I turned to look at the large panes of glass that were covered to block the sunshine in disbelief. "We're three stories up."

"Oh, I know. You were commenting how you didn't want the Chief to find you in your intoxicated state. I believe you referred to yourself as a 'Were-ninja.'"

Because scaling three stories of a residential building would totally fly under the radar. "What happened next?"

"Well, of course I had to let you in. For some reason, you seemed surprised to find me here in the room, and you decided to attack me."

My head snapped back towards him; I instantly regret the motion when my pounding head decided to punish me. Covering my face with my hands, I tried to fathom what he was saying. I had attacked him? What the hell? "Why would I do that? Are you all right? Did I seem upset?"

His smile went from amused to positively devious. "Upset isn't the word I would use, and I was perfectly all right with it."

My confusion lasted two and a half more seconds before the biggest blush I have ever had in my life overtook my face. "Oh. *Oh, God.*"

"I think you should really hang out with your friends more often," he mused casually. "It puts you in such a great mood."

"Oh, shut up. Was there anything else I did?" Was there anything else I *could* have done?

"No, no, after you pounced you fell asleep."

I sighed. "At least I managed to do something un-embarrassing last night."

My relief was short-lived. He chuckled again, and I just glared at him. "Well, I wouldn't go that far. When I say you pounced and fell asleep, I mean you *immediately* fell asleep." He looked down at me with hurt eyes. "Do I bore you that much?"

"That's it. I'm done." Face-to-pillow contact. "I've filled my humiliation quota for the day, better just to stay here."

"I'd be careful with that pillow," he suggested teasingly. "There's quite a bit of drool on it."

I didn't even raise my head to flip him off.

It was quickly retracted when my favorite aroma filled the room. I peeked as subtly as I could, and found that Daimon had somehow procured a mug of coffee and didn't seem ready to hand it over any time soon.

"That better be for me," I warned him dangerously.

"I don't know, it's quite delicious. Too bad I can't substitute it for blood."

I held out my arm and wiggled my fingers expectantly.

"Oh no," he chided lightly. "I know better. Get out of the bed, and you can have the coffee."

"You, sir, are treading very dangerous ground," I growled.

But he didn't back down, the meanie. "I won't have you be late on your second day of class, Professor."

I groaned and forced myself upright on the bed, eyes sealed shut. "You're lucky you're cute"

As my eyes were closed to the world, I was taken by surprise when he kissed me in a way that made my toes curl and my heart pound in my chest. By the time he released me, he had somehow managed to maneuver the mug into my hand and wake me up fully.

I blinked owlishly only to find his smug face right in front of mine. He tapped his knuckle under my chin, and I realized my mouth was hanging open. I snapped it shut.

"Awake?" he asked without a single doubt.

I casually took a sip of coffee, not even flinching when it burned my tongue. "Not quite. If that's all you got, it's no wonder I fell asleep last night."

He hummed suspiciously as I got up and began moving around. The coffee never left my hand as I picked clothes out of the closet and made my way towards the bathroom. My head hurt every time I moved and made walking in a straight line very difficult. I did, however, manage to make it inside and shut the door behind me before rubbing my forehead and wincing delicately.

It was funny, I thought, how I could force myself to get up and fight after being attacked by a knife made specifically to kill werewolves, but a little hangover headache had me pouting and moaning in pain.

Setting my coffee mug on the counter, I turned the water on to "just below frosty" and splashed my face to wake me up completely. When I looked up to take my first glance in the mirror, I couldn't help but pull a face. There were deep, purple bags under my eyes and a pale cast to my cheeks that made me look positively vampirish. I didn't even want to ponder what had decided to nest in my hair in the middle of the night.

Taking out my brush, I ripped through my long locks until they were untangled enough to put in my standard French braid. I had done it every day since starting training, and the process had become comforting. Closing my eyes, I deftly pulled the strands over one another and imagined it was someone else's fingers. After all, during our training days, it was always Kate who tied back my hair in the morning.

The sudden nostalgia had me pausing at the end of the braid and looking back up into the mirror. What would she say if she were here with me today? Could we have found Nikolai together by now? Would she be okay with Daimon tagging along?

Stop dwelling, I thought firmly, *she wouldn't want you to dwell, that's for sure. Remember all the happy memories you can and try to make more with the people you love. That's what she would want.*

"I still wish you were here," I whispered. "I miss you."

Taking a deep breath, I finished my morning routine and changed into my comfiest outfit, AKA baggy sweatpants and a tank top. It probably wasn't suitable for an instructor, but the hell with it. It wasn't like I signed on for this job anyway.

Exiting the bathroom, I did a round through the room, packing necessities in my bag and hefting it over my shoulder. Daimon was waiting for me by the door. I handed him the empty mug and stood on my tip toes so that I could brush my lips lightly against his.

"I'll be back later," I told him quietly. "I'm going to hit up the books after class and get some research done. Nikolai's not going to put up his feet just because Grandmother assigned me extra chores."

He brushed a loose strand of hair that had escaped my tight braid behind my ear. "I'm going out to dinner tonight. I'll leave as soon as the sun sets and come find you when I return. Have fun torturing your students."

I smirked. "Don't worry, I plan on it."

Slipping out the door, I made sure I heard it click shut before reaching into my bag. Now that I was safely out of Daimon's mocking radar, I could put on my sunglasses to combat the fluorescents that lit the entirety of this campus.

As I traversed through the halls, I saw the stares and knowing looks people sent my way. The sweatpants and sunglasses this early in the morning, if anything, were a dead giveaway, but, if Daimon's retelling of my return was true, then I'm sure there were plenty of other stories to be heard today.

Making a pit stop at the cafeteria, I waltzed into the kitchen to make myself my second cup of coffee of the morning, knowing fully well that it wouldn't be my last.

I was two minutes late when I kicked the door open to my classroom and marched inside. A second kick had it slam shut behind me as I strolled over to my desk and plopped down into the chair behind it. No one said anything as I counted the students to make sure they were all there and chugged my coffee at a disturbingly fast rate.

"Um, Ms. Maria," a hesitant voice called out.

Only lightning-fast reflexes saved him from the stapler I threw his way. He practically threw himself out of his chair in order to dodge it and managed to knock over the kid next to him as well. When they were both righted and settled, I tilted my coffee mug towards his horrified expression.

"Child. What is this in my mug?"

Confused, he sputtered, "Um, well, coffee I guess, but–"

The next projectile quickly stopped his rambling.

66

"That's right. Coffee." I addressed the rest of my beyond-disturbed class. "First lesson of the day: if there is coffee in my cup, you *do not speak to me*." A raised eyebrow. "Am I understood?"

Assurances sprung up from all over the room so urgently I couldn't help but grin. Returning to my beloved drink, I finished it in one solid gulp and slammed the mug down on the desk with a contented sigh.

"What good little children," I praised them. "You listen so well." Sitting up, I snagged the garbage can by my chair and removed the bag from it. Placing it in the center of my desk, I ordered the students, "Your overlord commands you to put your homework in this conveniently-located container."

They stared at each other for a moment too long and tested what little patience I had at this hour.

"*Now.*"

I smiled as they scrambled around one another. Some neatly folded their slips of paper and placed them inside while others, in a movement I believe was started by Chris, simply crumpled them up and tossed them from around the room.

After a short debate over who had managed to throw it from farther away, I called for order in the court once more. Settling myself in my comfy teacher chair, I propped my feet up on the desk and placed the bin in my lap. Dramatically shuffling the papers around, I took hold of one and pulled it out, unfolding it for my perusal.

It was at this time that the class realized I intended to read them all out loud for everyone to hear. For some, their barely-restrained horror was clearly displayed on their faces.

"Let's see," I began, turning the slip of paper the right way, "first question: 'What kind of training do teenage humans go through?' What an excellent way to start our lecture." Putting the bin next to me on the ground for the time being, I relaxed a little more and tried to think of a good starting point for my lesson. "The answer to that is pretty extensive, actually. You see, humans our age don't just have one type of, well…what you would call training."

With that, we began an in-depth discussion on teenage human life, which extended into adult human life, and continued to human life and society in general. When conversation began to lull, another question from the bin quickly fixed that. Surprisingly, everyone in the room was completely enraptured with what I had to tell them. They soaked up the information like greedy little sponges, and asked astute questions that were far more relevant than yesterday's failed attempts.

Telling them of the life I had left behind reminded me of another time I had explained all of this to someone. The first time I had visited Kate's family, her father and I sat down together and traded stories and information in a discussion that had a profound effect on how he viewed humans. Much like now, with these students, he was more surprised by the similarities between the two different species than the more obvious, drastic differences.

And, against my will, I found myself actually enjoying the exchange. What with my throwing staplers at people's faces and kicking over podiums, I expected my students to have the fear of God put into them at this point, but, as the class went on, it became more and more apparent that a sense of ease was befalling them, and that here they felt comfortable talking about a subject that had been largely ignored for the better part of their education.

The ease was almost transforming into fun by the time the chimes were sounded, signaling the end of our time together for the day. I was shocked to hear more than a few groans of disappointment. I actually had to shoo a few kids out of the room.

"Get out of here, would ya?" I admonished Marcella's pack in particular, going as far as to kick her butt when she lingered too long by the door.

Once I managed to get those misfits out the door, I turned, only to find that there was one lonely soul left in the room. Nestled in a seat towards the back, I found myself searching my mind for a name to match the face.

"Julien, what on earth are you sitting around for? You're going to be late for your next lecture!"

But he continued to sit, opening and closing his mouth like a little fish and fiddling with something in his hands.

I was at a loss, but I tried again. "Is there something you want to ask me?"

That seemed to snap him out of whatever spell he was under. Jumping up from his desk so quickly he nearly startled *me*, he stuffed what it was he had been fiddling with (it looked to me like a crumpled and torn piece of paper) in his bag, hastily gathered his books and, with a quick nod towards me, strode out the door.

I watched him go for a moment, thinking his indecision might have him turn around, but he didn't stop. As I moved away from the door, I found myself shaking my head. "Teenagers."

With a glance towards the clock, I returned to the desk for my belongings and left the room just as swiftly as Julien had.

My headache had eased enough with the coffee that I could walk around without my sunglasses, looking like a mess and a half. As I passed the cafeteria and smelled the lunch preparations, my stomach grumbled demandingly, but I forced myself to walk past it. Later, I told myself, I could eat later; I wanted to get a move on my Nikolai research.

However, as fate would have it, I pushed my way through the main doors of the building, and a gang of misfits were lying in wait.

I tried to turn right back around before they noticed me, already planning an escape through the rear entrance, but, as I spun on my heel, a hand snagged the strap of my bag and dragged me backwards.

"And just where do you think you're going," Austin asked suspiciously.

I tugged, but he didn't give any ground. "Well, you know, I have a lot of teacher things to be doing this morning. Because I have a class now. With students. And work. Yeah."

I was turned around sharply to see the rest of my packmates had assembled in a line facing me with arms folded across their chests, looking more than a tad bit skeptical.

"Ria," Cindy asked sweetly, "you wouldn't happen to be overworking yourself already, would you?"

"Especially not after we took you out last night to stop you from doing that?" Carter added.

"Who said anything about overworking? I'm like the queen of laying around, avoiding effort, and eating everything in sight."

And, of course, right on cue, my stomach let out a growl worthy of a Bengal tiger.

Everyone's eyes dropped to my tummy, then returned to my face with varying looks of exasperation and disbelief.

I, for one, looked down and accused, "Traitor. I literally just told you I'd feed you later."

"Not good enough," Vince made clear. Shit, he was in doctor mode. That meant there was no way to get out of this one. "You are going to step away from the work for a few more hours, put up your feet, and let us feed you the best post-hangover meal you've ever had."

"Who said anything about having a hangover? What a bunch of lightweights you are."

Cindy, at least, was amused now. "Ria, there are sunglasses hanging off of your bag."

Play it cool. Play it cool.

"So, what if it was sunny this morning when I walked to class?"

She gave me a look. "It's fall in Upstate New York, and you expect me to believe there was an ounce of sunlight this morning?"

"Guilty," Vince declared loftily. "Strike three for you, Ria. We're taking you back to rehab."

Realizing what this meant I shook my head and tried to backpedal. "Guys, wait, not again."

But it was too late. For the second day in a row, I found myself hefted onto Austin and Carter's shoulders and marched away, much to the amusement of everyone we had the misfortune of passing on the way to our destination.

"Where are we even going," I asked from my perch. "Should I be in any way concerned?"

"You know better than to ask, Ria," Austin scolded. "It's our traditional pig out spot."

"Tradition," Vince chimed in, "and therefore required, but you were going to miss it for *work*." Suddenly, his face popped up far too close to mine. "*Shame*," he hissed.

"*Shame*," the other's chorused.

"This is degrading," I whined, noting the pointed fingers and the people doubled over laughing. It was also killing my image. Feared Council Head killer dragged around werewolf campus by the miscreants she called her packmates. Twice.

"Well, if you had just stuck to the rules and come to us, we would be skipping arm-in-arm to breakfast, but no, Ria wanted to be all productive and miss out on friendship bonding time."

I couldn't help but wither a little at the blatant accusation. Did they really think I was ignoring them?

A squeeze around my legs had me craning my head to look towards Carter. "We haven't seen you in weeks, give us a few more hours before you retreat to your books."

"Yeah, what he said."

"I know, I know," I told them. "It's just – I can't let him get away from me, guys."

"We'll get the bastard, Ria," Vince swore. "However, seeing as he seems to have formed a creepy attachment to you, I don't think he's going to run away any time soon."

He did have a point. Nikolai had implied that I had a part to play in his future plans, but what really made my anger burn was the idea that he had had a hand in Kate's murder, or a fang as he had claimed.

There were bite marks on her just before she died, I remembered, *but why would he bite her and then kill her? It doesn't make any sense.*

Long ago, vampires had discovered that the blood of a werewolf was dangerous to them. It wouldn't kill them, but it caused them pain and made them sick, something that should have been impossible for an immortal.

The earliest vampires that tried to snack on werewolves were made weak enough to be killed quite easily, but, tit for tat, a vampire's bite was no mean thing. Sometimes it had a nasty effect on the werewolves bitten too.

I should have tried harder to find him right after taking down the Council, he would have been weakened by the werewolf blood.

But I could beat myself up over it later because we were walking over the threshold of someone's house. A few twists and peeks later, I immediately deduced that we were in Austin's family home, which made perfect sense; his house was the closest one to the campus due to the fact that his mother was an instructor.

I had thought, well, hoped, that the boys would put me down at the door, but we made it all the way through the front entrance, parlor, and halfway across the living room before our parade even stopped.

"What on earth do we have here?"

I winced, recognizing the sound of a voice I would always associate with too many pushups, sore muscles, and mysterious bruises.

Twisting so I could see her stern face, I sent her a sunny smile. "Oh good, someone who can boss this boy around. Mrs. Johnson, have mercy on your favorite ex-student?"

I was convinced that Mrs. Johnson had been a Marine in her past life. She didn't even crack a smirk at my plea. "For God's sake, Austin, put the girl down. She is more than capable of walking on her own."

"But not obedient enough to go where we want her to," Austin responded as he nodded to Carter to begin the descent.

I have never been happier to have two feet on the ground. One needed that kind of small reassurance when this close to Mrs. Johnson.

She was seated in one of the arm chairs in the room, reading a heavy book that looked suspiciously like human military history. Funny, I had never pegged her as a human sympathizer. She had certainly had no sympathy for my soft human upbringing.

"We're going to get the food started," Austin said while frog-marching me to the couch next to the chair. "Mother, if you would be so kind as to keep her entertained, we'll be done soon enough."

Before any protests could even make it past my lips, the losers managed to beat it out of the room, leaving me sitting next to a live dragon. She seemed impervious to my nervousness, though, returning to her reading as if I wasn't even there.

I'm not ashamed to admit I jumped when her voice cracked across the space between us.

Without looking up from her great big book, she asked, "Austin tells me you were just released from the hospital."

"Yes." I held up my bandaged arm; her gaze cut over to it for a moment, assessing, before returning back to the page she was currently on. "Just yesterday, actually; thus, the indignity of being *carried* across campus was apparently necessary."

She grunted in some form of response, and the room was painfully quiet once more.

Normally, I would have never interrupted someone in the middle of their reading; it was an unforgiveable crime in my book. The silence, however, was doing quite the number on my already-frayed nerves.

"So," I started awkwardly, "what do you think of this year's trainees, Mrs. Johnson?"

Very calmly, she turned her head and stared right at me. With deliberate, nerve-wracking slowness, she shut her book, never breaking my gaze as she set it down on the table and leaned back against her chair, arms crossed across her chest.

"Adequate," she finally responded, "they're a little lazier than other groups, but that won't last very long here."

It certainly wouldn't. Mrs. Johnson had more than one way to make someone work their butt off.

"The real question here, I think," she noted, "is what *you* think of the trainees."

Despite my well-honed sense of self-preservation when it came to dealing with this woman, I gave her a suspicious look and asked, "You wouldn't have happened to have anything to do with that class?"

Raising her eyebrows, she remarked, "I had plenty to do with it. I've seen firsthand the benefits of having you in Austin's pack. There's a reason you nutcases are sent directly into human civilization for many of your tasks so often." She tilted her head once in the direction of the kitchen, where we could hear said nutcases causing quite a racket. "Because of you, they have a unique understanding of humans. They could blend into human society if they had to. With the Council dethroned, much of the anti-human propaganda has died down and left curiosity. People are going to venture out, and if they do it without any previous knowledge, it won't be long until someone makes a mistake."

She had a great point, a few great points, actually. "So, were you the whisper in the Chief's ear, then?"

She shifted in her chair slightly, considering me for a moment. "You should know better than to think I'd resort to whispering, Maria."

"Oh, believe me, I do," I assured her.

"It was most of us, actually."

"Us being?"

"Your instructors, the Chief included. We recognized the human problem the instant you stepped onto this campus."

I shrunk into the couch. "I've heard that more than once."

"You aren't the problem here, Maria," she reproached lightly enough. "You're the solution to a problem that should have been addressed the instant we noticed how vast the human population has become."

"It's going to take more than one class of trainees to close the cultural gap between humans and werewolves."

She gave me another look, and I felt my mouth snap shut immediately in response.

"No, it won't solve everything, not unless you shout your lesson plans from the top of the main building for the entire campus to hear, but your students will go home at the end of the day or term, and share what they've learned with their parents, who have been just as deprived of information. Those parents will tell siblings, cousins, and their parents, who have also been kept in the dark."

"The ever-reliable gossip train," I whispered, astounded. She was absolutely right. I knew from experience how eager people were to learn about humans, and how quickly word got around here. What was said in my classroom might as well have been printed on a billboard for the entire werewolf world to see.

She nodded in agreement. "You're young enough that the human society you grew up in has not changed drastically, but old enough that the students won't see you as one of them."

"No offense, Mrs. Johnson," I added dryly, "but I don't think there was any worry that was going to happen."

She didn't need an explanation. For one inexplicably short moment, I actually saw her features soften from the stern grimace she kept on her face at all times. There was a mother's warmth under that fearsome exterior.

"Have people been behaving themselves," she asked with only a little bit of bite to her tone.

"Enough," I replied vaguely. "The looks and comments are unavoidable, and the rumors didn't get too out of hand like I expected them to. All in all, it's nothing I can't handle."

Not that I could have said that four years ago. The silenced rooms and wary expressions would have had me curling up into a tiny ball of insecurity and social anxiety, but four years of struggling, striving, and strengthening gave me the ability to walk on with my head held high.

"When people hear how you are contributing to the education of the trainees on campus, I'm sure their opinions will turn quite drastically."

That sneaky devil, I thought gleefully. I may have underestimated the cunning of the woman famous for her brute strength.

Before I could properly compliment her deviousness, the door to the kitchen burst open and Austin emerged. "Thank you, Mother, for keeping her occupied. You're welcome to join us if you want."

"J-Mom!" Vince hollered. "I've made my special omelets! You can't say no to that!"

"Pass," she immediately deadpanned. Gathering her book, she rose from her chair. When I stood up, she grasped my forearm. "Don't work yourself too hard, Maria. If you ever need to vent, my offer still stands to drop by my morning class."

I smirked. "I might just take you up on that."

She turned and walked away, avoiding the kitchen entirely; I heard her heavy steps walking up the stairs.

"Amazing," Austin murmured, "even my mother likes you. That's borderline impossible. Vince has been in the house since before he could walk, and he still hasn't gotten a handshake."

"That's because the first time he did step foot in this house he broke three windows, swung from the dining room chandelier, and ripped hundreds of pages out of books in the library. Don't worry, Austin," I muttered, strolling towards the kitchen, "there are plenty of people on this campus who are lacking a decent opinion of me."

His arm came up to settle around my shoulders in a way that never failed to comfort me. "They'll never know what they're missing."

Our brunch was splendid; my pack really outdid themselves, making a meal large enough to feed an army. Needless to say, it would be enough to hold us off until afternoon tea. When everyone was finished with their meal, Vincent got up and cured the remainder of everyone's headaches. It was times like this I could almost forget his smartass attitude and put him in the running for my favorite person in the world.

"Why didn't you just do this yourself this morning, Ria," he asked curiously. "You seemed to have grasped healing magic with surprising ease."

"I don't like any spells I have to aim at my own head," I told him matter-of-factly. "I only have one, and I'm rather attached to it."

"I don't know," he teased, "maybe it could use a magical kick-start."

I was real close to breaking Mrs. Johnson's "no fighting in the house" mandate when I heard Cindy's voice.

"Aren't you hungry, Carter?"

Within a second, all of us had turned to face him. His plate was, amazingly, empty, still clean of food, and his eyes were shut, as if his headache had returned full force.

"Are you all right," I asked concernedly, nodding Vince over to his side.

But his eyes opened before Vince could make it there. "Fine," he said in his usual measured tone. He stood up from the table. "I'm sorry, but I have to speak with the Chief."

"Is something wrong," Austin questioned, "do you want us to go with you?"

"I'm not sure." It wasn't often I heard Carter sound unsure of himself. It couldn't mean anything good. "I think I'll be fine on my own."

"I'll walk there with you," I told him. "I have to stop by the Kennel on the way there anyway. You guys don't mind taking care of the dishes, do you?"

"We're fine," Cindy was quick to reassure us over the sound of Vince's whining. "Go do what you need to do."

Just then, the door burst open, and in walked Marcella looking tired to the bone from a long day and shocked to see her brother's pack had stopped by for a visit.

Before I could even think to greet her, Vince called out from the sink where he had already started his work. "The midget has finally come home. Do you need help reaching for an after school snack?"

I couldn't help but smile at the way Marcella's face turned bright red. Vince never failed to find a way to tease Austin's little sister. Her height made her an easy target, but I knew better than to mock the just under 5' tall trainee. She could be a little she-devil in the training ring.

True to her reputation, she, somehow in the span of a few seconds, managed to wrestle off her shoe, wheel around, take aim, and nail Vince hard enough in the side of the head to send him sprawling to the ground whining like a baby.

You'd think he'd have learned by now.

With a huff of anger, she marched over to the cabinet and pulled out a protein bar all by herself. She kept her eye on the newly-righted Vince as she devoured the snack with a little more viciousness than was absolutely necessary.

I'd only seen these two interact a few times, but each time it was harder to contain my fangirling. I'd seen enough human sitcoms to spot Marcella's massive crush on her older brother's best friend, and, if Vince's teasing was any indication, that crush could be reciprocated.

Well, at least, that was what Cindy and I gabbed about when neither of them were around. A sneaky glance across the room let me catch Cindy's eye. She was giggling softly behind her hand.

Austin, of course, remained clueless.

"Ria," Carter called from the door, "are you ready?"

Ruffling Marcella's hair as I passed her, I bid the rest of them a fond farewell and strolled out of the house with Carter.

I let him have a few moments of peace and quiet after the craziness that is the pack brunch. It was a testament to our friendship that Carter sacrificed his preferred meditative silence for outings with all of us.

Looking up at him, I noticed his eyes were closed again and his dusky face seemed paler than it should have in the sunlight.

"Are you all right," I asked again, more unsure than the last time I asked.

He was quiet for another moment; I didn't think he was going to answer me, until then his hushed voice responded, "I'm not sure. Something is wrong."

I didn't have to ask how Carter knew this; it was linked to his inner magic. The magic of the tribes was kept even more under wraps than those of the clans. All we knew was that Carter just....*knew* things, in a way that was far different than the psychic abilities of Kate's clan. It wasn't something we questioned (it wasn't like Carter could tell us anything anyway). We just kind of went with it.

However, there were times, much like this was shaping up to be, when the price of Carter's magic became prominent. My guess was that his magic was deeply tied to nature, and, therefore, the magic that all werewolves drew from. After all, it was Grandmother, the Chief of Carter's tribe, who taught us how to harness natural magic in the first place.

"Whatever it is, I'm sure Grandmother can figure it out," I replied with as much confidence as I could.

"She will have to do it before tonight."

"Tonight? What, oh–"

I had forgotten, but tonight, when the sun finally went down, a bright full moon would light up the sky. All of my werewolf friends would revert to their true forms for the entirety of the evening, and I would be left one of the only human-looking people on campus. In fact, I would be left completely unable to Transform for the evening, as well.

The full moon was one of my least favorite things in the world.

I was surprised to find Carter's dark eyes looking down at me when I checked on him next.

"It's one night," he said nonchalantly. "It'll be done before you know it."

"It's so much harder without Kate here," I said sadly. "It's like I'm cut off from you guys."

It was true. Without Kate's telepathic abilities, I was completely unable to communicate with my friends. They could understand me, but I would have no clue what they were saying. Common sense told me it was one night, but, alone, it seemed like an eternity.

I was almost in wallow mode when Carter came to the rescue. "You'll never be cut off from us." His answer was curt, as if it was the most obvious thing in the world, and it was that ease that gave me comfort.

The bright yellow caution tape was still wrapped around the entire Kennel, making it quite easy to find at a distance. Waving off Carter, who was heading straight for the main headquarters, I took time looking around at the damage. The glass in the windows had yet to be replaced after the bombs had blown them all out. The building itself was still structurally sound, but pieces of concrete, glass, and other bits of debris littered the ground, but I was not in the least concerned. I was on a mission here.

I had to know what the man of the hour had been up to for the past 200 years.

Ignoring the "Caution" and "Do Not Enter" signs littering the entire premises, I strolled towards the slightly-decimated-but-still-hanging-by-a-thread front door of the Kennel and marched inside.

I was hardly noticed amidst the hustle and bustle of clean up and recovery. There was no denying the building had seen better days. Scorch marks were being scrubbed off walls, papers were recovered and reorganized, and prisoners were being shuffled to more secure locations.

It was inevitable that I was detected, though. A Kennel guard, seeing that I was not one of his lackeys, rushed over to, undoubtedly, lead me right out the way I came, but froze when he saw my face.

"Maria," he greeted me with a firm grip on my forearm, "already out of the infirmary?"

"And up to no good, too," I assured him, sneaking a look around. "How's damage control?"

His mouth tightened. "Painfully slow. I'm afraid it will be quite some time before I can tell you exactly what happened here."

Oh please, I thought, *if you only knew.*

"Don't worry, that's not what I'm here for." I ran my hands over a file on the table next to me and casually flipped it open, looking without reading. "I need information."

He paused before venturing cautiously, "If it's information you're looking for, why not check the main archives? They might have more of what you're looking for."

I gave him *the look*, which I reinforced by adding, "Oh please, I'm not a trainee anymore. You know exactly who I'm looking for. I wanna know what he's been doing and where, and my best start is here in his prison records. I know just how accurate these puppies are."

He surprised me with a gruff chuckle as he ventured over to a brand new filing cabinet. "I forget just how much you kids have grown. Maybe once all of this blows over, you should consider taking up work here in the Kennel."

This was a pretty hefty compliment around these parts. Kennel dogs had a whole lot of pride for what they did and were fully aware of their importance in the community. It was a shock to my system to be so openly accepted by this man, whom I had met only a handful of times.

"I'll think it over, Sir. Thank you."

Neatly picking through the files, he came to one marked with a red flag and plucked it out, but, though I stood with my hand ready to receive it, he hesitated for a moment.

"I want you to know something before you take this, kid. I know you know better than most that there's a whole underbelly of conspiracies happening behind the scenes. I know 'knowledge is power' and all that, but just remember it's also quite a burden."

It was as if his words made me remember what felt like the weight of the world on my shoulders and the lifetimes I had seen for my tender age.

"I never forget it, Sir," I told him quietly as I accepted the file from him, and, with a final nod, I turned on my heel and walked out of the Kennel, determined not to let anyone see the shadow of memory that lingered around me.

CHAPTER SEVEN

Situated in my room with a warm mug of hot chocolate and a comfy chair under me, I readied myself to open up Nikolai's file and peruse the thought process of a lunatic.

Definitely not looking forward to this.

Well, somebody had to do it, might as well let the girl halfway to the funny farm go for it.

Taking a deep breath and telling myself to buck up, I yanked the cover open like I would rip off a band aid. Immediately, I was assaulted with a mess of photographs, maps, and dates. It looked like Nikolai had been across the world and back. Literally.

Starting off chronologically, I followed his path from his eastern European home, to the Scandinavian region, to Italy and France, until he showed up in America and wandered up and down every nook and cranny it had to offer him.

The words were beginning to blur together by the time I got to dates I recognized, but, rather than be comforted by the fact that I was getting somewhere, a deep-set chill settled over me when I traced his path up to a part of the country I was very familiar with.

When my finger stopped at the entry from Rochester, New York, I nearly threw the entirety of the file into the roaring fireplace.

By this point, it was safe to say that I was in a permanent state of sick and tired that there was a hella big conspiracy loop forming around me, and I was not privy to what was happening.

"What in the seven hells were you *doing* there, Nikolai?" I whispered to his photograph. Even in a stilled frame, he stared out mockingly, as if knowing his web of activity was thoroughly confusing me.

But this brought on another chilling thought: had Daimon made contact with Nikolai while they were both in Rochester? Had he really lied right to my face after promising not to leave me out anymore?

"I have not truly spoken with Nikolai in many years,"

"Are you the one that poor Daimon is searching so desperately for?"

It was like they were just trying to play me against each other. Every day, I was running deeper and deeper into the labyrinth of lies and deceit that surrounded me, and it felt like I was no closer to finding my way out.

Caught somewhere between deep sadness – felt in the pinch at the back of my throat – and the anger that simmered inside me, I threw the file in one of the desk drawers and grabbed my cloak as I strode out the door to catch some fresh air.

As soon as I left the building, though, I came to the realization that today was just not my day.

I had spent more time than expected stalking Nikolai, and left the building just in time to watch the sun fall behind the horizon. The howls began just as the sky turned a deep hue of indigo and grew until I was positive everyone on campus had Transformed for the night.

Despite Carter's reassurances and my own common sense, a sense of complete and utter loneliness washed over me, and, as the full moon came out of hiding from behind the clouds, I felt my own change take place. As soon as the moonlight hit my face, I felt myself not necessarily weaken, but revert back into something, some*one*, I knew I wasn't anymore. I felt uncomfortable, trapped within my own skin.

Such a feeling, paired with all of the inner turmoil I already found myself facing, was just too much. So, I fled, running to the one place where I would always find some peace of mind, or at least a pleasant enough escape. I bolted for my spot, avoiding the friends I could not talk to and the problems I could not solve.

Curling up into a tiny ball, I rested my face on my knees and tried to ignore the sounds of yips, barks, and howls that seem to come from every inch of the campus.

It wasn't long before she showed up, the blacker my moods are, the faster she seems to find me.

"Would you like sad violin music to go with that face, little wolf?" Her tone was as impeccably sarcastic as usual, but even that wasn't enough to lift the veil of sulking that had overcome me.

I lifted my head to look up at her. Despite her usual greeting, the lines of her face seemed to run deeper tonight, as if something was troubling her. I had a few guesses as to what it was.

"Did Carter find you," I asked casually enough.

With a great sigh, she leaned back on her preferred sitting rock and stared up at the full moon that was currently at the top of my shit list. Something was definitely wrong, I noticed worriedly. Even my human eyes could see the heaviness of her shoulders, the way her hands trembled slightly, and the distant look in her eyes.

"He did, little wolf. He did indeed."

Grandmother always had a hint of worldliness in her voice when she spoke, and, more often than not, there was a bit of doom and gloom in their too. Tonight, though, there was more of a sense of impending disaster than I felt comfortable with.

I realized how ironic it was that I asked her the same question I had asked Carter. I was sure, like him, she wouldn't give me an honest answer, but I had to try anyway.

"Are you all right, Grandmother?"

"I'm fine, little wolf," insert eye roll here, "more confused than anything."

"A second opinion couldn't hurt," I suggested with equal parts concern and burning curiosity. Helping Grandmother with her problems could take my mind off of my own for a while.

She shook her head, though. "I wish more than anything that I could have your help at a time like this, but there are things little wolves cannot see, things that trouble me deeply."

"What Carter saw today," I guessed easily enough.

A nod was her answer as her eyes focused on the line of trees below us, as if she were seeing now what he had seen then. I looked, too, trying to find what had caught her attention so, but my human eyes revealed nothing.

"When morning comes, I'll have my real eyes back. I'll be able to help you then."

But all I got was another negative shake of her head. Expression grim, she never took her eyes off of the horizon. "I'm afraid that's just it. No matter what form you take, little wolf, there are some things in this world that you are happily blind to."

"Be my eyes," I told her. "Tell me what it is you see."

"Chaos," she rasped, stamping her staff once on the ground as if to dispel something, "chaos and darkness and evil that shakes the trees and smells like blood."

Wow. Sorry I asked.

"It will show itself soon," she warned, "that much I know, but in what form, I cannot begin to imagine."

"And you have quite the imagination," I noted glumly, "perfect."

"I am not the only one who came here troubled this evening," she reminded me, neatly taking the subject away from things little wolves couldn't begin to understand. "What is on your mind?"

"Lies and deceit and mysteries that grow as time goes on; I'm nowhere near an answer to this mess, and the web is becoming more tangled by the day. I just wish–" but I didn't know what I would wish for, even if it would come true: for Nikolai to take a sudden vacation? For Daimon to stop lying through his teeth?

For Kate to come home?

She stayed quiet while I organized my thoughts. "I don't know. I just hate sitting here clueless. I hate this feeling that a huge storm is coming, and I just have to batten down the hatches and hope everything doesn't blow away."

"At this point, no one is sure what Nikolai's endgame is."

"He's had centuries, Grandmother, to prepare whatever it is he's doing. If that's not an unfair advantage, I don't know what is."

Her voice changed then, the trepidation and uncertainty that colored it before was swept away, and the confident Chief I knew and loved returned. "The coming events will test you, little wolf."

"I think the events of the recent past have tested me enough, thank you very much." I didn't mean to snap, but fear had frayed my patience.

Her look was admonishing enough. "Those events were not to test *you*, but rather the rest of us. We merely rose to the challenge with your help. No, I feel what's coming is meant for you, little wolf."

I narrowed my eyes at her, assessing. "Sometimes I wonder how you know these things, but I'm guessing it's just one of the perks of your job."

Her small smile spoke of age-old secrets and hidden mysteries. "You could say that, I suppose, but, in any case, I know without a doubt that you will rise to such a challenge."

Her unwavering confidence always made me self-conscious. Could I really live up to the expectations she had set for me?

Before I could even think of asking her anything about my so-called "test", the sound of the alarm made Grandmother freeze and turn her attention back towards the campus.

But even in human form, I could hear the howling calls coming from the opposite direction, from far into the woods that my little cliff looked over. Leaping to my feet, I closed my eyes and focused, blocking out every other sound until all I could hear was the sound of the wolves in the woods.

"What is it, little wolf?" Grandmother asked with quiet urgency.

"Something's wrong," I responded, listening in horror to what sounded like distress calls dwindling, as if the wolves were being picked off one by one.

Turning towards the campus, I thought for a moment about what I could possibly do. Everyone would be heading for the alarm to get their marching orders, but I knew it would be too late for the wolves by then. I was probably the closest to the action, but I was stuck as a human.

As the howls faded drastically, I made my decision. Following steps I could have taken with my eyes closed, I skidded down the steep slope of rock, slowly and carefully, taking care to remind myself that my reflexes were no longer supernatural, until I was firmly settled on the grass.

"Where are you going?" Good Lord, did she sound *panicked*? "You'll only get yourself killed in that form!"

"Maybe, but I can mobilize a whole hell of a lot faster than the wolves all the way over on the other side of campus. By the time they get to them, there may not be anyone left to help."

Ignoring the rest of her objections, I ran for the surrounding woods where I could hear what remained of the howls become even more frenzied.

Something's really, really wrong, I knew instantly. *Is it Nikolai?* I instantly clamped down on the thought, not wanting to distract myself.

I ran and ran until, somehow, for the second time in just as many weeks, I found myself in the clearing where Kate had breathed her last. Strewn about the clearing, were the wolves I was looking for.

Immediately I rushed to them, looking for a pulse, the rise and fall of a chest, anything to check and see if they were still alive. To my great relief, they all were still breathing. Some were more injured than others, and they had all been knocked unconscious from the looks of it, but what mattered most was that they were still alive.

Reaching the last wolf, I laid a gentle hand on the side of its neck to check vitals. When I did, though, disturbingly familiar silver eyes snapped open, and its head weakly flailed about.

"You're safe," I crooned softly, not really worried at the moment about the identity of this wolf. The head stilled for just a moment, as one eye caught sight of me and widened. "I'm here, and reinforcements are coming. Your packmates are all alive, and whoever did this is long gone. You're safe now."

My reassurances didn't quite have the desired effect, though. The panicked look in its eye remained there, and, now more than any other time, I wished Kate were here so that I could understand what was causing this wolf so much distress.

It took me a moment to feel it, the insistent prodding that felt like someone was tapping my shoulder lightly. Maybe it was just because it had been so long since I'd last felt it, the mental cue to allow a telepath into my mind. Not since Kate's death and the Council Head's invasion of my memories had I allowed one of their clan into my head.

Hesitantly, I opened my thoughts to the wolf, and had to fight the urge to clamp my hands over my ears the instant I did.

"RUNRUNRUN," it practically screamed in my mind.

"How pitiful." I froze at the sound of the all-too-familiar drawl. "These wolves should really step up their training. A whole pack of toys to play with and I didn't have the least bit of fun."

Removing my hand from the soft fur of the wolf, I noticed it started struggling again as I stood up slowly and turned to face him directly, keeping myself firmly planted between him and the fallen pack.

Leaning on one leg with his arms crossed over his chest in his usual fashion, Nikolai looked like hell had made me a personal delivery.

"I was so hoping you would be foolish enough to come today," he said with glee as I glared at him. "You've proven my theory right. You're trapped in that beautiful human form of yours for the night while your brethren slip their leashes."

"Don't talk like you know everything about me," I snapped, angry beyond belief that I had once again played right into his hands. Would there ever be a time where I was a step ahead of *him*?

"Oh, but I know everything there is to know about you. At least, much more than you yourself know."

Creepcreepcreepcreepcreepcreep

"Wouldn't you like to know more about yourself, Maria, to know those little bits and pieces of your curse that not even you understand?" With a small smirk he dropped quite a bombshell. "Don't you want to know why the Council feared your creation from day one?"

Why was it still so tempting? At this point, I thought I had myself figured out well enough that his words should have filled me with apathy, but it was that curiosity that kept me coming back to the "why's" I still didn't understand.

Needless to say, "why" is my least favorite word in the dictionary.

But the knowledge that Nikolai offered me was one that came with strings attached, strings that I did not want to have anywhere near me. So, time to turn him off.

"I'm sure more information would be available if the worldly expert on such subjects had been more...selective in his choice for company."

His face became cold in an instant. He didn't like it when I knew something that he wasn't ready for me to know. "I see your paramour has been more forthcoming than I had originally expected."

Huh. Funny how he's known me for two years and can predict my every move, but the man he called "brother" and spent centuries with still takes him by surprise.

As if knowing what I was thinking, Nikolai's face became so menacing chills wracked up and down my spine. "You and I are astonishingly similar, Maria. It isn't hard to predict what move you will make next in this game."

"Well, this is all wonderfully nightmare-inducing, but this is the second time you've harmed my friends, and, regardless of what shape I take, I will not let you get away with it a second time."

He was as wide-eyed as a child feigning innocence. "That was not my doing. I swear, darling."

"Yeah? And next week we're canonizing the Council Head. I'm not in the mood for games, Nikolai."

He sighed tragically. "I suppose I am in a way responsible. I should have kept a better eye on my new pet."

My eyes narrowed. "I think Rowan is more than capable of taking responsibility for his own actions."

If Nikolai's smirk got any wider, his face would split open. I'd seen that look before. The storm was about to hit.

"Rowan? Hardly. He has not an ounce of humor. No, my newest toy is the jewel in the crown."

"Yeah? Well, I don't care if it's the Queen herself, bring him out here, he's got quite a bit of explaining to do." I could afford to be cocky; I could hear the reinforcements behind me, most likely sent by Grandmother.

His shit-eating grin hadn't faded in the least. "I would never hinder you from sharing your concerns in person." He looked over his shoulder in the dark woods, calling out to someone I could not see. "Darling, your sister is here to see you."

A thousand possibilities ran through my head, but they all led my thoughts to one person. Had Nikolai found out I had a family, a human one at least? Had Rowan told him about my only sibling, my little brother I had not seen in years? For me, nothing could possibly be worse.

But the thought came too soon because, out from the dark abyss of the encroaching forest was someone I never thought I would see again. Why?

Because, less than a year ago, I had held her battered and bleeding body in my arms as she died right here in this very clearing.

With eyes that were cold and dead, Kate looked without seeing me as she snarled, baring a new set of fangs in the process.

Chapter Eight

I couldn't move as she went to stand by Nikolai, couldn't even breathe. She didn't recognize me at all, and I barely recognized her in return. Her face was paler than I remembered, a pallor that reminded me of death. Her eyes, once a beautiful shade of silver, were black from lid to lid. All the life and vitality that had radiated from her – what I had loved most about her – was gone, replaced by this being in front of me.

"You're dead," I found myself whispering. "I watched you die. I went to your funeral and saw your body *burn*. *Who are you?*"

"I had a few vague ideas as to what your reaction would be," Nikolai mused, "but out of all the possibilities I never expected denial would be what you would turn to."

If he hadn't spoken, I would have forgotten him completely. As soon as I heard his voice, my head snapped in his direction, and, if I wasn't bound so thoroughly to my human side for tonight, I would have feared a wendigo transformation.

"You," I spat like a curse.

His smile was so evil the Devil would have pissed himself. "Me."

"What did you *do*? Huh? *WHAT DID YOU DO TO HER?*"

I would have rushed him, but one minute I was standing on my own two feet, and, in the next, I was flat on the ground with Rowan kneeling beside me, his arm keeping me planted there.

"Don't be foolish, human." Later, I would look back and be surprised by the statement. If I had been in my right mind, I would have noticed that he sounded off somehow, his voice filled with more unnamed emotions than I had ever heard from him.

But I was most certainly not in my right mind. My dead best friend was standing in front of me, and the vampire who was quickly shaping up to be my archenemy seemed to be pulling her strings.

"Oh please, Maria. My once-Maker was the foremost expert on all mythical creatures. It was mere child's play influencing this discarded game piece to serve my whims."

"What do you want from her," I demanded. Kate had suffered so much. She didn't deserve this. Why had this happened?

"It's not what I want from her; it's what I want from you and what she can do for me."

I could feel such a rage burning inside me as I'd never felt before. I'd never in my life met someone I hated more than this being right in front of me.

"I am going to *kill you*," I swore. "I'm going to end your miserable life and then dance on your grave."

His smile didn't falter the least bit. "I love it when you sweet talk me, love. Let her up Rowan, she can't hurt me tonight."

"Never underestimate a woman scorned, Nikolai." The instant I felt his arm let up pressure, I broke free and had him on the ground in less than 10 seconds. When he didn't fight back, I turned my attention to Nikolai.

He seemed to feel my homicidal desires because all he had to say was, "Don't even think about it. My pet has quarrel with anyone who harms her master, possessive little thing she is."

That was supposed to deter me? With a growl that sounded like it should have come from my wolf-shaped mouth, I took two threatening steps towards Nikolai, but, out of the corner of my eye, I saw Kate move and halted in my tracks. The closer I moved towards him, the closer she moved to the wounded wolves on the ground.

"It would seem your dear Kate is not afraid to fight dirty," Nikolai noticed amusedly.

I retreated back, determined to protect the pack, despite the fact that I wanted to rip Nikolai's smirking face from his skull. As soon as I did so, Kate moved to take a position in front of him in a very deliberate, protective way.

I couldn't believe my own eyes. "Kate? Kate, please it's me Ria. Nikolai did this to you, let me help you."

"I'm afraid she can't do that, love. You see, this version of your late friend is merely a shadow of the girl you knew, perfect in almost every single way except for one important detail..." His hands curled around her shoulders. "Her free will belongs to me now. It took a little practice to get it to work, but with a few noble sacrifices your wolf friends made, I think I've gotten it just right."

"The missing wolves," I whispered, finally realizing.

"Exactly."

"To what end?" I would not let my desperation leak into my voice. I couldn't leave myself vulnerable. "So you've made yourself a little puppet, that's all well and good, but what? To make me angry?"

"If only that were it," he said tragically, "I would have won already."

"Then why? I was under the impression that gloating was your strong suit."

"Your curiosity is simply tantalizing. Really, it just leaves me shivering, but I'm afraid it will have to burn for a little bit longer. I'm merely here to prove a point."

"What point? That you're responsible for my early hypertension? Or that you like playing at being God thinking that you can just fool around with people's free will?"

"I don't just think," his voice burned with an intensity that had me taking a step back before I could stop myself. "I've plotted and planned and worked until I *know*. However, you just don't seem to get it yet. So, as much as it pains me to do this, it seems you require a small...demonstration."

Curling his long fingers around her neck, Nikolai brushed the scars left by his fangs lightly with his fingertips. "Kari," he murmured softly in her ear, "help your dearest friend understand."

The thin line that Kate's lips had settled into parted once more to reveal gleaming fangs. Then, she let loose a growl she usually saved for enemies we faced together. I'd never realized just how terrifying it was until it was directed right at me.

I witnessed everything happening around me as if I were detached from my own body. I saw Kate's gaze settle over the silver-eyed wolf just behind me, saw murder in her eyes as she let loose claws black as pitch. A sense of understanding settled over me as she stepped forward, a dark sense of purpose in the slight motion.

Nikolai was going to make her kill an innocent wolf, I realized at once, one of her own kin, no less. If she did that, I knew no one would try to fight for her. No one would believe she had an ounce of herself left.

She would be as good as a wendigo in their eyes.

But there was something Nikolai didn't understand in this great big scheme of his: I would *never* stop fighting for Kate. Dead or alive, friend or foe, we had fought and laughed and cried and bled together. I owed Kate everything. So, I would do anything to keep her from harm.

It was with that thought in mind that I threw myself to the side, right into her path of travel, as she launched herself towards the defenseless wolf. I told myself it was for Kate as the tips of her claws caught my shoulder and raked up my collarbone, stopping just under my chin. It was all to keep her safe as the force of the blow threw me back until I collided with the wolf I was trying to protect.

The burning pain was so intense tears streamed freely from my eyes as I propped myself up on an elbow, unwilling to let myself be left vulnerable on the hard ground. Keeping my eyes on her, I held a hand to the skin of my neck and brought it to my face, feeling my heart drop to my knees as a single glance told me my fingers were already covered in blood.

A cold nose at the back of my neck let me know that the wolf behind me was still awake and unharmed, to which I breathed a sigh of relief. However, when Kate began moving again, I struggled to my feet once more, hissing in pain when the movement stretched my newest set of wounds.

"Kate, *stop*." A part of me leapt when she stopped suddenly, as if she were actually listening to me. "I know you're in there, you stupid bitch; so, listen up. The only way I'm going to let you hurt this wolf is over my dead body. So, go ahead and pick your opponent, Nikolai or me."

"You are too reckless by half," Nikolai snapped impatiently.

"Not quite." Though I talked to him, I kept my eyes on Kate, not wanting to miss any warning she might give. "As you've mentioned before, I play some part in your future plans, as distasteful as the notion is to me. Tell me Nikolai, what's Plan B if your newest 'toy' sees me as collateral damage?"

Nikolai was seething under the blank expression he put on his face, Kate remained motionless, waiting for her master's command, and Rowan watched from the sidelines, as if he, too, was curious to see how events would play out.

With an infuriated snarl that seemed very uncharacteristic for his usual playful demeanor, he called, "Kari, cease and desist at once. You've made your point, and, for once, your sister has played the right hand at the right time."

Kate returned to his side without another word, her face cool and impassive once more. I could barely contain my relief, or retain my tough girl act, for that matter.

If it had been any other night, I would have been able to brush off the scratch Kate had given me, but tonight there were already little points of light swirling around my vision, telling me that I'd lost too much blood.

Nikolai's head tilted to the side just so, assessing me with eyes I was convinced saw everything. In a matter of seconds, the raw fury that he had shown just a moment ago was swept away, and the overly-amused antagonizer had returned.

"In any case, this should work just as well in convincing your companions that your beloved Kate is far out of your reach." He reverted back to his usual smirk, and I almost missed his previous show of anger. "If it's any consolation, I'm indescribably happy that she missed your lovely face, my darling."

"Go to hell, Nikolai."

Even my dull, human senses heard the first drop of blood from my shoulder hitting the grass at my feet. The hushed noise seemed to awaken something dangerous in Nikolai. I saw the way he breathed in the air around him, taking in the scent of my blood. I watched as a feral cast overtook his expression.

It was easy to forget your foe was a vampire when he was having a simple conversation with you. Especially when he had never attacked me with his fangs.

"Fascinating," he marveled, his eyes glued on the wound at my neck. Reflexively, I held a hand to it, as if shielding myself from his gaze. "The curse has even been washed from your blood tonight."

As he talked, I had the misfortune of watching his fangs elongate. My heart sank to my knees.

"I wonder…does it taste human, too?"

A terrifying thought hit me: I had nowhere to run, and I was out of time.

The moment Nikolai took a single step forward, I thought it was all over for me.

"Not a step closer, Nikolai." I stiffened as my view of Nikolai was suddenly obstructed, but relaxed when I immediately recognized the shoulders of my savior. As subtly as I could, I fisted my hand in the back of his shirt for support I dearly needed. My hands were shaking, I noted deliriously. "It seems, once again, you have overstayed your welcome, quite a distressing habit of yours."

Daimon's presence seemed to knock Nikolai out of whatever spell he had been under. All the telltale signs of a hungry predator seemed to vanish within a few moments.

"Ah, so the noble Prince Charming has come. How picturesque. Where is your white horse and armor, brother? We can't neglect such important details."

I didn't have to see his face to know the very instant Daimon caught sight of Kate. My hand was against his back and felt the distinct motion, when his whole body seemed to reverberate with the shock of seeing her for the first time.

He even sounded like the wind had been knocked from his lungs. "What have you done?"

"Something you would never have the initiative to accomplish," Nikolai bragged. "You and our Master hid in your research, and still, *still*, you never learned."

"What are you talking about," Daimon snapped.

"You claim you sought knowledge, and, yet, you locked the most valuable treasures away where no one could find them, not even daring to look amongst their pages."

Okay. Totally confused as to what was happening here, but I knew better than to interrupt. I just had to listen and make sense of what I could.

"You are talking about dark magic, Nikolai, true evil our Master knew had to be kept away from the darkness of our world. He kept those tomes hidden for a reason."

"And that reason was never good enough for me. You should know better than anyone else, Daimon. This game we're playing is not like the others. I'm playing to win now, and all of my cards are being laid out on the table one at a time."

"I wouldn't pick up your prize just yet." I felt Daimon lean back closer to me, as if to block me completely from Nikolai's view "The wildcard is still in my hand."

"Not for much longer, brother. You'll see."

And without another word, Nikolai, Rowan, and Kate disappeared back into the blackness of the forest.

Despite their disappearance, Daimon remained perfectly still, waiting to see if they were really gone. When a few uneventful seconds drifted by, he reached back and untangled my hold on his shirt, placing the arm around his shoulders instead. With one arm wrapped around my ribcage and another scooped under my legs, I was lifted bridal style into his arms. Once I was secure, he began the long walk back to campus. Running would have jostled my injuries too much, and the danger was past us.

"The other wolves–" I protested as I caught sight of them over his shoulder.

"They are in good hands," he cut me off.

Confused, I turned just in time to see more wolves running towards us.

More than a few of them had silver eyes.

"Of all the reckless, rash misadventures you've undertaken." I noted for the first time that his jaw was clenched so tightly that the muscle was ticking. His eyes were glued to my shoulder, not full of hunger, like Nikolai's, but rather concern. "Maria, are you suicidal? Because I can assure you that there is a whole group of individuals on campus just lining up for a chance to throttle you before you run off again on some other escapade."

I tried to work up the willpower to retort (my pride may have been hanging by a thread, but it was still there, damn it), but, like a bad dream, it all came rushing back to me one piece at a time.

Nikolai and the fallen wolves.

Kate resurrected.

Kate's freewill in Nikolai's hands.

Kate *attacking* me.

Stopping mid-tirade, Daimon suddenly glanced down at me with worried eyes and held me even more tightly to him. "Maria? Maria, are you all right?"

It was only then that I realized my whole body was shaking now. From the tips of my fingers all the way down to my toes, I could not control the tremors that gripped me, just as I couldn't rid my mind of the image of Kate coming towards me with outstretched claws.

Stopping in his tracks, Daimon pulled me right up against his chest, so closely that my face was pressed to the underside of his jaw. It was all could do to unclench my hands enough to reach for the collar of his shirt, which I gripped tightly between quivering fingers.

It had been a long time since I had been held like this, like a child that needed to be comforted. It was the sort of thing that the warrior-trained, feminist part of me rebelled against with every fiber of my being. It was the same way my parents would hold me when I came to their room after having a nightmare.

Well, what I'd just seen could qualify as the worst nightmare I'd ever had in my life. So damned if I didn't get to be held like a baby, even if it did make my newest set of injuries burn like a bitch.

Daimon's voice interrupted my overly-emotional, traumatized thoughts. "I don't know what has been done to your friend, but I swear to you he will not get away with this, Maria."

"Kate," I whispered brokenly against the skin of his neck.

I closed my eyes as I felt Daimon nuzzle my temple and stroke my hair comfortingly. "She will find the peace she deserves when you and I are through with Nikolai."

With his solid support, quite literally, all around me, I was beginning to feel a little more like myself. "Good," I told him, "I call first dibs on strangling him with his own innards."

I felt his smile against my forehead. "That's my girl. We'll get him, Maria. You'll see."

And, strangely, I believed him.

He carried me all the way back to the campus and took me straight to the hospital wing. Though I protested I had spent far too much time there in the past few weeks, he remained unmoved by all of my pitiful whining. Unlike Nikolai, he had just hunted, and his hunger was kept at bay, but the sight of that much blood worried him for an entirely different reason.

I told him everything I could, and he was very patient with me. He listened carefully to my tale, holding my hand when I struggled to get the words out, and remained quiet, even though I knew he was brimming with questions, especially when I talked of Nikolai.

As he wrapped my wound in bright, white bandages, his jaw was set so firmly I was positive all of his teeth were going to be nothing but nubs.

"If you grind your teeth any harder, you're going to break your canines, and life will become very hard for you."

My jest had no effect on his mood. "He made her do this?" he asked tightly.

"Not quite," I answered quietly. His narrowed eyes told me he wasn't going to settle for that answer. "He originally intended for her to kill one of the wolves in the clearing." As quickly and quietly as I could, I avoided his gaze as I finished, "I couldn't let her do that."

Tying off the last of the bandage, Daimon shot up from his chair, and, in a movement that actually startled me, swung his hand at the table next to him and sent it careening into the wall. The sound of breaking furniture made a wolf peek its great head in, but one snarl from Daimon made him exit once more.

"*Of all the idiotic*–" His thundering reprimand echoed around the hospital wing so loudly I actually flinched. "Maria," he didn't continue until I met his gaze, which I was quite reluctant to do when he was like this, "are you *trying* to get yourself killed?"

"I was *trying* to save somebody's life," I yelled back, shooting to my feet. His anger had somehow managed to ignite my own, and, after all, it was so much easier to be angry than to think about what I had just gone through.

"I was *trying* to get through to my best-friend-turned-zombie. I was *trying* to stop whatever it was Nikolai wanted to get out of this meeting. That's all I've been doing for the past few months, Daimon. *Trying*! And what have I accomplished? Nikolai has been kidnapping wolves right under our noses, he infiltrated our campus and turned one of our best fighters against us, he,"

I sputtered for a moment, not even knowing what to make of what I'd seen, "he did *that* to Kate, whom he also had the privilege of killing right in front of me."

Absolutely deflated, I fell back into the chair I had been sitting in before. Daimon was strangely silent as my face fell into my hands.

"All I do is try." Goddamnit even my voice was starting to catch. "All I do is fail."

"Maria," he sighed, and I felt him reach out for me.

No, I couldn't handle any pity now, and I was not ready for comforting words. "Someone needs to tell the Chief what happened," I snapped acidly. His hand immediately fell away from me.

"You're in no shape to move anywhere yet," he answered, sounding thoroughly chastised. "Stay here and rest. I will tell her everything you told me."

I made no move to answer him, and, without another word, he turned and strode from the room, leaving me to my thoughts in the quiet of the empty hospital.

That quiet didn't last for very long.

I knew it was his doing, somehow. Within the hour, the door to the infirmary opened and I looked to find four, giant wolves making their way to my bedside. Four very familiar wolves.

I recognized Cindy first by the bright, blonde fur of her coat, and was surprised to find a note clenched delicately between her sharp teeth.

She came right up to the chair I was seated in and thrust the note in my face. Carefully unfolding it, I wished I could be back to my wolfy self so that I could properly growl at the words on the page

Your distress made me feel too guilty to give you the reprimand you sorely need. So, I'm handing you over to the professionals.

Chickenshit.

Looking up at them, I took note of their stern expressions – well, for wolves at least – and winced. "You're really gonna just sit here until you can yell at me too, aren't you?"

They all growled softly.

Great.

Looking out the window, I saw that the sky was already lightening. The day had been moving faster than I expected. It wasn't long before the sun was peeking over the horizon. I felt more of my strength return to me, and my four friends were restored to the forms I was used to seeing on a daily basis.

It wasn't long after that the tirade began.

"Do you have any idea how dangerous that was? What the hell were you thinking?"

"She wasn't thinking, that's what. One of those tenacious human traits sticking around, I imagine."

"Without even a single person for backup? Really? Even on a normal night you should have been sent back in a fancy feast can."

"That's a cat food brand."

"*Irrelevant.*"

"Maybe we should just consider locking you in the Kennel from now on during the full moon."

"And now you're bleeding all over the furniture. That's just great. I hope those intruders didn't swipe the bleach when they raided your room because these will be an absolute bitch to get out."

I let them all have their say. Even the standing peacekeeper, Austin, had his two cents, but I stayed quiet, trying to think of how the hell I was going to break the news to them about Kate.

Suddenly, I felt warm hands on either side of my face and experienced serious déjà vu as they maneuvered me so that my gaze met eyes black as pitch.

And other eyes for that matter. Everyone had come to an abrupt stop in their ranting and was staring at me with a serious face.

"We know this look," Cindy said as she came to sit next to Vincent who had somehow already managed to unwrap all of the bandages Daimon had spent time tying and was prodding my neck, examining it closely, "even if we've only seen it a few times."

"Yeah, that and the fact that you're not yelling back at us means that something that asshole-"

"Lunatic."

"-said struck a serious chord, and we wanna know what it is."

Carter's gaze had never left my face, even when his hands fell away to hold my shoulder firmly. "What happened out there, Maria?"

There was no getting around it now. However, before I could even take the breath to begin talking, the door to the room burst open to let in a very uncharacteristically pale and distressed Chief. Her eyes searched the room until she spotted me in the center of it all. "Is it true? What he's done, *is it true?*"

I felt nothing but absolute numbness as I turned to her and said, "I think I found your boogeyman in the woods, Grandmother."

This had my pack, already stressed and anxious, at their wit's end. I looked around at all of their faces and felt a part of me wither up and die inside. We'd all been through so much, too much really, to be fair. We'd worked so hard so that fighting would no longer be a necessary part of our lives, and I was about to kill all of those hopes that we'd built up together with a single sentence.

"Nikolai has somehow managed to resurrect Kate from the grave; she's turned into some kind of hybrid monster made to follow his command."

Talk about a bombshell. Yikes.

The very air in the room seemed to freeze in surprise, and all those who had been standing found it necessary to sit down.

And I wasn't even done yet.

Licking suddenly-dry lips, I continued on, "When I confronted Nikolai, he...he brought her out. She looked different, almost like a vampire, and she had fangs, but it was her." I held a hand to my throbbing wound. Strange, even though Vincent had set to work on it the instant I sat down, it hadn't seemed to close at all.

Vince drew his own conclusions. His hands jerked away from the wound and stared at it with newfound horror.

"Did she…" I saw his Adam's apple bob as he swallowed harshly. "Did she do this to you?"

I was trying to maintain my calm for their sake. As much as I wanted to fall apart, or even to be held again, I knew that it was their turn for comfort. So, I reached out and held Vincent's shaking hand.

"Yes, Nikolai seems to be pulling her strings and controlling her actions. A fact I wasn't willing to believe until this happened."

With a furious yell that almost made me jump from my chair, Austin wheeled around to the wall he had been leaning against and lashed out, much like Daimon had, punching a hole straight through it.

While I looked on in openmouthed shock, Cindy calmly got up from her place to lay a hand against his back and whisper something in a soothing voice by his ear. Vince pointedly ignored the whole outburst and set back to work with renewed effort, but soon after he started, he sat back shaking his head.

"It's no good, the wound won't close by magical means. It's gotta heal naturally."

First, Austin has a little rage outburst, and, then, Vince admits that he can't do something. What was going to happen next? Cindy and Carter would trade personalities?

"What's wrong with her," Carter asked from his seat next to me.

"It's not what's wrong with her. Kate was…is Ria's Maker. Even for werewolves, the bond is a significant one, for all that we don't know about it. What I do know is that if a Maker marks their progeny, they'll stay marked. We're going to have to clean this up the old-fashioned way."

He moved over to the nurses' station, and pulled out various bits of supplies with the ease of someone who had done this more than once. By the time he returned to his seat and was ready to patch me up, people seemed to have pulled themselves out of their shock and anger long enough to get the interrogation in full swing.

"Did Nikolai say how he did it?"

"Where did he learn how to do this?"

"Does he know what Kate has become?"

"Why does he need her?"

"Enough." I had almost forgotten she was here, but just the sound of her Chief Voice had me snapping to immediate attention. Pulling herself up from the chair she had been sitting in, she walked over to Carter's spot and immediately evicted him from it. Docile as a lamb, he vacated the seat so that she could place herself in the spot closest to me. "You are all like a band of chittering monkeys. No patience." Fixing me with a steely glare, she asked, "Now, little wolf, from start to finish. Tell me of what transpired between you and Nikolai. Do not leave out the slightest detail."

I did exactly as she said. From the time I ran from her and the safety of the cliffside – to which she responded by clocking me with her staff – to the point where Daimon carried me back to them, I told them every little detail, even as minor and insignificant as some seemed to be.

A thoughtful silence settled over the crowd as my tale came to an end, each person absorbed in their own thoughts.

"So," Austin sounded much calmer now, to my great relief, "the question is, what do we do now?"

As the others nodded in solemn agreement, I felt my hands clench into fists at my sides. "That's our biggest problem in this mess," I grit through my teeth, "too many questions and not enough answers."

But then I heard Grandmother's voice by my side, so quiet I doubted that the others could even hear her. "What would you have them do, little wolf?" To my surprise, the question sounded less like the reprimand I was expecting and more like encouragement.

I looked up at my packmates, at their determined expressions and steely eyes, as my brain began to work in overtime. I knew I couldn't possibly do this alone, and, what with Kate running around, we were all going to need each other more than ever. Just as it had been with the Council, this was our fight. This was personal.

"All right, listen up, 'cause I'm only gonna say this once. Now that Nikolai's up to something huge, we better be sure all of our bases are covered. Vincent?"

Without looking up from his meticulous stitching, he responded, "Yes, milady?"

"Your clan does autopsy reports as well as heath records, correct?"

"Affirmative."

"I want you to get your hands on every autopsy report you can, and I want you to check the health records for what happens to wolves bitten by vampires or if we've seen any hybrid-like creatures before."

If was surprised, he didn't look it. "Aye, aye, captain."

"Carter?" His gaze slid towards me, and I felt the full weight of his attention. "I need you to look into the disappearances we've been having lately, and, more importantly, I want you to see if there was any correlation between them and Kate."

Without another word, he nodded and left the room, following his marching orders.

"Austin?" Thought he hid it well, I had known Austin long enough to recognize sadness and anger hidden in his closed expression. I knew it would be unwise to leave him alone for a while. "Cindy? You too."

She seemed momentarily confused by the pairing up, but nodded understandingly when I flicked my gaze back to Austin meaningfully.

"The security around this place needs to be heightened considerably. So help me God, if I have to hear that alarm go off again there'll be hell to pay. Cindy? I want at least one member of your clan posted in each of the sectors, and Austin? I want them each protected by someone from your clan. I want an eye on every shadow. Nothing moves, nothing *breathes* without us knowing about it. Got it?"

"Got it. Let's go, Austin." Cindy tucked her dainty hand into the crook of his elbow while the newly-finished Vince clapped him on the shoulder. Together, they led him out.

I looked on with a fond smile. He would be okay. We all would, so long as we had each other to lean on.

As the door clicked shut behind them and I found myself alone in the hospital with Grandmother, I realized something I had looked over while I was doing my own thing issuing out orders willy nilly.

That was kind of her job.

As I turned to apologize to her, though, I was surprised to find her beaming proudly at me.

"I couldn't have done that any better myself, little wolf."

I shook my head. "I'm sorry; I honestly don't know what came over me."

"Don't apologize for such a thing," she said firmly. "Your pack has been leaderless long enough. You were Kari's second-in-command; it's time you took up you true place in that pack."

The statement didn't fill me with pride like it should have. Instead, I thought of a different leader, an alpha I would have followed to the very end, had fate let that play out for us. "I'm no alpha wolf, Grandmother, not in the least."

She laid her hand on my shoulder, and I immediately reached to hold it, seeking comfort now that the others were gone. "Give yourself a chance, little wolf. In time, you will see it too." Her voice changed from musing to brisk in an instant. "In any case, do you have a task for me?"

Originally, I had thought better than to order her around, but now that she was offering to do something, I couldn't merely pass up the chance.

"I'm sure Daimon gave you just as many details as I did." She nodded solemnly. "I need you to help me find out what Kate has become. Even with Vince going through his family records, there's no guarantee that he'll conveniently find a cure for her, that will only prove that something like her has existed."

"Where is it you intend to look for the information you need?"

I thought back to my conversation with Daimon, about how his Maker had once sent him on quests for information and ancient books of legends and myths. "Even the wildest of stories are first woven with a strand of truth," I whispered. "We'll start with the various Eastern European ones. That's most likely where Nikolai would have gotten the idea."

Grandmother looked as though her mind was a thousand steps ahead of where her body was. "I know just where to look, little wolf."

"Excellent." I paused, hesitant, before softly adding, "I know I may regret saying this, but Daimon knows many of the old legends by heart, and he and Nikolai shared a Maker. It may not hurt to ask him for help as well."

She certainly didn't seem very pleased by the idea. "I will if it is required. Anything else?"

I thought hard about my next request, knowing I was riding a very thin line between counseling my leader and telling her how to do her job.

Well, to hell with it.

My voice was as quiet as it was firm, letting her know I was serious. "I would call the Western Quadrant. If whatever Nikolai's planning is beyond our control, we have to find help to contain it now before it's too late."

Her eyes were as wide as they had been when she entered the room. "You believe it will come to that? Truly?"

"I believe we have a habit of underestimating Nikolai, and I refuse to be left picking up the pieces when his work is done. If Kate's current predicament is any indication, he's been preparing for this for a long time."

She stared me down for a moment, as if testing my resolve. "I trust your judgment, little wolf. I will send word immediately to the leaders of the Western Quadrant."

That was about as comforting as it was foreboding.

"What is it you will do first," she wondered.

I sighed, a crushing sort of feeling almost overwhelming me. "I've saved the worst job for last." I let my head fall into my hands and took a deep breath.

"You have the look of someone marching to their own death, little wolf," she noted worriedly. "Just what is it you have to do?"

My gaze didn't leave the floor. "While I understand that this is a matter that contains sensitive information, there are those who have been kept in the dark for far too long about it."

"What could you possibly be talking about?"

"I think it's time Samson and Sarah are made aware of just what has befallen their children.

CHAPTER NINE

By the time I walked through the door of my classroom later that morning, I was ready to crawl under the nearest rock and remain there for the rest of forever.

Grandmother took it upon herself to summon Kate and Rowan's parents, as I did my best to clean myself up and changed out of my bloodstained clothes. They greeted me with the same warmth they had once given their own children, and that just about did me in. I had intended to remain a strong support for them as I had for my own pack, but, somehow, as my story progressed, it was Samson's strong hand on my shoulder and Sarah holding my hand comfortingly.

It was with them that I finally let the floodgates open, that I finally let myself cry like a baby, and, by God, did I need that more than anything.

Unfortunately, I couldn't stay with them for very long. I had so many things to get done. Grandmother tried to convince me to take the day off from classes, but I knew that I needed a little normalcy in my day to balance out the calamity. It took some wheedling, but, eventually, I left her with Samson and Sarah, and made my way to my classroom.

I'm sure I looked like an absolute zombie as I strolled through the door. It was impossible to miss how the room fell into a dead silence when my students caught sight of me. Many of the faces that looked up at me were pale, and there was a fear that they didn't bother hiding, unlike so many of the other faces I had seen this morning.

I remained silent as I strolled from the door to my desk. My footfalls echoed loudly in the quiet of the space. You could have heard a pin drop.

I settled down stiffly in the chair, mindful of the bandaging Vincent had done with such care this morning. He insisted on having my one arm in a sling, so as not to aggravate the abrasions, and his argument was just too good for me to refute. Life was much harder with one arm, but it certainly helped with the pain.

So, with my free hand, I took a head count of my little ducklings, confused when I came up one short. I tried again, only to come up with the same result. It didn't take long for me to identify the absent student.

"Where is Camden?" I asked the class, getting anxious when people started exchanging nervous glances.

"Maria," my head snapped over to Marcella's table. Even she was just as pale as the rest of the class. "He's in the hospital wing. He went out with his sister's pack in her stead to do rounds last night."

"They were the ones caught in the crossfire," Madea finished when she couldn't.

The silver-eyed wolf, my mind supplied instantaneously. *It was Camden Kate almost killed.*

I couldn't help the way my hand flew to my mouth. It was all I could do to clamp down on the sick feeling that came over me with just the thought.

If I hadn't jumped in the way....

"Are you all right, Maria," one of my other students bravely asked.

It took everything I had not to laugh in his face at the absurdity of the question. How many times had I asked people the same thing over the past few days? How many lies had been my answer?

"No," I answered truthfully, "I most certainly am not. I'm going to have to go to the hospital wing for the second time today, and that, children, is the place I hate most in this world."

My banter seemed to put them a little bit more at ease, which, miraculously, had the same effect on me. It seemed Grandmother and Mrs. Johnson were right, despite my contrary opinions. This class really was good for me. This place was safe in a time when everywhere else was looking more dangerous by the day.

"I don't know what you heard about last night's happenings," I told them seriously, "and I don't know how caught up on current events you guys are, but let's get one thing straight: despite how unimportant schoolwork or lectures or rambling instructors may seem at times like this, it really is the stuff you learn in here that saves your butts out there. So, we're going to carry on in here as if nothing has happened because, if anything, this information has only become that much more important for you to learn. So," taking them by surprise, I hitched myself up on top of the front table, much like I did the first day. Making a show of settling down on the desk, I summoned up my sunniest smile and announced, "What are we talking about today?"

It just so happened that myths were the order of the day. So, I did my best to explain the difference between myth and all-out fiction, and tried to sooth their egos when it became apparent that the general human populace didn't believe they existed, and, therefore, didn't appreciate the back-breaking work they went through to keep them safe.

"Remember my story, about how the first werewolf was created," I reminded them seriously. "I think we, as a whole, more than qualify as something that humans would be afraid of, even if we are protecting them. It's for the better, then, that they don't think we exist. They're much more capable of defending themselves now than they were hundreds of years ago."

All in all, it was another productive class, and, keeping true to my words, when it was over, I went straight from my room to the hospital wing, eager to see how Camden was holding up.

The nurses ran in the other direction when they saw me coming, which made me happier than it should have. It didn't take me long to find him; they had sections of the hospital wing specifically for packs, so that they could all be close together. I wasn't friends with the wolves in this pack for obvious reasons, but I recognized them enough to find his section.

He looked to be the least injured among them, but was in his own gurney all the same. When I stopped at the end of his bed, he peered up and had the gall to look surprised to see me there.

"Maria, what–"

"So, you think a few booboos are enough to excuse you from class today?"

Peering around, I caught sight of the empty chair by his bedside, and helped myself to it. He was still struggling to sit up by the time I sat down, and I lifted a hand to put a stop to that.

"Oh please, don't tire yourself out. You are more than deserving of a break after what you saw last night."

He was not in the least bit subtle as he looked at the bandage wrapped around my neck and shoulder. "And you aren't?"

"Fair enough," I laughed, sitting back fully, "but that's not why I came to see your smiling face."

His brows furrowed together in confusion. "Then why did you come?"

"You missed lecture today! You think you're going to get out of it just like that?"

"You came to the hospital wing just to re-teach the lecture you finished ten minutes ago," he asked disbelievingly. If he rolled his eyes any farther, they would get stuck in the back of his head.

I allowed him his sass, but pointed an accusing finger right in his face. "Don't give me that look, you little shit," I teased him. "You can deny it all you want; I know that, secretly, my class is your favorite."

And, miracle upon miracles, the kid actually had it in him to smile, just a tiny bit.

"Then instruct away Miss…" he was confused again, obviously racking his brain for the last name he would never find. I made sure no one on this campus, or anywhere else for that matter, knew a thing about it. The more in the dark I could keep my old life, the safer the people in that life would be.

"Ew, just call me Maria," I joked. "Miss makes me sound so old, and you certainly missed some pretty interesting things today."

So, I retold the lecture, from start to finish. He had many of the same questions the other students had, and a few more that showed me he was really getting what I was saying. It was exhilarating to have Camden, who just a few days ago was Desiree's twin when it came to thinking about anything human, to this new and improved version of him, who was genuinely interested in what I had to teach him. Thank god I was determined not to hold his relation to Desiree against him that first day, or who knows where we would have been right now.

Looking down at my watch, I realized just how much time I had spent with him, certainly more than the hour I spent with my class. "All right, I think it's about time I let you rest up. I'm sure you're more than ready to get out of here by now."

A bit of highhandedness returned to his expression. "I'm feeling fine, but these nurses are determined to keep me here for as long as possible." He looked over at my bandaging again and petulantly demanded, "Tell me how you got out of here so quickly."

I couldn't help but smirk. "Tell them you're friends with me, and they'll kick you out the first chance they get."

With that, I stood up from the chair, stiffer than I would have liked, and was prepared to say my final goodbyes when another figure stopped just at the end of the bed. Looking over, I froze when a familiar face sneered at me.

"*You*," Desiree spat with all the malice in the world, "what are *you* doing here?"

I shrugged, determined to ignore her as best as I could. It only made her angrier. "Filling your brother in on the lecture he missed today. Wouldn't want him to fall behind the rest of the class, but, if you would excuse me, I have other appointments to keep today."

She didn't move, and I felt the stirrings of World War III beginning in the small hospital wing. "Just what do you think you're doing, filling my brother's head with human sympathies? Do you think this is funny?"

"Desiree–" I heard Camden from behind me.

"Stay out of this, Camden," she didn't even look at him. "She's obviously already polluted your brain with these fabricated stories of hers."

"Fabricated stories," I asked incredulously, "seriously? After years of you mocking me for being born a human, you think I would have to fabricate stories about humanity? To a classroom of trainees, no less?"

"No sane werewolf would sympathize with humans after just a few days of classes with you," she snapped impatiently. "Just who do you think you are, lying shamelessly to trainees, my brother included?" She stepped closer to me, getting in my face. I just narrowed my eyes, not backing down. "Keep your filth away from his education, or, so help me, I'll find a way to keep you locked in that Kennel like you really deserve, or did you think we all had forgotten how you *murdered* the rightful leader of every werewolf here?"

"Right after he abused his powers and murdered his granddaughter," I shot right back, "or did *you* forget that part?"

I saw as the whites of her eyes blackened, and thought of the last time we'd faced one another. It had been in an arena, with all eyes watching as the first human in a decade passed the second Trial to become a full-fledged werewolf and defeated her nemesis to get there.

The part of me that seriously needed a kick in the face when it came to matters of self-preservation was eager to prove her wrong again. Screw a half-mangled shoulder, I wanted to take all of her ill-conceived prejudices and shove them up where the sun didn't shine.

"You better watch yourself, *human*," she whispered dangerously, "or you might make me mad enough to teach you another lesson in respect for your betters."

My smile was just inviting trouble, and the growl building in my chest was becoming so loud it was hard to talk loud enough to hear past it. "Bring it on, bitch. I could take you with one arm done up in a sling."

I realized, then, that my growl wasn't the only one I heard. Our catfight was smack dab in the middle of a room full of her packmates.

Smooth move, Ria.

"Desiree, Maria, *stop this*."

Our heads snapped towards him at the same time. The stupid boy had actually gotten out of his hospital bed, even if he was still leaning heavily against it.

Desiree surprised me by shoving past me to be by his side. I refused to cry out when she hit my shoulder in the process, resorting to saying nasty things under my breath, but that quickly stopped when I watched as she tried to gently persuade her brother to lie back down and rest.

"Please, Cam," she beseeched him, taking his hands in hers, "you're still not well. You need to rest."

Was this really the same girl who had beaten me to a pulp as a trainee just for being born a human? Unbelievable.

"No, Desiree, not until you let this go." Laying his hands on her shoulders, I noticed that, though he was her little brother, he still had a few inches on her. "Don't you think it's time to put the past behind you?"

She stiffened and sent a dirty look my way. "You cannot just expect bygones to be bygones after what *she* did to me."

Halfway to yelling at her again, I was stopped when Camden pitched in, "Not even after she saved your little brother's life?"

Her anger was gone in a flash, replaced with disbelief and a bit of the concern I had seen before. "You don't really expect me to believe...the rumors–"

"Then listen to the facts," he cut her off. "Last night, your pack – with me as your stand-in – was attacked while doing rounds. The attack came so swiftly we could barely see the culprit in the dark, but when she got to me...I didn't want to see." He looked into her eyes as he spoke, even though she was already shaking her head uncertainly. "It's true, Desiree, what they're saying."

She backed away from him until she fell into the chair I had been sitting in moments ago. Her eyes were haunted by things that I, too, had seen, and more. The light from the lamp on the table reflected against the tears in her eyes. "You cannot mean to tell me that she..."

"Would I really lie to you? About this? About the cousin who taught me how to hunt in our backyard? About the girl you once called your best friend?"

Wow. Newsflash. Hadn't heard that one before.

Desiree was shaking her head again. "But why would she do that? The person I am thinking of would never attack a group of her brethren."

Camden opened his mouth, shut it again. I saw the plea in his eyes when he turned to face me.

Clearing my throat, I waited until Desiree's skeptical eyes met mine, and told her as calmly as I could, "It would seem that Kate is under an ancient spell that reanimated her and put her under Nikolai's command."

But she would have none of that. "So, you were there as well," she accused.

"No, I got this in a tragic knitting accident," I retorted, gesturing to my neck. "I'm actually just a gossip fiend who heard it secondhand."

Desiree got to her feet again, and Camden moved until he stood between us, his back to me. It was a very telling position.

"Yes," he said over her growl, "she was there. She was there standing between Kate and me." He turned his head just slightly, so he could see the bandaging. I recognized the guilt in his expression. "She was the one who jumped in the way and took the blow that was meant to kill me."

That was when Desiree's eyes shot towards me, and, in a single glance, I saw her world crumble.

A very frazzled-looking nurse chose that moment to clamber around the corner and give us a disapproving look.

"All patients should remain in their beds unless otherwise instructed by a nurse or healer," she scolded, right from the book, "and anyone causing the patients distress should leave the premises immediately."

I rolled my eyes and then turned away from the siblings. "Don't worry, I'm already on my way out."

"I am as well," Desiree added, helping her brother back onto the bed and even going as far as to fluff his pillow.

Eye roll number two. "Camden, if you find your way to class on Monday, there is an essay due on differences and similarities in the perspectives of werewolves concerning humans and vice versa."

"I don't get an extension?" he wheedled pitifully.

"Are you kidding? You'll have plenty of nothing else to do while you're here; consider it a blessing in disguise."

With a final wave, I strolled away, determined to get a head start so I wouldn't have to interact with Desiree in any way, but I could clearly hear her footsteps catching up to me by the time I reached the door.

I was debating whether or not to bolt, but she beat me to the punch.

"Maria, wait."

This woman was seriously testing the limits of my patience.

"Look," I told her, spinning on my heel to face her once more, "I don't really know why you've had it out for me since day zero, and, to be quite honest, I couldn't give a crap, but however this war thing," I said gesturing to the space between us, "however the hell it started, I've tried my hardest to keep your brother completely out of it. So, if you could kindly–"

"Thank you," she interjected.

It took me like a solid ten seconds to reboot my brain after that.

"I'm sorry. What?"

"You saved my little brother's life," she supplied simply, "as much as I dislike you, I believe that's deserving of a thank you." Lifting her chin, she returned to her haughty self, the one I was more familiar with, and began strutting down the hall.

I debated letting her go and waiting until our next catfight to interact with her again, but curiosity was eating away at me. "Desiree," I called.

She took a few more steps before stopping, but she did not turn to face me. "What? You have my thanks, what more could you possibly want?"

I debated again, but this time it was whether or not to go full wolf on her or walk away. Taking a deep breath, I told myself it was for Camden's sake. "You don't hate me just because I'm human, do you?"

She didn't say anything, didn't make any move to turn around, and I was sure that she would just walk away and ignore me, but, after a full minute of silence, she turned her head just enough for me to see her profile. "No, though it certainly doesn't help your cause. I hate you for less petty reasons."

Without another word, she turned her head with a swirl of her blond hair and strode off, leaving me alone in the hallway to my thoroughly-jumbled thoughts.

CHAPTER TEN

It was a relief, really, after the past few days I had endured to find myself back in the library.

There were few places on earth I felt more at peace in than when I was surrounded by the smell of paper and ink. Some of my fondest memories could be found in this place. There were good memories, like the exam week Kate and I had made a fortress out of books and successfully lived in it for two solid days, and then, there were other…less than great memories, like when Kate and I had our last fight, and I hid here rather than confront her.

I was trying – and failing – not to let my thoughts be consumed by those same memories, but rather to focus on the task at hand: finding any hint of Nikolai's game plan in one of the oldest books I had ever seen in my life.

The translation dictionary was open on my lap as I flipped through the ancient text in front of me, looking at pictures and maps, trying to find anything of use.

These people just needed to be introduced to Wikipedia. Seriously. One search engine could have found me an answer yesterday.

But there was something about leafing through the ancient tome, with its delicate pages and aged smell, that had a sort of novelty, one that was lost when scrolling down a computer screen.

"Is this how you spend every Friday night, you crazy party animal?"

I couldn't help but smile as soon as I heard that voice. "Enough of them. I was wondering when I would get to see you again."

Looking up from the book, I had to let my eyes do some adjusting before I could see her properly.

Tall and limber, she was built like a dancer, but made to be a warrior. Her skin was a warm, olive tone, accentuating green eyes and falls of dark hair. Even in the safety of the campus library, the distinct wrinkles in her shirt sleeves told me she was carrying her much-loved knives.

The last time I had seen her, we'd been fighting for our lives and trying to avenge the deaths of our loved ones, the people the Council Head had thrown away to better suit his plans.

Alessandra ambled on over to where I sat and embraced me heartily when I stood up, not that I was at all shocked by the warmth behind the gesture. Spending a night fighting for your life with someone certainly helps to bring you together.

When I settled myself down once more, comfortable in my chair with my book on my lap, I looked up to find that she had taken the seat across from me and casually propped her feet up on the table.

"So," I wondered, flipping to find my page once more, "how does it feel to walk around campus without being public enemy number one?"

"Makes me feel all warm and fuzzy inside. You, on the other hand, look like shit." Sneaking a peak up at her, I caught her thoroughly inspecting my appearance. When I simply shrugged, her eyes narrowed. "When was the last time you had a good night's sleep?"

Ever the serious one, I cracked a smile and honestly responded, "The last stay I had in the hospital wing."

Her frown deepened. "That doesn't sound promising."

"Things have been a little hectic around here lately."

"And that's why I'm here, kiddo." Swinging her legs off the table, she sat up and leaned forward so that her whispering couldn't be heard by anyone else. "Grandmother called me in, said you needed some expertise."

Oh thank God. Reinforcements. "Depends, do you enjoy leafing through dusty, old books for stories and legends that may not even be real until you can't see straight?"

Rather than respond to my quip in a similarly sarcastic manner like she usually did, I looked up to see that her face was one that I had seen too many times today. It was the look of someone faced with something too sad to be true. Alessandra reached across the table, holding the hand I had poised above my book.

"There are no words that can express how much I regret this turn of events," she told me quietly. "What Nikolai has done to your friend defies every rule the supernatural world adheres to."

"Well," it was getting easier and easier to make my voice nonchalant and distant; I couldn't figure out if that was a blessing or a curse, "I should have known life was getting too boring around here to leave alone."

Whether it was the bitterness of my words or the blasé manner I delivered them in, I could tell that something about my statement struck a chord in Alessandra.

Calmly as you please, she took the book out from under my hand. As she closed it and placed it far out of my reach, she said, "Look, I know the end of the world is approaching quickly and we have to figure this out sooner rather than later, but I'm not liking this whole 'doom and gloom, everything is hopeless' attitude you've got goin' on here. Don't let him do this to you, Ria."

"Do what?" I challenged.

"Don't let Nikolai change you. That's what people like him do. They isolate you; they turn you into your own worst enemy, and if you let him do that, there's nothing stopping him from winning."

"What if I need to be changed?" I wondered aloud. "Aren't these struggles supposed to change us until we become who we're meant to be?"

She chuckled softly. "I supposed you speak from experience."

"Well, I certainly wasn't like this when I got here. My fun-loving attitude and general optimism were just aching to burst free."

Yet again, Alessandra did not laugh at my dark humor, and I got the distinct impression that there was something bigger eating away at her.

"I've always felt guilty," she began, "for not being there for you in your training. For so long, I just sat back and let things happen, hoping you would be fine, that you would figure out everything on your own. Maybe if I had done something about it…"

"You were there when it mattered," I assured her heartily, "and that's all I could have asked for."

"But you must have had so many questions, been so lost and confused like I was, and no one was even allowed to help you. I just…I can't even imagine what you went through."

Come on, Ria, I thought, *don't let her feel all this guilt over something she couldn't have fixed.*

"It really wasn't all that bad. I found friends who were willing to risk everything to help me, and who did. They told me about you, they shared their clans' secrets to help me use magic like everyone else…"

I would have gone on, but, at that moment, Alessandra's now-wide eyes snapped up to meet mine, her face a mix of confusion and shock. "You can use magic?"

Wait. What?

"Well, yeah, everyone can," I reasoned. "I know you struggled with it like I did, Grandmother told me as much, and I'm pretty limited myself, but I did figure it out in the end."

"Ria," she sounded like she'd been punched in the stomach, "the only magic I can use is the ability to use my werewolf traits in human form."

"That's what I do," I told her, but she shook her head before I could continue.

"No, I mean that's *it*. I can't do anything else. No human can, or ever has been able to." Noticing that the volume of her voice was creeping upward, she took a deep breath and leaned forward to whisper, "There may not be much of a history for the human-born, but I was able to do my own research after I left, no human can wield magic like the supernatural-born are able to."

"But I'm human, I've always been human," I reasoned hopelessly. "What does this mean?"

"I don't know. I really don't." She seemed at just as much of a loss as I was.

Completely and thoroughly distracted from my original task, I plundered on. "What other rules are there for humans? I don't know anything about what it means to be a human-born."

"Well," she said, pulling herself together, "it's about time you learn then." She held up one finger in front of me. "Human-born cannot, or, at least, shouldn't be able to, wield magic." Another finger. "Second, humans are forced to revert back to human form on the full moon."

"I do that," I added quickly. "I've never been able to Change on the full moon. I'm completely human for the night."

"So, you still follow the rules on that one, good to know. Those are the only real weaknesses we are sure of, but there are some benefits to being a human-born."

"Really?" I drawled, "Please enlighten me."

She smirked. "Humans are capable of resisting certain levels of silver better than the supernatural-born."

"The knife," I whispered, reaching at my hip for the weapon I was so used to carrying everywhere with me, only to be met with empty air.

"Yes, I heard about that little escapade of yours," she noted drily. "You seem to have a distressing habit throwing yourself into near-death experiences."

I threw my hands up in the air in exasperation. "Everyone assumes it's like a lifestyle choice I make, like every morning I must wake up and think 'Gee, how can I attempt my imminent demise today?'"

"Something tells me human-born traits is a safer subject today."

"Give the girl a prize, she's guessed it right," I joked, holding the bridge of my nose between my thumb and my forefinger. "Any other details we've missed? Any life-changing revelations you want to throw at me?"

"There's only one other thing I can think of, and then you're in the clear, but don't worry, it's definitely a good thing."

"Oh thank God."

"The human-born will never be able to transform into a wendigo."

The words didn't register for a solid 30 seconds, but, when they finally did, I found myself slowly looking up from the table to Alessandra's face. Realizing something was not right, her expression lost its easy-going flair and settled into something more wary.

"That's not possible," I whispered. "Alessandra, it's…"

"Ria, please don't tell me…"

"I thought you already knew." I sucked in a deep breath. "That's why the Council signed my execution order when we first met. It wasn't for showing my rebellious side." I lost my words between the memories for a moment, and had to anchor myself in reality so as not to get lost in them. "I was there when Kate died, and, Alessandra, I lost it. I lost every shred of humanity I had. I should have Transformed, I should have become a wendigo that night, but I was pulled back."

"Ria," she said gravely, "the only thing more impossible than a human-born becoming a wendigo is a werewolf coming back from a wendigo transformation."

"You think I don't realize that," I hissed. "I don't know what's wrong with me, or even what any of this means. My situation was complicated enough to begin with." Feeling that stress and pressure that I had come to the library to avoid, I shut my eyes and collected myself until I could think straight again. "Look," I said more calmly, "I can only handle one mystery at a time here. Right now, this is just too damn much."

"And Nikolai takes precedence," she finished understandingly. "When he's wrapped up in chains and locked in a rubber room, we'll finish this discussion, Ria. I will help you figure this all out."

"That's a great comfort to me," I told her sincerely, and it was true. To have Alessandra's help and guidance was a blessing I never would have thought possible a few years ago.

"Time to get down to business, then." Reaching in her bag, she whipped out a few texts that made the books I was studying look like they were hot off the presses. Seeing the look on my face, Alessandra laughed. "If we're going to catch a criminal mastermind, we're going to need to whip out the big guns."

"Where did you find these," I whispered reverently as I brushed my hands over their worn covers. These books must have been centuries old.

"My family used to have a library that scholars flocked to," she told me. "Most of our collection was lost the night of the massacre, but a few of the rare texts were kept in the safe, and, thus, were protected."

"I'm almost afraid to open them," I half-joked. Knowing my luck, they would dissolve into dust the instant I tried.

"Before we do that, maybe it would be a good idea to narrow down what we might be looking for," she suggested. "We never got the full story, only the distress call and the bare basics that came with that."

I didn't miss the pronoun she used. "We? Who's here with you?"

She rolled her eyes at that. "The hubby, of course. Can't leave to pick up a gallon of milk without him tagging along. Like I can't handle myself."

"I agree with him," I joked. "Just think about it, you could have fallen up the stone steps and broken your face, or you could have hit a tree on the way here, and let's not forget the ever-present danger of untied shoelaces."

"I see you, too, are used to dealing with overprotective vampiric brats," she mused.

"Now, how could I live up to being your successor if I didn't have some scary vampire man to tote around?"

She let out a back of laughter at that. "Well, regardless, I got the missive from Grandmother, and Max just happened to be reading over my shoulder. He thought he could be of some help on the vampire front, so he was my plus one."

I heard what she was saying, but my mind was still caught up on one irrelevant detail. "You managed to hook yourself a big and scary vampire Elder...and his name is Max."

"Not if you want to keep breathing it isn't," she warned. "To you and everyone else, it's Maximilian, or 'Your Royal Scariness.'"

Side note: if she had said his name was Maximus, I probably would have absolutely lost it right there.

"I'll keep that in mind," I noted nervously. No one wanted to get on a vampire Elder's bad side. That was horror movie material. "Now, back to real business; I need your help finding out what Nikolai has turned Kate into."

She leaned back in her chair, but was by no means relaxed. A purely meditative look crossed her features, and I could tell she was already thinking. "Must be pretty out there if even Grandmother doesn't know. Give me a decent description."

"Nikolai has already acknowledged that he used magic to resurrect Kate, and I know that he bit her before she died and had her killed with one of the hunter's silver knives. He stole mine just before she came back, so he must have needed them in the resurrection spell. She maintained a human appearance when she saw me, but she seems more animalistic, and something tells me she could still shape-shift if she wanted to." I found myself almost growling now, still furious about what I had seen, what he had made her do. "Her free will, though, is completely under his control."

I wanted to say more, but found I couldn't find it in me. My free hand found its way to the bandaging at my shoulder of its own volition. I felt Alessandra's attention shift towards it, and knew she was connecting the dots herself.

"She really must be under his control if she did that to you," she accepted. "So, do you have any theories? Any ideas we can start our search with?"

I nodded. "Maybe a wendigo isn't the only thing a werewolf can become when things can go terribly wrong," I suggested.

Her eyes widened. "You mean another variation of the werewolf curse?"

"Something like that. Now, tell me where to start looking. The sooner we figure this out, the sooner I get to see Nikolai rot in a cell for the rest of his miserable existence."

And so, Alessandra and I got down to the nitty-gritty research that had consumed me for hours already. We sat in the library, for ages it seemed, fishing through the texts together. Growing up around this kind of stuff gave her the advantage. She had a basic understanding of the language they were written in, which made the process multitudes easier on me. However, when the sun began to set outside the windows, we knew our day had to draw to a close.

As we collected up the books, the sounds of an argument drifted towards us.

"Whatever problem you may be having, dear, now is simply not a good time. She is in the middle of some very important research."

"She's the only one who can help! I just need to see her for a second!"

"I told you already…."

Peeking my head around the corner, I saw the old and wizened librarian barring the path of a familiar face. After a moment of searching, I recognized her as one of my own trainees Kelly.

Maybe she needed help on the essay I had assigned or something. It wasn't like I had office hours when the kids could just swing by, or even an office for that matter.

I stopped gathering up my books for a second to walk over to their side of the room. Strolling right up to the librarian, I laid my hand against her shoulder, nearly sending her out of her skin in surprise. With a kind smile, I assured her, "It's all right. She's one of my trainees. Thank you for your concern, though; I appreciate it."

Nodding stiffly, she turned her eye back to the girl. "Now you watch yourself, Maria is a very busy person, and her work is for our benefit. Don't keep her away from it for too long." With that being said, she marched back to her domain with her chin held high.

It took all I had not to laugh in the little librarian's wake after seeing the less-than-impressed look on Kelly's face.

"Crazy, old dragon never liked me," she muttered.

"Maybe sometime I'll give you dragon-taming lessons, but I don't think that's what you came here for. Am I right?"

Within a moment, she became unsure of herself. It was almost as if she was suddenly rethinking her visit to me. Casting her gaze about the room nervously, she caught sight of the other scholars who shared the space with us. "Is there anywhere more private we can talk?"

Well, that threw me for a loop.

"I'm guessing this isn't about the essay," I noted as I threw my arm over her shoulder and led her to one of the empty private study rooms, away from prying eyes.

I felt her shoulders sag under my arm. "It's Malachi."

Uh oh. This couldn't be good. "Your packmate? The one who got up close and personal with Nikolai?"

She nodded. "We're technically not packmates yet, but he's my friend and I'm – well, we're all concerned about him."

"Say no more," I told her. "I'm quite familiar with the feeling. Just tell me what's going on and we'll figure it out, kay?"

Gathering herself, she nodded and took a deep breath. "It's just that, well, we thought he would be back to normal by now. We've given him time and tried to help him as much as we could, but he's just not right. I mean, he wasn't the liveliest of people to begin with, but he used to be more outgoing and now, now he's no better than a zombie."

Malachi, of course, was in my class too. I hadn't seen what he'd been like before Nikolai invaded his life, so I had no real comparison, but I could at least understand where she was coming from. Malachi never spoke in class unless he had to. He never misbehaved or was involved in the shenanigans the others attempted. I tried to think of a time where I actually saw him speak casually to one of his classmates, but couldn't picture it.

I was going to ask what she wanted from me, but she beat me to the punch. "We wanted to go straight to the Chief, but we were worried she'd lock him up again. We tried talking to him together, but he just brushed it off."

She was starting to ramble; I saw the panic taking hold in her eyes. Resting my hands on her shoulders, I waited until she stopped talking. "You want me to talk to him," I guessed as much as offered.

Her wide, hopeful eyes stared up, and a part of me heaved a great sigh, knowing there was no way I was getting out of this now. "Would you? You're the only one who could possibly sympathize with him. You're one of the only people on campus who has survived an encounter with him."

"A fact I become more aware of every day," I muttered. "Don't you worry, Kelly. We'll have Malachi skipping around this campus in no time."

Amid her showers of thanks and praise, she gave me the location of his room, which he apparently never left anymore.

I opened the door of the study room and walked her out. She followed me back to the tables where Alessandra and I had spent our afternoon. I found Alessandra leaning against one of the bookshelves, the books she was devoted to reading cover-to-cover safe in her arms.

"I gotta take this," I told her as I collected my own share of literature. "Mind if I run?"

She waved her hand at me. "I know how it is. Go do what you gotta do."

Looking back at Kelly, I saw that she had frozen in openmouthed shock staring at Alessandra. Not surprising, really, she was practically a fairytale character around here. Just saying her name on campus had been forbidden under the Council.

Seeing Kelly's gobsmacked face, Alessandra cut her eyes to me and winked. "What," she asked, "did I forget to brush my teeth today or something?"

I shrugged. "Kids these days."

Alessandra smirked. "Until later then. Hey kid," she said turning her attention to Kelly, "know where I can wrestle up some decent food around here?"

I stood shaking my head as Alessandra led the sputtering girl out of the library, laughing quietly to myself. Poor Kelly could barely put one foot in front of the other. Alessandra was probably going to have to lead *her* to dinner.

I would have loved to stay and watch for amusement's own sake, but I had a nasty habit of selling all of my free time. Taking my books, I ran to the building next door to drop them off in my room.

I opened the door as quietly as I could, in case Daimon was still sleeping. It wasn't necessary, though. As soon as I was in the room I could hear the shower running in the bathroom. I contemplated waiting to talk to him when he was finished – we hadn't spoken since I yelled at him in the hospital – but that conversation would take time, and I wanted to talk to Malachi as soon as possible.

So, dropping the books on the bed, I plucked my cloak from its hook by the door. The days were getting colder, and the night wind was starting to bite. Winter would be here soon enough. Here in Upstate New York, winters were dark, long, and damned cold. The sun would disappear for so long it would be a surprise to find it shining at all until March, at least.

That, of course, made it the perfect time for vampires to come out and play.

Swinging the heavy fabric over my shoulders, I clasped the front of it, somehow feeling more comfortable with its familiar weight spread across my shoulders. Once I managed to tuck it around the arm done up in the sling, I walked right back out the door, onto today's next mission.

The campus was pretty quiet at this time of night; instructors were heading home, trainees were heading to dinner, and only a few stragglers remained roaming the sidewalks.

According to Kelly, Malachi hadn't seemed too inclined to join them for dinner lately. There was a good chance I'd find him in his room.

I walked into the training dorms and was met with a humdrum of activity that was the polar opposite of what was happening outside. Friday nights were pretty lively in the trainee dorms, I remembered with a smile. Trainees stopped when they saw me, but, whether it was from me being their instructor or my previous reputation, I couldn't tell. It probably didn't help that the cloak I was wearing made me look a tad more imposing than I usually did.

Regardless, they parted like the Red Sea when they found themselves in my path of travel. Conversations would stop for a breathless moment, and then continue with the sound of my name drifting everywhere. This continued through the lobby, down the hall, and, finally, up the main staircase.

Luckily, Malachi's room was on the third floor; I didn't have to climb very far, and it wasn't long until I found myself in front of his door.

"Well," I whispered to myself as I reached up, "here goes nothing."

I knocked firmly on the wood of the door and waited. Enough time passed that I considered coming back later, thinking he might have gone to dinner with his pack after all, but, just as I took my first step back from the door, it slowly swung open, and I found myself smiling at the man of the hour.

He and his friends sat in the back during my class, and, due to his general lack of activity, I didn't find my attention falling on him much. Now that I was close up to him, I saw the sallowness of his cheeks and almost felt the gloomy aura that surrounded him. When his blank eyes met my gaze, I struggled to bring a smile to my face.

"Hello, Malachi," I greeted warmly.

"Maria." He nodded woodenly, though he did seem a little surprised to find me on his doorstep. "What brings you here?"

I leaned towards him and lowered my voice, as if sharing a secret. "A little birdy told me that you need a good talking to."

If he hadn't had a serious case of "Emotionless Robot Disorder," I imagine he would have sighed. "Kelly," he guessed easily enough.

"She's worried about you. All of your friends are." Taking one look at his gaunt cheekbones and pale face, I immediately felt guilty I hadn't noticed this sooner. "I'm starting to see why."

"There's no need to worry yourself." Even in his messed up state of mind, he was playing the tough guy card; one that I had seen too many times to be fooled by. "They're just overreacting to recent events."

"With good reason," I assured him, "it's no mean thing you've accomplished."

"And what's that?" He was a bit confused now.

Good, I had to try to get any emotion I could out of him. That seemed like a good first step.

"You survived an encounter with the boogeyman." Turning from his door, I took three steps down the hall before gesturing for him to follow me. "Come along, trainee, and I'll tell you all about the monster hiding in your closet."

It was a leap of faith; I was more surprised than I cared to admit to find him trailing just behind me.

If I thought the looks and attention were bad on the way up, it was nothing compared to how it was on the way back with Malachi in tow. People openly stared, and all activity stopped when we passed by. I was hoping to get a glimpse of Kelly or her pre-packmates, but they must have been at dinner.

We made it through the swarm of unwanted attention and out the building. It wasn't until we were free of little trainee ears that I attempted talking to him again.

"How are you liking your classes, trainee? Everything going well?"

Again, it was as if he were surprised by my attempt at small talk rather than interrogation.

"I'm doing well in all of my classes and have enjoyed the new material brought on by yours."

Well, I wasn't expecting that bit of flattery. In fact, when I looked at him, he seemed a bit sheepish he had admitted it himself.

I smiled conspiratorially. "Don't worry, Malachi; I won't expose your nerd status to all your little friends."

If anything, that only made him more embarrassed.

And, like many of the other guys I spent time with, he was more concerned with getting to the point of my conversation. "Aren't you going to ask me questions about him?"

His direct question was one I couldn't help but scowl at. "I know why you must think that. I can't even imagine how many people have interrogated the hell out of you about this – about him – especially after all the shit he's been pulling lately, but I'm more than aware that that's not going to accomplish anything."

"What makes you so sure of that?"

I couldn't help but smile. He obviously didn't understand what I was trying to do, even if he put on a shrewd façade. My little brother, Seamus, used to do the same thing. Being the big, strong brother, he couldn't have his sister outwitting him – even if I was older than him.

Where had that come from? I thought disconcertedly. I hadn't really thought of him in–

But I stopped the lie before I could even think it. I did think of him. I thought of Seamus a lot, but it had been awhile since someone had reminded me completely–

"Maria?"

I found myself snapping back to attention. Goddamnit, I couldn't have this kid think I was ignoring him. Save the angsty thought arguments later, Ria.

"Sorry, I have a nasty habit of getting lost in my own thoughts. What was I–"

"Nikolai. You aren't going to ask me about him?"

Ah, yes, that.

"No, not really. I'm sure everyone else has thoroughly beaten the subject to death. If you had any more to say about him, I'm sure you would have said it by now."

"So, what are you…"

"Doing here? Moral support. Not including the pack taken down last night, you and I are two of the only people who have survived meeting Nikolai one-on-one. Congrats."

He smirked just the slightest bit, his lips barely moved a fraction of an inch, but I saw it, and my heart recognized the expression again. What was it about this boy that reminded me so much of my little brother?

"I didn't realize that was something worth congratulating."

"Oh, believe me, it is. I might have even brought balloons, but this was a little last minute."

We continued walking in the dark, meandering slowly down the road next to the trainee living quarters and down the beaten path attached to it.

"In any case, I'm sure you know just as well as I do at this point that Nikolai doesn't just leave your head when he's out of sight. He kind of just…lingers. It's the creepiest thing, and it's totally unsettling."

He tilted his head to look down at me, curiosity alight in his eyes. "You think so too? But you seem so unafraid of him?"

The snort of laughter that came out of me was completely unintentional, and it confused the hell out of him. "There's a big difference between being afraid of someone and being afraid of what someone is capable of, what they'll do." I stopped walking for a moment and looked him dead in the eye. "I am not afraid of Nikolai. I never have been, and I most certainly never will be. What he is, is a bully with a brain. He's too damn smart for his own good, and he knows how other people's minds work like the back of his hand. That's really what you have to watch out for."

Pausing for a moment, I walked down the remainder of the path until we found ourselves at my spot, the place where I usually found myself when I resembled Malachi even the slightest bit.

As he took a moment to appreciate the view, I suddenly found myself remembering the conversation I had just had with Alessandra in the library.

"Don't let him do this to you, Ria."

"Do what?"

"Don't let Nikolai change you. That's what people like him do. They isolate you; they turn you into your own worst enemy…"

Laying a hand on Malachi's arm, I waited until he turned to face me to say, "Nikolai likes to run rampant through your brain until you're afraid of your own shadow. It seems like one of those battles you have to face on your own, but you don't. As cheesy as it sounds, all of your friends are right there behind you, just waiting to lend a helping hand."

He had that sheepish look on his face again. "Yeah, I think you're right," he whispered.

I smacked his shoulder. "Of course I'm right, you little brat. Once they promote you to an instructor, you can never be wrong."

For the first time since I'd met him, a true smile stretched across Malachi's face, a bit hesitant, a bit unsure, but it was there nonetheless. At that moment, recognition slammed so strongly into me that I found it hard to breathe for a moment. I caught his look of surprise just before I turned away from him to face the horizon.

"Maria, are you all right," he asked almost worriedly.

I took a deep breath and shook memory away from reality. "Just fine, trainee."

"You know," he started hesitantly, "you keep getting this look on your face. Like you're looking at me and seeing someone else."

I turned to face him, marveling at how astute his observation was. "You're right. You remind me a lot someone, someone who was very dear to me."

He seemed immediately repentant. "Someone who died?"

"No, no," I corrected, "just someone I haven't seen for a very long time. You act a lot like he did. He'd be just about your age by now, too."

"Who was it," he asked curiously.

I felt my face shut down immediately, the reaction I always had when people asked me about my past, my human life. My lack of forthcoming facts usually turned people off the conversation right away. He just seemed taken aback by my sudden change in countenance, and I cursed my momentary lapse in warmth. I was here to try and help him, damn it.

"I'm sorry," he almost frantically backtracked, "I didn't mean to–"

"No, it's not your fault," I assured him, schooling my expression back to one of kindness. "I just try to be careful, you know?"

He nodded. "I don't know why I even asked, you don't have to feel pressured to tell me, Maria." He turned back to look towards the trainee dorms. "I should head back soon, I still have some work I want to get done tonight."

Shit, one little thoughtless reaction and I successfully managed to scare him off, even when he had been doing so well.

He turned back to face me, but didn't meet my eye. "Thank you for taking the time to talk to me. I appreciate it."

There was a silent war taking place in my head. Torn between the need to protect my family and the need to comfort a young mind who had glimpsed the horror that was Nikolai, I struggled to form a complete sentence as he was spinning around to return to his hidey hole.

He's just a trainee, Maria. He takes your class. He's been scarred by Nikolai. Don't make him feel like he's done something wrong; that's the last thing he needs.

So, closing my eyes as tightly as I could, I admitted a secret I had only revealed to my packmates. "My brother," I blurted out. When I finally found the courage to open up my eyes again, I saw him looking back at me with shock on his face and more emotion than he had shown thus far combined. "You remind me of my little brother."

"You have a family?"

"Had," I corrected firmly. "I had a family, a human one."

I'd confused him again. "But you just said he wasn't dead."

My smile was sad. "I don't get to call them my family anymore, not if I left them behind."

Still hesitant from my initial reaction, he paused before continuing. "What was your brother like," he asked carefully, obviously not sure if I would shut down again.

"He was the golden child," I told him honestly, "perfect at anything he did, and a real pain in my ass." My eyes were wetter than they should have been. "I love him very much, even now."

There was an almost sympathetic look in his eyes. "Thank you for telling me."

"Don't sweat it, kid. You caught me on a sensitive day, but I trust that that little tidbit is gonna stay between you and me, hmm?" He nodded quickly. "Good. Run back to your trainees, Malachi, and get your essay done."

There was definitely a little bit more life in him as he waved goodbye and walked back home.

That was better than could be said for me.

I felt like I was trapped in an endless stream of my own thoughts as I made my way back to my room.

Would Malachi return to normal after our talk?

Would I regret spilling the beans about my family?

Would he tell anyone about my brother?

How was my brother doing?

I made it all the way up through the campus, into the building and to the entrance of my room without interacting the slightest bit with another person, barely having the presence of mind to open my door once I got to it.

I only came back to myself when I was greeted with the sight of Daimon sitting cross legged on the bed, his hair still wet from his shower, one of the ancient books I had left behind in his lap. Like me, he had a pen and paper beside him, and I saw half of a page already filled with notes (It wasn't like we could pull out a highlighter with these books anyway).

Shutting the door, I leaned my back against it and watched him for a moment, not wanting to disrupt his focus. He hated it when he had to stop reading in the middle of a page, anyway.

Sure enough, when he finished the page he was on, he set the book aside and looked up at me, only to be taken aback at my appearance.

"Maria? What's wrong?"

I laughed softly. "So much for those lessons in hiding emotions."

"That's the kicker, though," he pointed out as he unfolded his long legs and got off of the bed, "now when you're upset, you put on a blank face."

"Better than a sad one," I tried to say it lightly, but it came out sounding tragic.

He was standing in front of me now. His hand came to rest on my good shoulder for a moment before slowly running down my arm, all the way to the tips of my fingers. He wound his own around them, and rubbed his thumb against the back of my hand.

"Not while I'm here," was his quiet avowal. "Don't hide from me, Maria."

The longer I stood in front of him, the more I felt that mask I'd learned to wear slip away. "I don't think I ever really could, even if I wanted to."

He smiled softly at that. "I won't pretend that doesn't make me happy. Now, what has upset you so?"

I almost wished I could hide from him, especially as I opened my mouth to talk, only to feel my lip tremble slightly. Biting my lower lip, I took a deep breath, knowing it was fruitless trying to speak again, and simply threw myself into his arms.

There were things we needed to get straight between us, misunderstandings, dishonesties, and whatnot. He had lied to me, he had spoken about me as if I were no better than a game piece in front of Nikolai. I was positive he was trying to keep me in the dark as possible. He had a nasty temper when I did (in some people's opinions) stupid things, he took up more than half the bed…

But right here, right now, this was the man I loved; the only one who could possibly understand the demons that plagued me and the faces that haunted my dreams. I was sure as hell not going to let him push me around, but I could take care of that later.

"I miss them," I mumbled into his shoulder.

"Ah, I should have guessed as much."

I looked up at him with teary eyes. "But I never talk about them."

"No, but you keep that picture under your pillow. You pull it out sometimes just before you go to sleep. I've seen you." He brought his hands up to my face. "You may never speak of them, but you've kept them in your heart and in your thoughts," he stopped for a moment, brushing my cheek with his fingertips, in a comforting matter, "just as you've remained in theirs."

"Really," I breathed, amazed, "but how would you–"

"I used to visit them regularly," he said easily, "just to check on them. They're all doing just fine, and they talked about you all the time."

Holding the collar of his shirt tightly in my hand, I couldn't look him in the eye as I asked him something I hadn't questioned in a very long time. "Did I make the right choice, Daimon? Am I terrible for leaving them behind?"

Daimon just wrapped his arms around me, holding me tightly to him. He stroked my hair softly and rocked me back and forth. I wasn't breaking down like I had with Kate's parents. This was a slow burn, an ache that had been a part of me ever since I walked out my front door.

"You did what you needed most," he murmured into my hair. "This is the path you were supposed to take. I'm sure of it. You were meant to be here, and I'm sure they would be very proud of the woman you've become. They were always so proud of you."

"But I *miss* them," I protested, my voice barely a whisper.

"That's not a crime," he reasoned. "It's just the price."

He held me for a long time, and we didn't say anything more to one another. Everything else could wait for now. As dejected as I was, I wished I could take that moment and stay forever because I knew they were going to be few and far between in the near future.

We stayed like that until I could barely keep my eyes open. When he felt me lean against him with more fatigue than sadness, he scooped me up in his arms and carried me to the bed, where he held me still, keeping me safe from the sadness and loneliness that he had seen consume me once already.

If I wasn't careful, I might have asked him to never let me go.

Chapter Eleven

I slept in the next day, the well-deserved reward on my first day off. It wasn't until the early afternoon that I finally decided to leave the room and take my books down to the library again. I left the still-sleeping Daimon a note and gathered my materials, including the notes that he had taken, loading them in my bag before walking out the door.

Knowing I would be mocked for having coffee this late in the day, I stopped by the cafeteria and picked out a nice tea instead. I kept my hands firmly wrapped around it as I walked outside, and almost debated going back for my cloak. It was cold, even colder than it should have been this time in the season, but I hustled to the heated library and shook off the chill there.

I usually sat at the same table every day to do my research. By now, people knew not to sit there unless they were with me, but, when I turned the corner, I saw it was already occupied.

"She lives!" Vincent cried, only to be immediately reprimanded by the librarian.

"We were just debating whether or not we were brave enough to try and wake you up," Cindy laughed.

"I can tell you right now that wouldn't have ended well," I told her, taking the seat across from her. "Especially if you had sent him." I pointed a finger at Vincent, who did his very best to look affronted.

I nodded "good morning" to Carter who spared me just a glance from his text. My eye traveled farther down the table to find someone I didn't expect to see with my misfits.

"I see you guys have made a new friend."

Alessandra winked at me as Vince stretched an arm over her shoulder. "Yeah, you know us. You make friends with one of the human-born; you make friends with all of them."

"Good enough for me," I laughed as I pulled out the book I hadn't finished reading yesterday. "I'm guessing you're all here to help?"

"We're not on the schedule for rounds today. So, we might as well," Austin spoke, not looking up from the text he was sharing with Cindy, who I noticed was sitting *very* close to him, closer than usual. Hmm....

Commence fangirling.

Cindy, though, had her full attention on me, and watched as my eyes shifted back and forth between the two. When I raised an eyebrow at her, her cheeks immediately turned pink, and I fought the urge to actually giggle. So, there *was* something there.

"Well, the more the merrier," I said happily, as I pulled out Daimon's notes and began perusing them. They were neat, orderly, and well thought out, the notes of someone who was used to doing extensive research and piecing together facts. Considering who his Maker was, it was no wonder he was good at this sort of thing.

The day was an easy one compared to the hellish week I had just endured. I fell into my well-oiled research rhythm with no trouble at all. Every once in a while, I would have a break in the form of trainees who came to the library to do research for their assignment and found me instead.

I opened up my own table for questions, one that Alessandra eventually joined in on. They were hesitant to approach her at first, but her laid-back attitude and obvious expertise attracted a small crowd of curious minds.

I had been worried about her coming to the campus to help us. It wasn't that she bothered me. I loved the woman, and her experience and knowledge made her an irreplaceable asset on our little team, but, though we shared a similar history, she had been a social pariah in this community for almost ten years, her name completely besmirched by the Council.

Whereas my indiscretions were justified to the public right away, people had spent years thinking Alessandra was a traitor, and that kind of judgment didn't just fade away overnight.

Watching the trainees eagerly vie for her attention, I felt a part of me breathe a sigh of relief.

"You seem quite pleased with yourself, Maria."

"Indeed she does. Is this your work, young wolf?"

Startled, I spun around to find two vampires standing right behind me, Daimon with an easy-going smile, and His Royal Scariness stoic, yet somehow mildly amused at the same time.

Walking up to Daimon, the much less scary vampire, I smacked his shoulder. "You know I hate it when you sneak up on me."

He snagged the hand that I had hit him with and brushed it with his lips, every inch the gentleman. "I'm sorry, my love, but sometimes you just make it too easy."

I debated hitting him again, but I didn't want the vampire Elder to think I was ignoring him. So, I settled for sending him a scowl before turning to face his companion. "Good evening, Maximilian."

He nodded in greeting. "Good evening, Maria. Have you foisted your students off on my mate?"

My smile returned instantly. "They foisted themselves. This is practically a once in a lifetime opportunity in their eyes. I don't think they're going to waste a second of it."

Daimon's smirk widened a spec. "How does it feel to be demoted to the second most famous human-born on campus, Maria?"

"Refreshing," I replied, which immediately earned me his laughter.

It was then that the trainees seemed to notice there were newcomers, and, when they caught sight of Daimon and Maximilian, they looked about two seconds away from peeing their pants. This was probably the closest they'd ever come to vampires as powerful as these two.

"Is that–" one started to say, but when their attention turned to him, his eyes widened and he seemed to swallow the rest of his own sentence.

"Don't worry, children," Alessandra told them, pulling her feet from where they'd been resting on top of the table and standing up. "These two are tame." She took a look at their skeptical faces and amended, "Well, mostly tame."

"Do not spread falsehoods, Alessandra," Maximilian warned. I'm pretty sure a few of the trainees just wet themselves at the sound of his voice. "It will do them no good."

Suddenly, I heard Vincent's voice rise up from the table. "Is anyone contemplating how trippy seeing this is?"

When the rest of the table nodded robotically, I turned to Alessandra, but she looked just as confused as I was. We simultaneously looked to our vampire counterparts to see if they, too, were stumped, but the knowing looks they were sending us said it all.

Daimon craned his head towards Maximilian. "As ever, they seem unaware of their own renown."

Even Maximilian nodded and said, "It is remarkable, really."

"What," Alessandra pressed, "the hell are you talking about?"

"I believe I can be of service here," Vince enthused as he sprung up from his seat and dashed towards us. Facing the trainees, he began his lecture. "Look here, kiddies, this isn't something you get to see every day, even if you're as experienced and worldly as I am." Gesturing widely to Alessandra, he continued, "This is the ever-famous Alessandra, who, at the time of her training was the first human-born in almost a century to complete all three Trials. Behind her, looming rather forebodingly, we see the vampire Elder who revealed the truth of her past to her, leading her to break away from the Council and allowing them to unjustly brand her as a traitor."

Sliding over to Daimon and I, he spread out his arms in front of me. "Fast forward ten-ish years and we have another human-born join the party. Changed illegally by her best friend, Maria faces the prejudice of werewolves and the general bad opinion of humans they have. She, however, kicks everyone's judgmental asses to the curb and comes out on top, second in our trainee class, which I am definitely still bitter about. When the Council Head tried to force her to become a part of their conspiracy, she laughed in his wrinkly face and, with the help of some super strong and brilliant werewolves and the rest of this ragtag group here, overturned the power-hungry bitches and saved the day."

Vincent seemed quite proud of himself, and the trainees looked as if they'd been brainwashed with a little case of hero worship.

Turning to face the rest of the "ragtag group," I remarked, "I've never heard it put quite that...poetically before?"

"He does have a way with words, that one," Alessandra laughed.

Vincent's mouth dropped open. "You still don't get it; you really don't get it. You guys are like living legends, and you still manage to shrug it off."

True enough. Alessandra and I looked at one another and shrugged as eloquently as we could.

Daimon chuckled behind me, and I felt his hand come to rest on my shoulder. "I don't think even your powers of speech are capable of making them see such, Vincent."

"My breath was simply wasted," he bemoaned, making his way back to his seat.

"So, why have you decided to grace us with your presence this evening," Alessandra asked her vampire.

"We heard you could use assistance in researching," he answered, composedly as always. "I'm sure you will find it much easier with the help of two people who were alive when these books were written."

I watched as everyone took a moment to examine the aged tome closest to them, and then look up to marvel at the vampires, who were suddenly even more impressive in their eyes.

"That would certainly help," Alessandra noted. "All right, you and I get this one."

She returned to her spot at the table and he followed her like a shadow. I felt more than saw Daimon start heading in that general direction, but quickly diverted him. "My table is over here. I was going through that book."

He didn't question my sudden instruction, thank God. As he sat down in front of the book I had been going through, I stole a look at Cindy out of the corner of my eye. Her eyes were peeled on Daimon, though, who would have had to sit in front of her, had he gone to the same table as the others. The last thing I wanted was for the dam on her self-control to burst, or to cause her any more pain.

She eventually noticed me looking at her, of course. It was then that she sent me a small, grateful smile that nearly made my heart break.

"Maria," Daimon called, wondering why I was still standing in place.

"I'm coming."

The rest of the evening was blissfully uneventful, which was more than I could have asked for. Even with Cindy and Daimon in the same general area for the first time in a long time, we got a lot of work done with no damage done to the surrounding area.

Well, unless you count the patience of the poor librarian who was on duty. I think we very nearly drove her up the wall with our constant chatter and, well...Vincent.

We adjourned to dinner together, vampires and Alessandra included, and had a grand ole time, chatting, joking, and relieving some of the tension that the past few days had brought upon us.

Yup, it was more than I could have asked for, a picture perfect evening.

Too bad it didn't last very long.

CHAPTER TWELVE

That night, I dreamed about Kate again.

It wasn't like the dream I had during my hospital stay, the one where I'd seen Kate sitting in the chair next to me. No, this was a memory.

It just wasn't how I remembered it.

I was back in the field where I had found the fallen pack and taken watch over them before Nikolai appeared. However, this time I was seeing it from the other side, from where Nikolai and Kate had been standing.

I saw my own face in this dream, horrified and awestruck. Nikolai was speaking behind me, the same words that I had heard him say days ago.

I knew what was coming. How could I not? I dreaded seeing this happen again, but, suddenly, the dream went from bad to worse.

Nikolai's voice was soft in my ear. "Kari, help your dearest friend understand."

No, *it was Kate's voice I heard now, though it wasn't spoken out loud.* I can't.

Kill the wolf. *His voice was the same as it always was, but its affect was astounding. I felt the sheer weight of the command grip all of the muscles in my body. I felt myself move forward to do just what he said.*

Please, not him.

Do it, *he repeated, patient and unrepentant.*

There was no ignoring him. Quick as lightning, I darted towards the fallen body of the wolf I now knew to be Camden. Rowan, Ria, someone help me.

Little did I realize I had actually answered her request.

The Ria across from me threw herself in front of my attack, just as I knew she would. A sick feeling settled in my stomach when I actually felt the claws attached to my hands cut through my own skin. Ria was thrown aside; I heard her cry out.

Horrified, I looked down at my hands, at my claws.

They were covered in blood. Ria's blood.

No, no, no, no! Ria, I didn't mean to!

Well done, you've marked your best friend, your own progeny. I wonder, *that terrible, horrible voice spoke again,* **would you kill her if I asked it of you?**

That was when my eyes shot open. Throwing myself upright in the bed, I held my hand over my mouth to smother the scream that lingered just behind my lips. The marks at my shoulder felt as though they were aflame, and, if I wasn't mistaken, my whole body was shaking.

When my eyes focused on something, it was silver, and I thought I was dreaming again.

Then, the silver blinked.

In the farthest corner of the room, hidden in shadows, all I could see was the bright silver of her irises; I watched as they disappeared momentarily every time she blinked.

I couldn't believe what I was seeing. Shock immobilized and muted me for countless moments, enough time for her to step out just far enough for me to see her outline in the gray light of the coming dawn. I opened my mouth to say something, anything, but she held a finger up to her lips. Striding across the room, she stood in front of one of our giant windows, which I hadn't even noticed was opened, and nodded her head in a "follow me" gesture.

Then she jumped.

A strangled cry broke free of my lips as I rushed to the window and hung out of it precariously to look down. Where I expected to see a pancake, Kate stood watching me make a fuss. Then, calmly as you please, she turned and began walking towards the outskirts of the campus.

I don't know how long I stood gawking, but Daimon's husky voice made me jump.

"What is it?"

"Nightmare," I answered quickly, "I woke up and noticed we left the shade open."

"Trying to fry me in my sleep?"

As I ran around the room looking for something to wear, I saw Daimon prop himself up on an elbow and rub his eyes. I must have woken him from a pretty deep sleep.

As I sat back on the bed to tie my boots, I felt his lips by my neck and his hands on my shoulders. "Just where do you think you are going? You have hours until you need to be anywhere and it's frosty outside. Come back to bed."

Sorry, honey, I just had a little nightmare about seeing through my dead best friend's eyes as she viciously attacked me. Then, she showed up in our room and told me to follow her, so that's just what I'm gonna do.

Turning around, I laid a soft kiss on Daimon's lips and smoothed his hair back into place. "Go back to sleep. I just need a short walk to clear my thoughts."

He hummed softly and lay back down on the bed. I continued to stroke his hair and whispered the only sleep spell I knew as I laid soft kisses on his head.

"I'm sorry," I breathed into his ear. "I'll be back soon."

Rising from the bed, I buckled up my sling and threw my cloak over my shoulders, making my way out of the room and through the building as quickly and quietly as I could.

He was right, the frost had taken over the landscape outside, and I immediately regret not putting on a good pair of jeans. My little pajama shorts were not having this weather, but that really didn't seem to be too high on my priority list right now.

Searching the tree line, I was halfway to believing she had been another dream when I caught sight of a fluttering cloak. Running towards her, I followed the tracks I could now see in the frost until they stopped just where the forest butted up against the campus.

She was there waiting for me, the emotionless mask I had seen her wear still on her face. She looked me up and down, but remained completely and utterly silent.

I couldn't bear the silent treatment for very long. "What are you doing here?"

She looked up into my eyes, then. The familiar sight of silver put an arrow right through my heart. They still weren't back to normal, the whites of her eyes were blackened the way they were when we took wolf-form, and she still had an air of unnaturalness around her that chilled me to the bone.

But that face, Kate's face, the face that I thought I'd never see again. How could I just turn around and go back to bed when she was here in front of me?

She didn't answer my question, but rather began walking away deeper into the forest, as if expecting I would follow, but, despite how glad I was to see her, I wasn't an idiot, and I was by no means naïve. Nikolai had resurrected her; Nikolai's command was the reason my arm was trussed up like a Christmas present. She was going to have to give me some sign that it was safe to follow.

Eventually, she noticed I wasn't trailing behind her, and she slowed to a stop before turning to look at me. This time, though, her face was different. It wasn't the blank mask she had had on earlier. There was a spark in her eyes; there was feeling in her expression, something I had felt her incapable of in my dream.

"Please, Ria," she beseeched. "Come with me."

That was a call I simply could not ignore. I was bound by the rules of best friendom to listen to her.

So, with a single nod, I jogged until I was next to her and fell into step with her renewed walking.

She led me through the woods for a long while, and, after some time, I saw places that were familiar. Was she lost? Or were we just going around in circles?

Eventually, though, we came to a house that I had never seen before in my life. It was an old monstrosity that looked halfway between "in need of renovation" and falling in on itself.

Not deterred by the state of the structure, Kate marched right up the front steps and held the front door open for me. Pausing for a moment of uncertainty, I looked Kate in the eye and held her gaze as I stepped into the house.

It was dark inside. Not a single lamp was lit, and the dark clouds outside prevented any natural light from reaching the place. Channeling my magic into my eyes, I sharpened my sight to see in the dark and instantly regret it.

Seated in every chair, standing along the walls, and blocking all possible escape routes, stood vampires upon vampires. When a single lamp flickered to life, I saw the boogeyman himself emerge from the shadows and take his place on a large, raised chair that reminded me of the Council Head's place of honor.

"At last," Nikolai greeted, "welcome to my humble court, Maria. I'm so pleased you could make it."

"I must have missed the engraved invitation. Maybe it got lost in the mail." As I spoke, I subtly glanced around, taking note of my situation and looking for an emergency exit.

All I managed to glean was that I was in some pretty deep shit.

"A pity. Here," he purred gesturing to the seat next to him, "please come sit. There's a place right here next to me."

Conveniently enough, it was the only free seat in the room. It might as well have had my name embroidered on the cushions.

"What am I, your new court jester? Sorry to disappoint, but I can't even juggle."

He laughed. "Not quite. You, my dear, are going to be my left hand."

My eyes narrowed. My trainee years had made me a student of history, myths, and legends. I knew my symbolism well.

"Destruction's not really my thing, Nikolai. You might find it easier to rent a bulldozer than put me on a leash." I took a step back, easing towards the door. "Have one of your new friends look it up. In the meantime, you've interrupted my beauty sleep, so–"

But one more step had the vampires at the door hissing like cats. So much for the easy exit.

Nikolai simply tilted his head and sent me a sunny smile. "My dear, if you were any more beautiful, I wouldn't be the only vampire vying for your attention."

"Oh, save it for somebody who gives a crap, Nikolai," I warned him. "I am not in the mood for your bullshit tonight."

My biting tone did nothing to tame him, though. While more his cronies began snarling at me, his gleeful laugh echoed around the room. "Temper, temper, Maria. Do you always let your feelings lead you around?"

"Only on special occasions," I spat. I was so tired of seeing his stupid smirk centered on me, and, unfortunately, he'd found me on a night where I was mad enough to do something about it.

"Indeed, it seems you have found yourself caught in my web by those same feelings, little butterfly. Yet again, you come to me by your own choice."

"And just like all the other times, I'll find myself walking free."

"Hmm," his smirk sharpened until it the look of a predator took over his face. "You'll find this time to be quite different."

That was when I heard the door slam shut behind me, and all the vampires locked the windows and stood guard in front of them. Nikolai had me trapped.

Well, he thinks he does, I thought, *I might as well get some info out of him while I'm here, and then I can just do what I do best and beat feet it out of here.*

"So, what, you use Kate to lure me out here so you can compliment me to death and offer me a really comfy chair? Doesn't seem like a very relevant plan there, Nikolai, especially when I've been known to cause some damage breaking free of your traps."

"You seem very confident for a woman trapped," he drawled. "I doubt even your Prince Charming will be able to get you out of this little snare."

I felt a grimace cross my face. I was no fairytale princess who needed to be saved. "I don't need his help when it comes to you."

"Is that so? That's certainly interesting, I thought you totally enamored by his web of lies. Has he not told you all kinds of terrible things about me?"

"Is this the part where you're going to deny all of them?" *Keep the man talking, Ria. You need as much information as you can get out of him.* "Like killing your own Maker, perhaps? Or maybe you just don't want to give your new buddies any ideas. It's certainly tempting."

I took note of how a few of the vampires surrounding me closed in on Nikolai, protecting him from any less-than-pleasant ideas I had.

"Children, children, there's no need for that," he chided them lightly. "Our dear Maria is still lost and confused. Remember, a devil in disguise whispers in her ear."

"You're certainly calling the kettle black, Nikolai. You happen to be the devil I know."

"I have no reservations about hiding my true nature from you, love. It's my brother who wears a mask; it's my brother who shields his actions with lies."

Info time. "Like what," I asked innocently enough.

His pleased expression warned me to tread carefully, though. I had to be skeptical of everything that came out of his mouth. "It's true. I did kill my Maker. I broke the greatest rule of all vampire kind for one simple purpose, to free Daimon from the control he was under. The poor boy didn't even realize it."

I can smell the bullshit from here, I thought cynically. "It's all a matter of perspective."

"Perhaps, but his retaliation was certainly clear enough."

I felt my jaw lock down hard in order to keep my curiosity from showing on my face. "Oh really?"

I've only seen Nikolai look angry or serious on a handful of occasions, so seeing the mirth wiped clean from his face always made me freeze in preparation. A gleeful Nikolai I could sometimes follow, a serious one was totally unpredictable.

"We all have one great love in our lifetimes, Maria, even 'monsters' like me."

"Make your point," I snapped, getting impatient.

He looked down at me, his eyes thoroughly examining my face. "Her name was Iskra, and she was a vampire I met shortly after I was Turned, during my time with my Maker. She helped me escape after I killed him, and Daimon took out his anger on her." Nikolai slowly stood from his chair until he seemed to loom over me. "He cut her down in cold blood in return for my service. I set him free, and he murdered the love of my life."

I let some of the surprise that was simply bursting from inside of me show. I had to let Nikolai think he was getting me somewhere if I wanted him to keep talking. Maybe if I stalled long enough, I could get some reinforcements to come bust me out, but that wasn't a plan I could rely on.

Nikolai's humor was slowly coming back. I could hear it growing in his voice as he said, "You see, Maria, I need you for my plans, I always have. It's the reason I have you now, but what happens when one brother has a shiny toy and the other is empty-handed? It is the way brothers are. Daimon's only reason for loving you is to keep you away from me."

As much as I told myself that it was a lie to keep me here, the accusation poked at old wounds. It had been my deepest insecurity in my relationship with Daimon, when I was human, at least: *why does he love me?*

But I saw what Nikolai was doing, which made me think back to my conversation with Malachi. I couldn't let Nikolai get into my head.

"So, that's what you need me for," I guessed, "to finally get your revenge against Daimon for killing your woman all those years ago?"

"You're thinking too small, love, far too small. If I had wanted you dead, you would have been dead after your Trial match."

Shit. He had a point.

Didn't this guy read his diabolical villain handbook? This is the part where he's supposed to tell me his plan in great detail and I creatively kick butt and escape.

"I see you are well and truly stumped. Well, don't you worry; you'll have plenty of time here to do your best to figure it all out."

Something changed in the air the instant the words left his mouth. The vampires who weren't stationed in front of a window steadily began to close in around me. Letting my eyes travel around the group, I took note of the look in their eyes and the manner of their approach, instantly identifying them as newbies.

Piece of cake.

Continuing to stare them down, I let a smirk spread slowly across my face as I reached up to unbuckle the sling that held up my arm. I forced myself not to show any pain on my face as I let it fall to the ground and kicked it aside.

Switching my gaze to Nikolai, I let my magic out completely, savoring the feel of claws on my hands and fangs protruding from between my lips as my eyes were turned as black as Kate's.

Between one second and the next, I let myself loose on them.

It was second nature going from one vampire to the next and systematically taking them down, as easy as breathing, even injured as I was. Ducking, punching, twisting, clawing; I never even had to switch forms before there were seven bodies on the floor, and I was all out of opponents. I did a quick check all the way around me to make sure no one was attempting a sneak attack before returning my gaze to Nikolai, challenging him with just one look.

His eyes seemed to be alight from within, and he now sat on the edge of his chair watching me. "Extraordinary, I forgot what it was like to see you in a real fight. How utterly breathtaking."

"Oh yeah?" I dared, "Why don't you come down and get a little taste, then?"

Three seconds later, I came to the realization that that was probably the worst thing I could have said if I had plans to leave tonight.

Leisurely, he stood up, and I had the vague image of a coiled snake, no, a crouched panther, calm and collected, poised to strike.

"I thought you'd never ask," he purred, and then he pounced.

I had almost forgotten what it was like to fight with Nikolai, like *really* fight him. He was faster, stronger, and more cunning than the average vampire, and that made for quite the frightening package. It was all I could do to fight him off and not get cornered into a group of his minions.

In a movement that was faster than I could track, he had his hand on my throat, and suddenly my back was firmly planted on the floor. "You know," he mused, leaning over me. "I never did tell dear Daimon about our last scuffle. Do you think he'll mind I've had a taste of you? He doesn't seem to share very well."

"Piss off, Nikolai," I spat in his face.

He bore down a little harder, and, suddenly I had to fight to breathe. "That's not very ladylike."

And just when I thought I was done for, there was a great crashing from the ceiling of the house. Pieces of roof fell to reveal five faces I was very, very glad to see.

"How about my foot up your ass," I heard Alessandra first and actually smirked. "Is that ladylike enough for you?"

"It's about time you clowns got here," I called up to them.

The persistent force at my throat increased until I was spluttering. "Quiet now, dear, and let the adults talk for a moment."

Uh oh, looks like someone wasn't happy we'd been found. Whoopsies.

"You are the other human-born," he guessed on the first try.

"And you are the scum of the earth, pleased to meet you. Now, if you would kindly let my friend up? She's turning purple and it's clashing terribly with her outfit."

Someday I would find that joke funny. Now? Not so much.

"Hmm." Nikolai didn't seem angry yet, more like mildly annoyed by this setback. "Kari," he called, "come play with your friend for a moment while I take out the trash."

And, with that, he let me go. I gasped for air and found myself heaving on my hands and knees as my friends dropped to the floor and began to mow down everything in their path.

I couldn't think about that, though, because, suddenly, there was a pair of boots stopped right in front of me, and I didn't need three guesses to figure out who it was.

Thinking fast, I held myself up with my arms and swung my legs around to knock hers out from under her. When she crashed to the floor, I put my knee to her back and twisted her arm harder than I had ever done when we were sparring together.

The sound of a window breaking took hold of my attention for a second too long as Kate twisted out from underneath me. She reached out and grasped my shoulder in a firm, unrelenting grip; I found myself crying out at the pressure she placed on my injury. As I attempted to make her let go, though, she got in a solid right hook to my face.

I forgot how good she was at those. I was going to have a fantastic bruise there tomorrow, and that pissed me off enough to return the favor with an added bonus.

When she reached for another punch, I deflected her and sent an elbow into her eye. While she stumbled, I held her shoulders and put my knee into her stomach and finished with a solid blow to the back of her neck.

As she collected herself on the ground, I heard someone call out to me, "Ria! Time to go!"

"Working on it," I yelled back just as Kate regained her footing. When she aimed a solid kick at my pelvis, I grabbed her leg in both of my hands and sent her flying to the opposite wall, but it was not nearly far enough. She had landed in a crouch, giving her the perfect opportunity to lunge and knock me flat on my butt.

As I struggled to right myself, her hand found its way to my shoulder once again. My struggles were immediately halted by a wave of burning pain at the small contact. When I looked, though, I saw she wasn't doing anything; she was literally just touching the skin of my shoulder.

So, why did it feel like she was taking a flamethrower to it?

Suddenly, her weight was propelled off of me, and I looked up to find Carter's face right above mine.

"Boy, am I glad to see you."

"I bet you are," he said, his voice strained. He reached down to my outstretched hands and pulled me to my feet. "We gotta go. We're never gonna finish off all of them."

"Strategic retreat it is." Looking towards the door I had come in through, I noticed a clear path through the fighting. "That way."

"Make the call," he told me as he bolted.

Using my magic to switch to my wolf vocal chords, I let loose the ear-splitting howl my friends would know to mean "retreat" and followed Carter to the door.

"*No!*" I didn't turn to see who had hollered, I didn't have to. By now, I knew not to pay attention to Nikolai when he used that tone of voice; I knew to book it.

The instant we were out the door, Carter and I Transformed and ran for the campus. Eventually, I heard the familiar sounds of my packmates running beside me, and, even without looking around, I could identify all of them.

I didn't have time to be relieved, though. We had to make it back to headquarters in one piece first. I had no doubt in my mind that Nikolai would chase us to the very last border. Luckily, we had Cindy to lead us home. Kate had led me around in circles for a reason; I had no idea where I was.

The instant the forest became familiar, and I saw the stone buildings of home, I could have cried with relief.

The very second the boundary line was crossed and we had the home team advantage, I Transformed back only to find I couldn't even stand up. I had never run so hard in my entire life. I heaved on the ground until a water bottle was forced under my face, and I drank the whole damn thing in one sitting.

When I could maneuver myself to a sitting position once more, I noticed my packmates were in the same boat I was. Vincent was the closest to me, sprawled out on his back on the grass beside me. I dribbled the last few drops of water on his face.

"You owe us," he rasped without opening his eyes. "You owe us for, like, forever."

"Don't I know it," I conceded without a fight. "How did you know?"

"Someone saw you leave campus," Austin seemed to be in a little better shape than the rest of us, which wasn't that surprising. He was doing his best to fan Cindy. "They came and found us immediately."

"We knew shit was going down when we couldn't wake up lover boy," Vince added. "As happy as I am you had such a great sleeping spell taught to you by the most skilled spell caster of all time, please find a better occasion to use it. I'm begging you. I can't feel my toes. Speaking of which, though, you might want to steer clear of vampboy for a little while. He was a wee bit put off when he woke up."

"A wee bit put off," I repeated.

"You also might notice a draft in your room. Don't blame any of us, he was the one who put his fist through the wall...well, more like arm. Regardless, there's now a 10x10 foot stretch of wall that needs to be replaced."

I cringed. Yup. Avoiding that conversation for a little while.

"Anyway, it was quick work from there getting Cindy to find you. We even had some volunteer service."

Alessandra cracked a smirk from her perch against the wall of a building. "I haven't had that much fun in *years*. I'm hopping on this bandwagon more often."

"We live to please," Cindy gasped.

"All right, missy," Vincent now had his eyes open and was glaring right at me, "you've got some explaining to do."

"Seriously, Ria, what was it this time," Cindy asked, seemingly exasperated. "Every time he puts up a welcome sign, you seem to be the first one in line."

"Kate, that's what happened." They all froze for a moment. "I don't know. I was dreaming about her, and suddenly I woke up and she was at my window. I was properly skeptical, I promise, but, guys, she talked to me. She looked normal again."

"We won't be fooled by that a second time," Carter swore. "We have to agree not to believe anything Kate says under any circumstances. It's too risky."

We all solemnly agreed.

"Just what did he want from you, Ria?" Austin asked breathlessly, "He seemed pretty bent on keeping you this time."

"He was," I told them. Thoroughly frustrated, I fell back against the grass and covered my eyes with my hands. "And I still have no idea why."

CHAPTER THIRTEEN

I could not even count how many times I had been forced to regale my night's events, or the number of reactions that involved me getting either unappreciated judgmental stares or being hit upside the head. By the time my sorry butt found its way to Grandmother, I was beyond ready to curl up in a ball in my bed and not emerge for days.

Seeing this, her hardened expression softened somewhat. She looked me up and down and, seeing slumped shoulders, bags under my eyes, and an overall bleak disposition, she decided to show a little mercy.

"I will have someone show you to your temporary room," she crisply informed me. "Get a few hours of rest so you can explain this to me at a reasonable time of the day."

I found myself nodding mutely, and turned to follow the poor wolf she had serving as her lackey this evening, but, suddenly, there was a hand on my shoulder holding me in place.

To my surprise, it was Vince; I had thought that he'd left with the others.

"First, Ria is going down to the infirmary. During the scuffles she's been involved in tonight, she somehow managed to lose both her sling and the security of her bandaging, and I am almost positive she's ruined my stitches."

Grandmother raised a single eyebrow. "And you needed my permission to treat your packmate?"

"Oh, no," his grip turned to steel, "I just needed to say it in front of you so there's no way she can brush off the medical attention she so obviously needs."

I rolled my eyes as Grandmother smirked. "I have to say, Vincent, there are days I underestimate your intelligence. Today was one of them, and you proved me wrong."

"Aw, shucks, Chief, does this make up for the one time I accidentally set your classroom on fire?"

Her dubious expression wasn't promising. "That is precisely the reason why I have no illusions about your intelligence, Vincent. Rewrap your packmate's wound. I shall speak to you tomorrow, little wolf."

Vincent never relinquished his grip, frog-marching me all the way to the infirmary, with Grandmother's poor lackey in tow. I didn't say anything the whole way there; it was enough that I wasn't arguing.

When we finally reached the hospital, Vince was quick to shoo away the nurses stationed there and sit me down in the nearest chair. I listened with half an ear as he ranted while gathering supplies.

"Honestly, Ria, you have to take better care of yourself. What would have happened if Nikolai had really managed to get his hands on you? What if he had seriously injured you when you tried to escape?" Suddenly, he was sitting in front of me, looking serious, which he almost never did. "Ria, can you please just promise me you won't go running off like that again?"

Vince knew how I felt about promises; he knew the weight behind the innocent request. At least, I hoped he did because then he could understand why I couldn't say yes.

"You know I can't promise that, Vince," I whispered, not sounding angry or reprimanding, just worn out.

He took it in stride, though, gathering his supplies and sighing deeply. "Fair enough, can you at least promise you'll knock on my door before you leave next time?"

That earned him a little laugh as I tilted my head, allowing him room to work on my neck. "What, you want to be read the riot act too," I asked.

"I don't know, might be more fun than just scolding you all the–"

He not only stopped talking, but I felt his fingers freeze on my shoulder. I craned my head just enough to see his face. He looked like all the air had been knocked right out of him.

"Vince, what is it? Am I growing another head?"

He didn't take the bait, though. He just stared at my shoulder, the disbelief on his face only growing.

"Vince, please, my blood pressure is through the roof as it is."

Inch by inch, as if he didn't want to take his eyes off of it, he turned to face me. Thankfully, it wasn't fear I saw in his gaze, but rather confusion and awe.

"Ria, it's healed."

I had barely registered the words before my hand shot to the skin of my shoulder. What had been inflamed and bleeding barely an hour ago was now whole, my skin was all in one piece. I felt the ridges of scars and peered down to see newly-healed pink skin. I ran my fingers along the four lines of claw marks, starting at the area just around my arm pit and ending under my jaw, just centimeters away from my face.

"Vince, did you do something new, a different spell," I tried, not knowing how to comprehend what was right in front of me, "or maybe one just needed a little time to kick in?"

He shook his head. "Nothing I tried could have done this. Ria, you were marked by your Maker, and only your Maker–" He swallowed his own words.

My mind instantly went back to the fight that had just taken place. Kate had said no words like incantations; she'd barely spoken at all.

Then, the memory of being held down surfaced. She had held her hand to my shoulder, right on top of the wound. The way it had burned was nowhere near normal. I tried to remember the injury hurting me after I managed to shimmy my way out of her grip, but couldn't.

My gaze met Vincent's, and I knew, with a single glance, that he understood what had happened without me putting it into words.

"Maybe she's not as lost as we originally thought," he whispered.

"My dream," I told him as quietly as I could, "before I left, I saw the fight I had with her – when she marked me – through her eyes. I heard her thoughts. She was fighting him. Maybe that was more than just a dream."

"Well, this is good, right? This means Kate can be saved somehow!"

But it didn't. There was not a drop of hope in my voice when I answered, "No, you didn't feel it like I did. In the dream, I felt the weight of Nikolai's command on her. There's no escaping magic like that. All this means, is that the Kate we know and love is trapped doing and seeing things that go against everything she is."

I spared a glance at Grandmother's assistant, but found him talking with a nurse, completely ignorant of our conversation. Leaning in towards Vince, I dropped my voice even lower, so as no one could possibly hear us.

"Nothing has changed, and the others will not find out about this. It'll only hurt them. I wish there was another way, but, goddammit Vince, I am not going to let her suffer like that." I reached out to hold his hand between mine; they were oddly cold. "If you see her, put her out of her misery, for her sake."

His face was set in stone, and I could see that my request went against every hope that he had built up for Kate. I knew the feeling; my hopes were quickly crumpling as well. I was worried for a minute he might refuse when I felt him grip my hands in return.

"It's our secret, then, but I stand behind you on this, Ria. We're not gonna let that monster rule her forever."

Seeing as I had no more wounds to heal and no desire to spend any unnecessary time in the hospital wing, I waved over the assistant and told him to lead me to my new room in triplicate. He was quick to obey, and, before long, I found myself trailing behind him, absently following his footsteps until a key was placed in my hand, and my new room stood before me.

With a gusty sigh, I walked through the door and turned to close it, resting my forehead against the frame and resisting the urge to beat my head repeatedly against it. After all the stupid shit I'd done tonight, I most certainly deserved it.

I don't know how long I stood facing the door, or how I could have missed his presence at first. The instant I stopped wallowing enough to take note of the surrounding world, I felt his rage and disappointment fill the room like a gathering storm.

I bit the inside of my cheek hard, knowing that, if I didn't, tears would slip out. Once I was composed enough to speak, I offered the explanation he was obviously looking for, but obviously didn't want to hear.

"Kate came. I had to go."

The storm broke, and I turned to face an irate, halfway to homicidal vampire.

"So, that's it," he seethed. "Kate makes one appearance and it's enough for you to forgo any scrap of common sense you have to follow her. Tell me, what did you think was going to happen? Did you think she had just magically broken free of Nikolai's control? Were you really foolish enough to believe that things would just get better because you wished them to?"

"I am *not* a fool," I whispered.

"Then what would you call it? Blind optimism?"

"Being. Human," I snapped, breaking through my mental exhaustion enough to feel the anger slowly rising to the surface in response to his accusations. "Am I not allowed to make mistakes anymore?"

His jaw was hard with an anger I had only seen once or twice before, and I knew, instinctively, that this was going to be one of those arguments I could never win, simply because his stubbornness would not allow it.

That didn't mean I was just going to give up and let him talk down to me. I recognized what I had done was stupid, and I loved him, sure, but I had promised myself a long time ago I would never let someone put me down without putting up a fight.

"No, it's about more than making mistakes," he responded. "It's about living in a dream world where you can magically fix everything. Well, you won't be able to fix anything if you just waltz into Nikolai's domain and let him capture you."

"Don't you *dare* talk to *me* about living in a dreamland," I hissed, "not when you sit here and feed me lies on a silver spoon." I saw understanding dawn in his eyes, and that only made my rage grow. It meant he was perfectly aware of his little white lies. "Did you think I would never find out? Or did you just prefer I stay in the dark for as long as possible?"

"Have you ever stopped to consider that Nikolai merely told you more lies to sow dissention between us," he casually asked.

"*Enough*," I yelled, finally at my breaking point, "I know you've been lying. I've given you time to make up for it. Stop trying to cover your own ass. I'm not an idiot, despite what you seem to think."

"So, what is it you seem to think you know all about?"

"Do you want the subjects alphabetically or in chronological order? Gee, I guess we could start with the fact that you and Nikolai showed up in Rochester just about the same time. That's certainly odd seeing as you told me you hadn't seen or heard from him in ages. That was a mystery I was left to solve alone this week, but in tonight's events I guess we have the whole Iskra thing. If you had at least *mentioned* her I could give you some credit, but I never even *heard* her name before tonight."

He looked taken aback for the first time since I started yelling at him, and still, *still*, he didn't back down. "She was an unimportant detail."

"Unimportant!" I couldn't help it; I shrieked. "All of a sudden, murdering someone is an unimportant detail? You must be out of your mind!"

"Were you there," he accused. "Did you ever meet Iskra yourself? She was the one who poisoned Nikolai until he became the vampire you see today! She was the one who convinced Nikolai to kill our Maker for her own selfish purposes! Tell me then, what kind of person you think she was, to have produced such evil?"

I couldn't even imagine what kind of person it would take to unleash Nikolai upon the world, but it wasn't her I thought of. There was someone else I *did* know, someone who had been murdered by those same hands. There was still pain in Cindy's eyes when she had to sit in the same room as her sister's accused killer.

"You're right, I didn't know her, but there have been others. All those other packs you massacred when you found me, all those families you tore apart looking for me." I was clenching my fists so tightly now I could feel blood under my nails. "Cindy is still bleeding from the wound you dealt to her. She was closer to her sister than anyone else on this earth, but that didn't stop you did it?"

His anger dissolved quickly into confusion. "What are you talking about? Who do you think I've killed now?"

"Don't you remember, Daimon, because I do. Clearly." I took a step towards him before realizing I didn't want to be on the same side of the room as him. "My pack was sent to hunt you down and execute you for the murder of wolves loyal to the Council. Packs of wolves you *demolished*, and one of those wolves was Cindy's sister."

Incredulity shone so strongly from him that I almost second-guessed myself. "Do I really strike you as a person who would needlessly murder dozens of wolves? I interrogated several packs trying to find you, yes, but I didn't go into a killing frenzy when they didn't tell me what I needed to know."

I shook my head; his words just seemed to bounce right off. "You know what? You have lied to me so much that I don't even know whether to believe you or not. I don't even know what you're capable of anymore."

"What I'm *capable* of? Is that what it's gotten to now? I am not a killing machine, Maria. I am a *vampire*. Did you never stop to consider that I had blood on my hands before today?"

"What, you think I've never had to take a life? Grow up. At least I can show an ounce of sympathy towards those lives that I've had to take." I sneered, "Does that disgust *you*? My humanity? That I don't have it in me to be a ruthless killer?"

His voice suddenly turned quiet, but I knew better than to think it meant his rage had cooled at all. "It was a human I fell in love with."

The words made me recall the last part of my conversation with Nikolai.

"What happens when one brother has a shiny toy and the other is empty-handed? It is the way brothers are. Daimon's only reason for loving you is to keep you away from me."

"Did you," I accused.

With widened eyes and a quiet gasp of surprise, he actually took a step towards me before he paused and demanded, "What did he tell you, Maria? *What did he say to you?*"

Was that it then, I thought, watching as his anger accumulated once more. Was this the big secret he really didn't want me to find out? Was this the final ruse?

"When did you end up meeting Nikolai in Rochester, Daimon? Before or after you met me?" I watched him freeze, shock-still. "Was our first meeting really in the park that day? Or did Nikolai's interest pull yours too?"

As the possibilities popped up in my head, the despair sank in deeper and sucked away what little hope I had left. I hadn't really allowed myself to think on it before, but now the pieces clicked together with frightening ease.

A bitter smirk pulled at my lips as I continued, "It must have been so simple to make a pathetic little human fall for you, easy as breathing, and I believed you so wholeheartedly. You had me wrapped around your finger in no time."

"What on earth are you talking about," he demanded furiously.

"You and Nikolai have had centuries to build up this little 'brother rivalry,'" I informed him plainly. "Was that your goal the instant you noticed him taking an interest in me? 'I'll ruin his little plans by getting her to fall in love with me.' Just like taking a new toy away."

Even in my distraught state, I saw Daimon move faster than a human eye could catch, and, by the time he took his place by the door where I had been standing, I had deftly avoided him.

When I saw him get ready to move again, I held out my hand and shook my head. "Do not. Come near me."

"That's it then," he snapped. "One night of lies, and Nikolai manages to turn you against me."

No. that wasn't even true. There was no way Nikolai could rip apart something I thought so strong in the span of a single evening. It shouldn't have been possible, but I knew that, and I knew the real reason why this had happened.

"No, you have been lying to me, repeatedly and continuously, for years, Daimon, *years*! I even gave you more than one chance to make up for it, to tell me the truth before something like this happened." A sad chuckle escaped my lips before I could stop it. "What am I doing," I wondered aloud, shaking my head. "I can yell at you about trust all day, but it's pretty damn clear you don't even trust me to begin with."

"Have you ever stopped to think, amidst all of these assumptions, that I lied to protect you? To keep you as safe from Nikolai as I could?"

"Knowing what I was facing would have kept me safe," I countered. "Knowing I had someone I could trust and count on would have kept me safe. This? Lying and keeping me in the dark? All you've done is blindfold me and tie my hands behind my back."

"You should have never gotten involved in all of this," he insisted fiercely. "You should have been kept out of it completely."

"Well, that's not your decision to make," I informed him bitterly. "I came back to you, but I sure as hell don't belong to you. I am not a child to be coddled and kept in the dark, and I refuse to be a piece on anyone's game board. Not the Council's, not Nikolai's, and most certainly not yours. I deserve better than that."

"Is that it then?" He asked disbelievingly, "Will you not even let me defend myself?"

I looked up at him, knowing somewhere in my mind that this was a memory of him I would never be able to shake, no matter how hard I tried. I had loved him for so long now, spent years of my life mooning over him like some lovesick ditz, and now I was facing the fact that this man may have never loved me back.

What does one do when their supposed soulmate doesn't feel the same way?

"I'm not even sure I would believe anything you had to say." Raising my chin, I looked him dead in the eye as I lifted my hand to my neck and told him, "In any case, I don't want to hear it. The first time you lost me, it was because of my rash decision. This time, it really was by your own folly."

That was when I ripped the silver locket from my neck with a painful tug and threw it at his feet.

For the first time since our fight actually began, I saw Daimon show some other emotion besides anger or shock. Fear and despair were plain to see in his eyes as his gaze shifted between the locket and me. I could see that disbelief had its hooks in deep as he shook his head and pled, "Maria..."

"*No*, Daimon," I told him firmly with only a slight quiver to my voice. *It's for the best* I told myself as my heart broke in two. "We're done here. I think you'd better go."

For a moment, he looked as if he would choose not to listen to me, and some deep part of me encouraged him to stay, to make it better. However, seeing the resolution on my face, he slowly crouched down until he could pick up the locket, something I had worn continuously for four years of my life.

His touch was so gentle it broke my heart completely.

But I deserved better, damn it. I didn't deserve to be lied to about things I *had* to know; I didn't deserve a relationship constantly torn apart by different personalities and morals; and I most certainly did not deserve to be second-guessing myself at every turn just because he was so "perfect" in my eyes.

So, I said nothing as he stood up fully. I didn't react when he held the locket to his heart and closed his eyes with a deep, shuddering sigh that could have been a repressed sob, and I chose to do nothing when he finally turned to leave the room.

When I heard the resounding click of the door shutting and was sure he had gone, I let myself fall to my knees and sob in the newfound stillness of the room.

Chapter Fourteen

Strangely enough, it was Cindy who showed up in my room a few hours later. I had managed to move from my spot on the floor to the bed, but was still a complete emotional wreck. She came bearing chocolate and comfort, and we laid on the bed talking, crying, and holding hands until people came looking for us later in the day.

Even two weeks after that final argument in my room, I carried an ever-present ache in my heart that refused to let up. I had not seen hide nor hair of Daimon since then, he had already come back at some point to remove his things from my room. It was strange, having someone who had only a short time ago meant everything to me, to having him simply plucked from my life.

But, of course, that was a pain I was used to bearing.

I threw myself into work those following two weeks, keeping myself distracted from the real world in my classroom and library corner. My little trainees were pivotal in helping me heal, slowly but surely. They had, no doubt, heard about everything that had transpired – sneaky little gossips that they were – but they did their best to make no mention of it. They, too, seemed to absorb themselves in the material I taught, and their enthusiasm filled me with a sort of pride that I guess came with being a teacher.

It was funny how, at first, I had resented this load Grandmother had stuck me with, but now it was a part of my life I couldn't imagine living without.

I hated it when she was right.

At the end of another eventful lecture, when the kids were packing up and filing out of the room, I found myself contemplating how I could get around admitting to Grandmother that this was becoming my favorite job.

That was probably why I didn't notice at first. The sound of someone clearing their throat startled me, and I looked up to find that one of my trainees was still here.

There, sitting in his regular seat in the back, was Julien, nervously folding his hands together and staring straight into the pile of books set on the desk in front of him.

He did this the first week of classes too, I recalled suddenly, but he had nothing to say then. So, why was he here now?

"Julien, your next lecture is going to start soon. Hop to, before your instructor comes in to drag you there."

I could see, even all the way from the front of the room, the way his jaw was working and how he took deep breaths, as if to steady himself.

What on earth?

"I have to talk to you."

I raised a single eyebrow. "You are talking to me, kiddo."

"No, not like – I mean," he broke off with a frustrated sigh, and let his head fall into his hands, rubbing his temples.

Done teasing him, I stood from my desk and meandered over to where he was sitting. Sliding between his table and the one closer to the front of the room, I pulled out a chair and sat in it backwards, resting my head on the back and settling my gaze on him.

"What up?" I asked easily enough.

He didn't lift his head up to face me; his muffled voice was hard to hear. "I just – I don't want to lay anymore problems at your feet. I know you have enough on your mind already."

Poor kid, it was obvious he was just looking for someone to confide in. God knows I could relate to that.

"Julien," I told him frankly, "if you can take my mind off of my own problems for a full minute, I will teach you what a human lottery ticket is and give you a winning one."

"Still–"

"Julien, if you don't fess up, I'm going to drag you by your ear to my pack, and, believe me, they can make anyone talk."

Suddenly, his face popped right up off the desk. He seemed a little frightened at the prospect, which was kind of amusing. My pack had quite the reputation around these parts, but all I could see when I looked at them were the biggest bunch of misfits I had ever had the privilege of meeting.

"Okay, okay, just…let me figure out how to say this."

"Take your time," I encouraged him, "I literally have nothing to do after this. You are saving me from an afternoon of dust allergies." However, after a few minutes of him still struggling to form any cohesive sentence, I figured he needed a little help. "Maybe you can start by explaining why you're coming to me for help? Is it something you could ask your parents or other instructors?"

That answer seemed to be easy enough. "No way, you're the only one I can go to with this."

"Okay, so why is that?"

"Because it has to do with humans."

That didn't sound promising.

"Okay, Julien, here's the thing," I told him, folding my hands together and pinning him with a good glare from across the table, "patience? Not really my strong suit. So, if you don't start talking within the next two minutes, I'm going to find my way to your combat class tomorrow morning."

Now properly terrified, he seemed to find his words quite quickly. His question, burst from his mouth with such haste that I knew it was something he had been asking himself for a long time.

"Are there humans that know? About us?"

It seemed like an odd thing to ask, I was sure we had covered this at some point in my lectures.

"A select few higher-ups are aware that a supernatural world lives a stone's throw away from theirs. There is no way we could exist, even in hiding like we do, without that."

It was true. While worldwide knowledge would most likely send people in a frenzy, a community as large as ours would have no way of hiding in the modern world. The world was much bigger back all those years ago when we were created. I'm sure the witch wasn't thinking about hiding us from GPS centuries ago.

But, during all of my musings, I didn't even consider that Julien's question could be any more than the curiosity of a confused student. I didn't expect it to be so much more than that.

"If they did know, the humans, would they hate us?"

That made me look up at him and give him a good stare down. Despite my suspicions, though, I was determined to give him an honest answer.

"Remember when I told you that story, about how werewolves were originally created?"

To my insurmountable shock, Julien actually paled slightly. "The humans in that story killed the poor man's wife."

I nodded, keeping a careful eye on his reactions. "It is a natural, human instinct to fear and hate what they cannot control or understand, especially when it's dangerous to them." His face fell immediately, as if he was personally crushed by this revelation. "However, there is one human you are forgetting in the story."

His brows furrowed together in confusion. "The witch?"

Shaking my head, I sent him a small smile. "The man's wife, the one who loved him so much, despite the rumors that he had handed his soul over to darkness. The one that was willing to do anything to protect him."

"But...she died."

The urge to roll my eyes was almost overwhelming. Boys. "Exactly, her love and devotion was put to the ultimate test, and, even then, she pulled through."

He took a moment to thing about this. His fidgeting had all but stopped and a pensive state had overwhelmed him.

Placing myself in his strayed field of vision, I snapped him out of it. "You wanna tell me what this is all about?"

Though I could tell his attention had returned to me, his thoughts were obviously still somewhere else. This became even more obvious by the tone of his voice when he spoke.

"I met a girl."

This time I really did roll my eyes. "Dude, that's an entirely different talk. If you wanna know more about all that, you should probably be asking–"

"She's human."

My heart stopped. I swear to God it did. It was a testament to how impossible this situation was that I didn't understand what he was trying to say for a few seconds. Without even thinking, I threw up a hand towards the door and didn't even bother looking as it slammed shut and locked with the help of a little magic.

I cannot begin to emphasize how big of a deal this was or how dire his circumstances would end up if anyone were to find out, a fact he seemed to read well enough on my face.

"She doesn't know," he added quickly. "She doesn't have the slightest clue as to what I am."

"When did this happen, Julien? How long have you known her?" I tried not to sound accusatory, but fear was making my tone harsh.

"I met her for the first time when we were ten."

That long? It had been going on for almost a decade?

"She was on a camping trip with her parents near here, and I was practicing Transforming away from my family compound." I saw his ears burning when he caught sight of my raised eyebrow. "I had trouble with it, and my cousins liked to tease me. I wanted to practice on my own."

"Fair enough. Continue."

"Her family loves the wilderness, they weren't really interested in going to a campsite, so they came to the woods close by my house, but she wandered away from their camp and got lost in the woods." Every child's worst nightmare. "I heard the sound of crying and went to investigate. I found her sitting alone just as it was getting dark."

"Did you know? When you found her, did you know she was human?"

He shook his head firmly. "I couldn't tell at first. I had never even been close to a human before. I just thought she smelled weird." My lips itched to smile at that, a child couldn't tell the difference between two races so estranged that one thought the other was merely a myth. "It wasn't too long until I put two and two together."

"So, what did you do?" I asked curiously, enthralled by his story.

"I wouldn't talk to her. I wish I had now because she was just so scared, but I just listened for the sound of her parents calling her name, and led her through the dark to them."

My fears were beginning to give way to confusion. "And that's it? That was the big human encounter that nearly gave me shock? Kid, there is an ulcer forming in my stomach now because of that one little bombshell."

"That's not it," he confessed. "I came back to the same place the next day, determined to really work on Transforming, but she was there again." He shook his head slowly, as if he still couldn't believe the sight. "I was beginning to see why my grandfather thought humans were dumb when she thanked me. Her parents made her bring a little talking device with her so she wouldn't get lost, but she wanted to thank me for getting her back. I was so terrified my cousins were going to pop out of nowhere and see me consorting with a human that I was unable to speak around her, but she talked enough for the two of us."

"Did you ever see her after that?"

He nodded. "She came to that spot the whole week her parents were here, and has since convinced her parents to visit the campsite often."

"Have you ever spoken to her at all?" I was trying my hardest to gauge how much he had let on, or how much she could have put together. "Julien, have you ever said anything that could let on what you are?"

179

"No, I swear I've never said a single word to her. I've been too scared to give her even just the slightest hint."

Something about the way he was presenting this was off. "You're not scared for yourself," I noted curiously, sitting back in my chair.

His face was more serious than I'd ever seen it. "I know what happens when wolves break the rules. I would never put her in that kind of danger," he stated with such conviction that I nearly fell out of my chair in shock.

"You love her," I whispered, mind reeling.

He looked like he wanted to refuse for a moment, probably still seeking to defend her, even from the person he had sought help from. His face turned bright red for just the slightest moment before a small, shy smile made its way to his features. It spoke of such affection and happiness that my heart physically hurt in my chest.

I knew what it was like to have a smile like that.

I knew what it was like to have that smile taken away.

"Is it even possible? To love someone I've never said a single word to?"

"I've seen stranger," I said fondly. "I once knew a werewolf who fell in love with a vampire. What a weirdo."

I could see the stream of apologies I was about to endure. Not feeling the pity party, I held up a hand, proactively stopping him.

"This little pow wow is all about you, bub. We don't have nearly enough time to talk about all of my problems. I don't think anyone does at this point." He backed off and I put my hand back down. "Now, tell me what changed."

"What?"

I gave him a look. "What changed? You've been talking, or not talking, to this girl for almost ten years and not told a single soul about it, and now, suddenly, you're saying you need help. Obviously something has changed."

Yeah, watch out, I'm a perceptive little bitch.

"She said she's leaving soon to continue her training. She's moving to a new state because she was accepted to a training program there."

It took me a minute to figure out what the hell he was trying to tell me. "College," I realized, "she's leaving for college."

He nodded. "That's what she calls it too. It's just, I've gotten so used to having her in my life, I can't imagine what it would be like to not have her."

I squeezed the bridge of my nose, taking deep, yoga breaths. As adorable and romantic as this all was, I was now finding myself, by default, in some pretty deep shit with this boy. I was a glutton for punishment, of course I was going to end up taking him under my wing.

There was no way this could ever end poorly, right?

I hate my life.

"So, why come to me, Julien? I'm flattered you place such trust in me, but I'm not really sure how I can be of any help to you…"

"I came to you for advice," his voice was so quiet that it was really a whisper, "because I don't know how you could be of help to me either."

My mouth was covered by my folded hands as I thought on that for a moment. "I might need time to think about this one, kiddo," my muffled voice told him. "Besides, you have almost a year really until she leaves for college. So, we're not in a rush quite yet."

He nodded. "I feel better just having told someone, even if there isn't something we can do."

"There must be something." I almost winced as I unwittingly promised something I wasn't sure I could deliver. "Now, let me write you a note so that your next instructor doesn't decapitate you."

"Thanks," he said, unaware as to what I had in mind.

When I didn't accept the small piece of paper he offered, he was confused. When I pulled out a permanent marker from his writing utensils, he became suspicious.

When I put him in a headlock and started writing my note on his face, he acted like I was tasing him.

"Dear lovely academic instructor," I narrated as I wrote, "I humbly apologize for the tardiness of this particular student. So full of enthusiasm was he over the workings of human society that I could not bear to send him away until the hour grew far too late to arrive to your class in an acceptable manner. A thousand apologies are sent your way. I dearly hope his enthusiasm remains constant throughout your lecture as well."

With any luck, the instructor would find enough humor in my little love note to forgive his tardiness and not ask any questions, and, with a little more luck, he would be able to wash that of his face by the end of the week.

As soon as I finished the makeshift late pass, I kicked his whiny butt out of my classroom, leaving me to my chaotic thoughts.

How could this have happened, now of all times? How?

But, even as I nearly beat my face against the desk in frustration, a thought occurred to me. Was this really face-beating worthy? The kid had managed to form a genuine attachment to a human. Wasn't that what I was trying to promote?

Was that so terrible? Being a werewolf did not define their relationship because she didn't have the slightest clue, and what he had done was take the ignorance and prejudice his family had probably thrust on him for *years* and completely disregarded it in favor of falling in love with a human based on her own personality and his own heart.

It was like every classic forbidden/unorthodox relationship written and heard about. As terrible as it seemed to everyone involved, it was exemplified by society because it was beautiful. I was halfway to going into full philosophy mode with literary examples and motifs included, when the door to my room opened, and I heard footsteps shuffling just outside the jamb.

I sighed. "Julien, if it's really gonna bother you, you can take the marker off of your face with nail polish remover, but I really wouldn't recommend it. You have no idea how pungent that shit is."

"What the hell did you do to your poor students now, Ria?"

My hand flew to my heart as I turned to find Austin's big, bulky frame standing not a foot away from my chair.

"How does such a large person have such a quiet step?"

Austin, not having the same quippish nature as his best friend, just laughed in response and took Julien's old seat across from me.

"What brings you to my humble hideout?"

"Is that what you're doing here, Ria? Hiding?"

My eyes narrowed suspiciously at his not-so-innocent question. "That has the beginnings of an accusation in it."

His face was halfway between reprimanding and exasperation. "Sheathe those claws of yours. I'm not here to accuse you of anything."

I immediately felt bad for my biting tone. "Sorry, apparently my claws are never fully sheathed."

"That's not entirely accurate," he mused. "I've seen what you look like without them bared. It's just been a long time." My expression simply begged him to continue whatever tangent he found himself on. Without a single ounce of hesitancy, he said, "When Kate was still alive; you were much more willing to open yourself up."

I very nearly guffawed in his face at the sheer ridiculousness of his statement. "Yeah, okay, sure I was all touchy feely when Kate…when I was in training."

"It's true," he insisted. "Everyone can see it."

I rolled my eyes. "Oh boy, is this what everybody talks about when I'm not around?" I began gathering together all of my things so that I could escape to the library and begin the research part of my day.

Diligently ignoring Austin's not-so-subtle stare, I walked over to my desk and pulled out my bag, looking to make sure I had everything I would need. To my dismay, my ancient book of the day was nowhere to be found.

I distinctly remembered dragging it to class this morning – it probably weighed the same as a small child – and the translating dictionary I needed was stuffed in one of the pockets of my tote.

I was beginning to feel a little more than irritated as I found myself turning over my desk for the book. It was so damned big; how could I have possibly lost it?

Austin's helicopter parent aura was also quite grating, and, even though I was sorry I had snapped at him, I ended up doing it again.

"If you're going to hover like a nervous mother hen, you might as well take a seat. I can't go anywhere until I find this damned book."

"I am not the one who hurt you, Ria. You have no right to be angry with me."

I closed my eyes and set my jaw as my anger, left as a shield over my sadness, rose to the challenge. When I was convinced that it was only human teeth I was doing my best to blunt, I opened my eyes and turned my head to meet Austin's steady and fearless gaze.

"You can either have the Kate or the Daimon talk today. No way in hell I'm doing both. So pick."

He raised an eyebrow in such a way that would have looked natural on my own face, but was foreign on his. Under the well of anger and sadness inside of me, there was a distant sense of shock. Austin was, and had always been, the teddy bear of the group. He was a head to rest your shoulder on and a hug whenever you needed it.

So, why was he acting like the Grand Inquisitor today?

Despite the fact that he could clearly see my formidable temper rising to the surface, his gaze was as level and perceptive as it had always been. I briefly wondered if he would simply ignore my request and prod at both sets of emotional scars.

I should have really known better, though. After another few beats of staring, he nodded his head once and ambled on over to one of the front row seats. Even when he was sitting, Austin still seemed taller than anyone else in the room.

"All right, Daimon it is then,"

"'He jests at scars that never felt a wound,'" I quoted as I sat down at my desk to search through its drawers for that damn text.

"What was that?"

"Nothing, please continue with your counseling, sir."

He didn't seem pleased by my sarcasm. Unfortunately, he didn't seem completely put off by it either, despite the fact that my head was submerged under the desk, and it appeared as if I wasn't giving him the time of day.

"Have you talked to him at all?"

"Why on earth would I do that," I commented distractedly as I opened the bottom-most drawer, and, lo and behold, there was the threadbare cover of the missing book and the key to my escape.

"Come on, Ria, you know why. It's been almost two weeks since your fight." I turned to see Austin lean forward on the desk and stare me down. "This is the man you risked your life to love not even a year ago. Are you really just going to let him go just like that?"

Mimicking his actions, I leaned forward on my desk towards him and narrowed my eyes. "Your concern for my romantic life is touching, really, but I would have thought that you would all be jumping with joy by now. The family wasn't exactly pleased when I brought a vampire home."

Hefting my bag over my shoulder, I proceeded to make my way towards the door, realizing, at this point, that Austin was going to follow me, whether I liked it or not. True enough, I heard the sound of his chair scraping the floor just as I was slipping out the door and exasperatedly held the door open for him.

"Sure we weren't happy about it, but you love him, Ria, and he makes you happy. That was good enough for us."

"Well, he stopped making me happy, Austin," I informed him tightly. "So, I ended it, and that's that."

"Ria, have you ever stopped to consider that maybe Daimon did what he had to in order to keep you safe?"

Are you kidding me?

I couldn't take it anymore. Spinning on my heel so quickly he almost barreled right into me, I stood my (much shorter) ground.

"Why the hell are you suddenly on his side? He lied, he kept information from us, he is Nikolai's blood brother, and Cindy's sister's murderer. I should have done this a long time ago."

He was quiet for a moment, searching my face while deliberating something.

"What if he didn't do it?"

Now I was all sorts of confused. "What? Didn't do what?"

Maddeningly, he hesitated for a moment, and, when he did speak again, his voice was pitched so low I'm positive no passerbys were meant to hear what he was saying. "What if Daimon was telling the truth? What if he didn't murder all of those packs?"

If I had been drinking something, I would have been surprised enough to spit it in his face. Luckily, for him, I just found myself blinking up owlishly at him. "Excuse me?"

Taking a quick scan of the area, he subtly leaned closer until he was almost speaking right in my ear. "Cindy told me about your fight, about everything that you said to one another. I think he might have been genuinely confused about the pack murders."

This couldn't be happening to me. Not now. "This is ridiculous. This happened *years* ago, Austin, why is this even up for debate?"

"Think about it, Ria. Does Daimon really seem like the type to mindlessly massacre whole packs of werewolves who had no fault against him? Were there any survivors to confirm that he was the one responsible?"

He didn't have to tell me all the facts. In my guilt, I had gone over them again and again trying to make sense of something so senseless. Something just didn't sit right with the whole thing, but I had always ended up convincing myself that I was just trying to justify the fact that I was in love with someone who had done horrible things.

"Even if he didn't do that, there are other things he's guilty of, Austin, things that, when piled up, I'm not so willing to forgive. There are only so many chances you can give someone before you just become a way-too-trusting idiot."

With that, I continued walking to the exit of the building, hoping, *praying* that he would take a hint and leave me alone, seeing as I was at my limit for the day. But I almost punched something when I heard his footsteps and longer strides quickly catch up to me.

"Ria, you can't always walk away from me, from us,"

"Watch me, Austin," I snapped acidly, throwing open the main doors and marching out as fast as I could.

"Ria, please, talk to us. We know you're hurting and we know you're trying to shrug it off and keep going, but you're only going to end up hurting yourself more."

I stopped mid-step, felt my hands ball into white-knuckled fists. "Do you have any idea how *irritating* that is?" When I turned to face him again, I found him slightly taken aback. "'Ria, come talk about your feelings.' 'Ria, why do you let your stupid, human emotions lead you around all the time.' 'Ria, your humanity is what makes you special.' 'You better learn hide those human emotions, human.' *I'm sick of it*!"

At this point, I was almost shouting the words right in his face, and it was definitely gaining some attention, but I couldn't possibly give a shit. There were so many feelings sitting in my chest, and so many thoughts churning in my head; it was starting to drive me insane. I had kept them bottled for so long, way too long really.

"Ria, if this is about the running off to Nikolai thing, we're not mad at you. We were just scared."

"If it was just the Nikolai thing, I wouldn't be so crazy, but that's all I've ever heard for the past four years, Austin, four *years*! Do you have any idea how exhausting it is? Become someone new, but be yourself, but you have to change yourself. Well," I told him, holding out my arms as if putting myself on display, "here's what you get. This is what this life has made me, and you all might just be stuck with it. So, sorry if it's not exactly to your liking."

"That's not the point, Ria. You can't just go around pretending like nothing's wrong," he tried arguing, but it ended up coming out more like a plea. "Ria you have so many people here to rely on, so many people who care about your health and happiness."

It was then that I started laughing out loud, as if what he was saying was the funniest thing in the world. It was at this point that I realized I was most certainly not okay. Not at all. And I think Austin finally understood just how badly I was faring mentally.

"So many people, he says," I almost joked, "so many people, as if there's a small army waiting for me with open arms when I get home. Look around, Austin. Look around and see who I have left," I told him, holding my arms open to the empty air.

"Let's start with the basics, shall we? I don't have a family anymore, for one. Well, technically I do, which makes it all the more fun, thinking all the time in the back of your head that you've either caused them unimaginable pain, or maybe even done them a great service by vacating their lives. Gee, at times like this, the love and support of the girl I called my best friend for years sure would be nice. Oh, but wait, she was murdered in a plot to get to me, and I managed to let her killer roam free. Double trouble. At least the man I love is there for me. Oh! My mistake, he may have never even loved me in the first place.

"So, you see Austin, it's really just me, and, at this point, why would I want to rely on anyone else? If anything, I've learned a valuable life lesson: people don't stay in your life forever, and if I just keep handing out pieces of my heart to everyone I love I'll only end up losing more and more of myself as time goes on, and, quite frankly, it just doesn't seem worth it to me anymore."

Then, all at once, I found myself very nearly surrounded by Austin's big bulky frame, as he embraced me so hard my toes barely touched the ground. The tears that had pricked the back of my throat and made it hard to keep my voice steady were already coming to my eyes, even before he spoke.

"I know we're not them," he told me quietly, solemnly, but with so much feeling I couldn't doubt anything he said, "and that none of us will ever be able to replace her, but you can't just throw up your walls and suffer in silence, Ria."

"Says who," I muttered petulantly.

"You have a whole support system here, Ria. Don't ever forget that. You don't have to go at it alone all the time."

"I can manage myself," I found myself snapping without any real bite. "I'm not a child."

"No, you're not. You're a grown woman who has earned the love and loyalty of a lot of people, and those people would be willing to do anything for you. Sure, we lose people; they move, they drift away, they may even die, but that's no cause for throwing in the towel. Kate is irreplaceable to you; we all know that, but, if you can find the strength to reach to others for help and support, you are the type of person who will always have at least ten hands reaching back."

I tried to take his words to heart, I really did, but all I could think about were the hands I could no longer reach for. There were occasions in life where I needed certain people more than others.

There were days I needed the love and protection of a parent.

There were days I need the camaraderie and the no-questions-asked support of a sibling.

There were day I needed to spill my guts and share things that I could only share with a best friend.

And there were days that I just needed the friendship and affection of someone who loved me just for being who I was.

Almost naturally, I found my arms reaching up to hold him just as tightly as he was holding me. "I'm not so sure I have that kind of strength," I whispered.

"And that's something only time can fix, but it will be fixed, Ria, you'll see. This sadness will not last forever."

"How can it not?" But, before he could answer, I gave him a little squeeze. "Thank you, Austin. Despite what I thought, that was just what I needed to hear."

He let me stand on my own two feet, then. Keeping his hands on my shoulders, he gave me a once over, as if to see for himself whether or not I was okay. When his usual, gentle smile returned to his face, I knew I must have checked out.

"Now, in return for stealing from my precious study time, you can be my research assistant for the day."

His only response was to laugh and throw his heavy arm over my shoulder as we walked to the library.

Chapter Fifteen

I had found out over the past few weeks while studying, that Austin was my favorite out of the pack to research with. Vincent, well, for obvious reasons he was less than helpful. Carter tended to be too quiet; a little socializing wouldn't kill him. Cindy didn't take to reading as much as I did; she preferred to be outside or doing something more hands-on.

Austin was a good mix of the group. He could spend hours sitting in one place reading and deciphering information. He could stand a good joke every once in a while, and he knew how to sneak coffee past the dragon at the front desk, much like he was doing now.

I smiled up at him as he placed a steaming mug in front of my book, careful to avoid spilling on any of the various piles of papers I had strewn around me. "She didn't even look up this time. Impressive."

"I've lulled her into a sense of misguided trust," he answered cheekily, taking his own chair and starting back in on his work.

I didn't, though. "So. Austin." He didn't look up, but I saw him raise his eyebrows. "I've done my fair share of gut-spilling today. I think it's time you did, too."

That certainly made him look up. "I'm not sure I like where this could be going."

My mask of innocent curiosity didn't fool him in the slightest. "I won't ask anything embarrassing. Promise."

He sighed and took up his coffee. "I suppose it can't be helped. Go ahead, ask whatever it is you clearly already have in mind."

My smile could have been confused for one of Nikolai's chilling leers. "How's Cindy doing, Austin?"

I couldn't help but laugh as Austin's eyes widened just before he found himself suddenly choking on his coffee. The librarian sent us a chastising look, to which I just shrugged.

"I'm sure I have no idea what you're talking about," he rasped as he reached in his pocket for a napkin to wipe his mouth with.

Tilting my head to the side, I gave him a look that clearly said I wasn't buying it. "You know, I would have assigned you guys to work together sooner had I known something like this would be the result."

"It's not...I just...oh God." His head fell in his hands. "There'll be no end to the teasing, will there?"

"Nope, but I promise to make it less painful if you give me all the details first."

Sighing once more, his forehead made contact with the wood of the desk. "What do you want to know?"

"Oh, only everything." I threw my pencil at him. "Start from the beginning, Casanova."

Lifting his head just enough for his chin to sit on the desk, he began his confession. "Fine. From the beginning it is. Contrary to your belief, I don't think it started when you put us together for sweeps of the campus."

"Really? Do tell?" It was all I could do to keep from squealing in girlish delight over the adorableness.

"No, not for me at least. I've always kind of admired her, really. Her happy personality is so infectious and welcoming. I guess it just draws people in. It drew *me* in. I think it's a real testament to her strength that she always manages to keep a smile on her face, and she's always trying to keep everyone around her happy too."

He looked over only to find me grinning ear to ear and covering my face with both of my hands.

"What? *What*?"

"Oh my God, this is the cutest thing in the entire world."

He rolled his eyes and his forehead was once more planted firmly against the desk. However, that did nothing to hide his burning ears. "Go back to work, Ria."

Laughing softly, I turned back to the pages in my book. "That's all I get? After I had a full mental breakdown in front of you? I just get to hear things I already know about my own packmate?"

God, I wish these things were written in English, or that I least spoke…whatever the hell they were written in. Going back and forth between the translation dictionary and the text was giving me a headache.

Luckily, with all the studying I had done already, a few of the words on the page were familiar to me. I could usually decipher the more obvious ones by now. You know, like "vampire", "werewolf", "moon", "blood", and "death, destruction, and mayhem."

As I searched through the foreign words on the particular page I was on, I happened to find a few of these familiar words and more than a few I did not recognize. Flipping through the dictionary, I reached for my writing pad to scribble down a sentence in the middle of the page.

I could hear Austin still talking; I found myself listening with half an ear. "I guess I really starting liking her more than a friend by the end of training, and Kate always had us doing runs together when we were posted off campus. I've only noticed it lately, though, I think."

Naturally, while the dictionary was extremely helpful in cases like this, some of the finer nuances of the work were lost, but it was just enough to help get the message across.

'Vampire bites are not normally dangerous to werewolves…darker magic…full moon…bite of fang and silver.'

Wait. What.

"Ria, are you even listening to me?"

'Curse of a vampire passed onto a werewolf… a creature that has walked through true death…cannot maintain two curses…thrall…'

"Oh my God," I whispered.

This time it wasn't impatience that colored Austin's voice, but rather curiosity and concern. "Ria, what is it?"

"This is…"

"Maria?"

Both of us turned to face the newcomer, obviously a trainee from Grandmother's tribe, who looked like he had run around the world in under a minute to get to us.

"What is it," I demanded, frustrated at the interruption.

"You're being summoned to the formal congress room. They said it's urgent. You must come at once."

Austin and I stole a look at each other. I noticed that, like me, he was suddenly sitting up much straighter in his chair and looked mildly surprised.

The only person who really had the authority to "summon" me was Grandmother, and she had refused to use any of the formal rooms of the Council ever since the night they were dethroned. On top of that, there was a sense of urgency?

This could only spell trouble.

I looked back at my book and fought the urge to scream; just as I was getting somewhere too! If only I could will it to just drop its much-needed information in my noggin.

"Maria," the trainee ventured uncertainly.

Knowing I wasn't about to get out of this, I turned back to the trainee and nodded. "Lead the way, kid."

With a sigh of relief, the trainee began a serious speed walk out of the library, leaving Austin and I to follow behind.

Sensing the urgency that came with the discovery in my hand, Austin waited until the trainee was close to the front door before bending to murmur close to my ear, "What did you find?"

"I'm not sure, yet," I answered honestly, casually checking for witnesses around me as I ripped a page out of a priceless text, "but I need you to find out what's going on. This doesn't look good."

With a single nod, Austin moved to catch up with the trainee.

That being taken care of, I brought myself back to the task at hand. Unfolding the paper in my hand, I skimmed the page to the best of my ability as I moved to follow them. It was much harder now without the translating dictionary, but I hadn't devoted myself to all of this research for nothing.

The words that had become so familiar to me over the past few weeks now only filled me with a sense of dread and foreboding. It was just as we were approaching HQ that I finished the passage with a looming sense of finality. Endless connotations began to spring up in my thoughts. This meant...

"Ria!"

Brought back to Earth by the sound of Austin's voice, I quickly stuffed the page in the back pocket of my jeans, and looked up to see him hustling towards me. Uh oh. "What is it? What's wrong?"

"Nothing yet," he said hesitantly. "Just get ready. The trainee couldn't exactly confirm it, but it would seem that we have guests from the Western Quadrant."

Really? Everything just had to happen at the same time? I didn't even get five minutes of time to come up for air?

"Just what I need," I muttered, massaging the ache already building in my temple, "a new crop of old farts convinced they rule the world."

"Yeah, well you need those old farts to help contain Nikolai," he warned. "So, you might want to try a different title."

"Austin," I turned to face him, showing him I was completely serious, "I'm capable of swallowing my pride enough to ask for help, especially now. This has to end."

He examined me for a moment, saying nothing before nodding his head approvingly. "Well, let's just hope they're in the mood to offer it."

The trainee was still there, leading the way, though we really didn't need it. This was a walk I knew well.

Memory melded with reality as I remembered taking these same steps to a war council, thinking of Vincent's reaction when he realized he had to call me "General" from now on. We were planning an all-out war against vampires then.

Funny how these things end up, isn't it?

Back in reality, I found myself facing a pair of wooden doors that held the same elegance as those forever closed on the Council's favorite room. This, however, was not a room the members of the Council would find themselves visiting often. No, they left others to do their dirty work for them.

But I had to push those thoughts away for now. I had bigger fish to fry.

With very little preamble, the doors to the formal congress room opened before us, and we strode in, heads up, eyes alert, and ready to go.

The room was large and spacious, an optical illusion enhanced by high ceilings and windows that reached all the way up the wall. A grand fireplace stood to one side of the room, and I could already hear a roaring flame within it, but it was the great, round table in the center of the room that served as the centerpiece.

It was a magnificent table, made of a familiar mahogany hue artfully carved in a manner similar to the doors of the Council's main chamber. It was circular, with a diameter that spanned almost twenty feet long, dominating the space. The legs and outer rim were the only parts composed of mahogany. In the center, there was a sweep of marble that was not as it appeared.

This marble was unique, and perfect for the war chamber. The rock itself was spelled to imitate whatever landscape the caster desired. This made it an incredible asset when it came to strategizing.

But I had a feeling that's not what we would be doing tonight.

The usual suspects had already gathered; the rest of our pack was already here, along with Grandmother. Beside her, I recognized Alessandra and Scarius Maximus, most terrifying couple on the planet.

There was another vampire standing next to him, but I didn't meet his eyes. I didn't have it in me at this point.

However, as my eyes traveled to the other side of the table, I found myself encountering faces I had never faced before, but recognized instantly.

These were not just guests.

The Western Hemisphere, in the world of werewolves, is divided into four different "quadrants" of territory, north, south, east, and west. Our Eastern Quadrant (AKA the Eastern half of the United States) is, or at least was, known for being under the unwavering control of the Council, one of the most fearsome groups of werewolves ever gathered.

One of them.

Just as the East handed over the mantle of leadership to the Council, the West has been led for just as long, if not even longer, by a collection of werewolves who instilled the same kind of terror-filled respect. However, where it took 12 wolves on the Council to do so, it only takes three in the West.

This was the Western Troika.

When I suggested that Grandmother send for help in the West, the last thing I expected was a personal visit. Judging by the look on her face, I'd say she thought the same.

But here they were in the flesh, and they fit the picture I had painted in my mind perfectly. Stern, wrinkled faces turned to face us newcomers with a critical gaze that examined us from head to toe, and I don't think they were that impressed with what they saw.

"Honored guests," Grandmother was in Chief Mode as she introduced us, "this is Austin and Maria, the final two members of the Elite pack. I have called upon them, as well as their fellow packmates, to share with us their expertise on the enemy we face."

It certainly seemed legit, but, as I took note of the distaste clearly visible on the faces of the Troika, I came to the sad realization that this was going to be much harder than it should be. I searched my mind, trying to recall the lesson where I had had to memorize all of their names, but they just weren't coming to mind.

Oh, well, I'd have to improvise.

"A warm welcoming for a murderer, Honored Chief," one of them spewed; let's call him Grumpy. I set my jaw and reverted to the mask Kate had taught me to wear in situations like this. "We do not live in ignorance. You have sent the killer of the Council to speak with us."

"An assassin with the experience of a trainee," the second chimed in (Bigoty, my mind immediately supplied)."There is no wisdom in such youth, merely recklessness."

The last looked me over only once before turning to Grandmother, writing me off completely. "Perhaps it would be better if you called on another to tell us of this so-called 'threat,' and leave the girl where she is useful in her research."

Oh, this one was definitely Bitchy.

I could see out of the corner of my eye the way my pack stiffened in anger, the way Daimon's and Alessandra's heads snapped towards the Troika with looks of pure disgust, and the way Grandmother's hands tightened on her staff slightly, but I was only left with a feeling of surprise. I had been filled with such anger and irritation not ten minutes ago, and, yet, now it was completely gone. Even provoked by the kind of people who had talked down at me for so many years, I was not in a rage, not even close.

No, it was a heavy sense of weariness that came to rest on my shoulders. Would this really never end? Could we not put the provocations, the prejudice, or the bigotry aside even in such a moment as this, when we were going out of our way to warn them of something that could potentially bring harm to them in the near future?

And it was that same weariness that allowed me to have some semblance of calm as I tried to put my thoughts into words. I stepped forward and began to speak before anyone could stop me. "Honored members of the Great Western Troika, it was I who asked the Chief to call you here, but it was not in an effort to explain myself or to provide you with excuses for my previous actions. That is not the true issue at hand today."

"You would place this alleged threat above the mutiny you engaged in, then?" Grumpy asked dangerously.

"Does it matter what she thinks?" Was the outburst from Bigoty on the far side of the table. "How presumptuous you are, speaking without the permission of your Chief!"

"I place the highest trust in Maria," Grandmother cut cleanly across him. "In this situation, she knows the enemy best, as he targets her as personally as he targets this quadrant. She is also the only one to have escaped his grasp, and has done so on more than one occasion. Therefore, Honored Troika, she speaks as freely as I do here."

So, put that in your juice box and suck it, Troika.

Bitchy remained pensive, absorbing Grandmother's words before directing his question at me. "And what is it about this threat that you have seen fit to summon us to the Eastern Quadrant to discuss it? What makes this vampire different from the threats we face every day?"

"A number of things," I told him clearly, "in the several encounters we have had with Nikolai, it has been made abundantly clear that he is in the midst of setting in motion a plot he has been constructing for hundreds of years. He is cunning, but, more importantly, knowledgeable, which is what makes him a real threat to us. He possesses information on the supernatural world that is nearly unparalleled, and, thus, we are not prepared to counter him. He is feared amongst his own kind and has proven dangerous to our own, and that is the reason that I saw fit to warn you of such a threat."

"I'm flattered, darling, really. I hadn't the slightest idea you thought so highly of me."

In retrospect, I really should have seen this coming.

In the split second after he had spoken, everyone in the room moved. My pack moved to protect Grandmother, and the Troika, similarly, had their own bodyguards stationed around them.

Nikolai sat perched in the topmost open pane of one of the windows that lined the wall, one leg propped up and the other swaying casually against the wall. I had to give him props, he seemed completely at ease staring down at a room full of his enemies. He even took the time to examine each of their faces before his gaze met mine, and he gave me a quick wink.

Not perturbed in the least, I strode closer to him until I stood almost directly under the window he had taken up residence in. Unfortunately, this put me at a close proximity to someone I had been actively avoiding for the past two weeks. However, he stood firm next to me, and even turned himself to be at an angle where he could block an attack from Nikolai.

It was a small comfort.

Surprisingly, it was a member of the Troika who spoke to Nikolai first. Not moved in the slightest by his little appearance, Bigoty's tone was akin to the scolding of a parent. "So, this is your *great threat.*" He actually scoffed. "How absurd."

I could have rolled my eyes. I was completely convinced at this point that these guys just wanted to prove me wrong and revel in my inferiority.

With a wicked grin, Nikolai faced what could be his newest set of opponents. "So, this is the Great Western Troika. How utterly fearsome. Maria, you have really outdone yourself with these reinforcements; I am just aquiver in my boots."

I saw their eyes flash dangerously with the insult, and the little hairs on the back of my neck lifted. With every insult, I knew they would be more willing to help us hunt him. This might actually work out in my favor. Taunt away, Nikolai.

"Watch yourself, vampire," Bitchy warned gravely. "You are a miscreant in these parts and, yet, you face us alone. A fool's move."

"Well, age has certainly given you some wisdom, good sir," he acknowledged jovially. I felt my eyes narrow immediately at that tone. "My mother always did tell me to take the words of an elder to heart. I suppose I shall obey just this once."

All it took was a smooth snap of his fingers, and, suddenly, Nikolai was no longer alone.

In every window stood one or more vampires, some I recognized from the house Kate had brought me to; others were new, probably replacements for the ones we took care of on our way out. Without thinking, my eyes searched, but Kate was not here with him, or, at least, had not yet made her appearance. I would have to simply bide my time on the Kate front because, for now, there were bigger things to worry about.

Nikolai had our little room completely surrounded.

I stole a glance at the Troika, but, even now, they looked unmoved.

"And now you have centralized your coven," Grumpy remarked as if he were commenting on some play in a football game. "There is a certain lack of soundness in your strategic decisions, vampire."

"I thank you deeply for your concern," Nikolai professed, "but you need not worry about me. There are others much like these ones, but they are not here with me."

"And where are these unseen forces you claim to have?"

Nikolai looked positively cheeky at this point. "Oh, here and there. Over the country and across the world, marching across those little lines in the sand you have drawn between your quadrants. And not just these ones either." Moving with speed that was almost unmatched, Nikolai leapt from his little perch to the center of the great table we all stood around.

Observing the marble under his feet with great interest, he swept his hand through the air until it hovered over the table's surface.

"Show me the world as they see it now," he commanded the stone.

He shouldn't have known how to do that, I thought incredulously. How does he know how the table works?

I watched, amazed like every other time I saw it, as the marble shifted and molded until it became a map of the world.

What was Nikolai playing at here?

"You may think that the entirety of the mythical world is firmly in your grasp, werewolves, but it is merely a delusion. In all of these lands, far and wide, you have stationed your brethren and minions," he looked up at the Troika and dropped his bombshell in a hiss that sent shivers up and down my spine, "but, then again, *so have I.*"

"For what purpose," the Troika tried again. "As you said, we are spread to the four corners of the world. What good is it to have vampires in regions where we already reign?"

Maybe the Troika thought they were being super clever asking Nikolai all these questions just to have him turn around and reveal all of his plans to us, but I knew better by now. Nikolai had his bragging pants on today, and we weren't even close to the scary part in the story he was so interested in sharing.

"It's simple, really," he assured calmly, "a reason which you are not anywhere near prepared for, though you may think otherwise. For hundreds of years, the mythical creatures of the world, like me, have been subject to the whims and control of werewolves, like you, and, following the example of my favorite werewolf over here," he said with an admiring glance in my direction, "we have reached our breaking point, but have no fear, our wrath is not saved merely for you, but rather the entirety of your kind."

Again, he turned his attention to the table. "Show them the world they have created." With another elaborate sweep of his hand, the map transformed again until I could see little figures on each of the continents and countries. Little wolves and, what I assumed were, vampires littered the landscape, still for a moment, but, after a few seconds, they began to move. Vicious fights broke out between the two different species all across the world. I had never seen the marble do this before.

Nikolai's quiet intonation was the perfect narration for such a scene. "Over time, you have, on several occasions, done your best to wipe vampires from existence, but you failed. You have always failed, and now? Now it's our turn." Finally, he reached out and commanded, "Show them what I will do to their world."

Just like that, the tide turned from the apparent stalemate on the map until, with eerily silent expressions of pain and terror, the werewolves fell one by one and sank back into the map, leaving only the vampires to roam the world.

Overcoming my horror, I glanced up at Nikolai wondered aloud, "How is it you plan on doing this? Even now, you are just as spread out as we are, and, as you said, neither species has ever been capable of exterminating the other. So, what's your big game changer?"

With a sigh of admiration, he shook his head amusedly and looked over his shoulder at the Troika. "See here, Elders? Take note. Maria always asks the right questions."

"Perhaps it is because she knows what questions you wish her to ask?" Bitchy's accusation was barely veiled, and I stiffened at the very idea. How dare he-

Nikolai's laugh was loud and boisterous, it filled the whole room and vaguely reminded me of our Trial match when I had pleasantly surprised him. The sound should have been pleasing – it was still a laugh, for crying out loud – but it brought goosebumps to my skin and a chill to my heart.

"You abandoned my company for this? Darling, I'm beginning to think you have poor taste. Alas, foolish Troika, Maria leaves me to pine heartily. She has not yet willingly joined my side of the fight." His gaze settled on me once more, and his smirk was made entirely of anticipation. "That will soon change, though."

"Feel free to hold your breath until that happens, Nikolai," I invited him fearlessly. I'd heard this story before.

His chuckle was low and quiet, like there was some inside joke I didn't quite get. "We'll see about that, but, because you asked so nicely, I'll answer your little question." Once more his hand passed over the map, and the werewolves returned to the fray. "There has always been a thin line between the real and supernatural worlds, despite how closely we live. Werewolves and vampires make up the bulk of the supernatural world, but there is another force to be reckoned with. Show them what they have failed to see."

All of a sudden, more people sprung up all across the world; hundreds of little humanoid figures took their places on the board in between the werewolves and the vampires already there.

My stomach sank to my knees.

Nikolai was right about one thing; for centuries upon centuries, the supernatural world and reality had rested on two sides of the same coin, separated, but undeniably connected. It was the great unspoken rule to all things mythical: never reveal the paranormal world to the humans, and for good reason too. Back in the days of old, when the two worlds were meshed, one could hardly tell where one ended and the other began. That was when humans were weaker, less populated, and not so formidable in the eyes of monsters everywhere.

Now, the world was in quite a different state.

Whereas we had simply retained all of our scary traits and abilities, humans had grown and expanded their knowledge. It was simply a matter of self-preservation to keep them from going all gun-ho and wiping us all off the map.

Nikolai couldn't even be considering changing that. Not even he could be that stupid.

I heard the hiss of surprise from Grandmother and knew she was thinking the exact same thing. "You cannot possibly think to involve the humans–"

"But I can."

I shook my head, still in a state of disbelief. It wasn't possible. Apparently he *was* that stupid. "It won't ever work," I told him seriously.

He tilted his head sideways, the way I had seen so many dogs do, and his smile widened. "Tell me why, my love. I do so enjoy the way your clever, clever mind thinks."

Ew. God, just blech.

"You want the humans on your side." It wasn't a question.

"Keep going," he encouraged.

I scoffed. "Take it from a human's perspective, Nikolai. When given the choice of vampire or werewolf, I have a feeling most people will go for the species that doesn't see them as a meal."

He made a low sound of agreement. "Point taken, but I have thought this through. The solution is really quite simple. Do you not see it yet?"

"Are you going to make us go through hoops for an answer?" I was surprised to hear Daimon speak beside me. I hadn't heard the sound of his voice in over a fortnight, but even I knew the question was unnecessary. Nikolai was just itching to spill the beans on his plans, which made me all the more nervous.

True to form, Nikolai answered, "Maybe I'll spare you just this once, brother." He turned away from us then, and began to slowly stroll around the edge of the table. Each step echoed forebodingly around the entire room, and filled me with a sense of dread before he even said anything. "It's true that, in the grand scheme of things, it is the vampires that hunt and, therefore, are threatening to humans, but what if we make them see differently? It is all a matter of perspective. After all, we all know the truth," he assured, gesturing up to the vampires that surrounded us. His coven laughed and jeered along with their leader. "Werewolves are dangerous, unstable creatures, capable of ten times the destruction and harm of vampires. The humans will be made well aware of this fact before any more damage can be done. After all, if they've recently Changed one human, what's to stop them from Changing more?"

"I left my humanity behind willingly, Nikolai," I told him clearly, not allowing him any ammo, "and no werewolf would intentionally harm a human. It's not how we work."

"But they do not know that, do they? I will simply have to convince them otherwise."

"You have no proof, and we won't give you any," I argued.

"Ah," he paused in his steps and looked out into space, as if pondering such a fact. "That is a bit of a problem, isn't it? Untrustworthy humans, always looking for facts, and always looking for the evidence to support them. Wherever will I find a werewolf to comply with my plans if you won't give me one?"

I realized his train of thought just a few moments before he leisurely turned his head to face me, a slow, sly smile curling at the corners of his lips.

"Oh, that's right. I already have one."

"Kate," I whispered to myself. Was this his plan for her all along? Then why...?

"The werewolf you spoke of in your missive?" One member questioned Grandmother. I noted that even he was beginning to sound a little nervous.

Wasn't that just great.

"Just think, Maria, if your dearest friend was able to scar you in such a horrid manner, what else is she capable of under my control?" Out of reflex, my hand ran over the scars on my neck and collarbone. I didn't even have to search for them with my fingers anymore.

I refused to answer him, a fact which only made him laugh again.

"Exactly, and once the humans get a glimpse of a feral werewolf, they'll do anything to protect themselves. In other words," he glanced around the room, looking into everyone's eyes, "you will find yourselves faced with an enemy you can neither outman nor outrun."

How could this have happened? I wondered as the strength left my legs; I had to grip the edge of the table to keep from toppling over. How could we not have seen this coming?

It was like I had told Grandmother the night Kate was resurrected: no matter what I did, what I thought I knew, Nikolai had had hundreds of years to prepare this whole plot of apocalyptic proportions. There was only so much I could do.

We couldn't give up, though. Not yet.

We had to think of some way out of this. Like now.

Nikolai's deep, thrumming laugh caught me off guard. "Oh, just look at you; all of you serious, stoic menfolk practically wetting your pants, and all because of some measly little humans. I should have tried this angle hundreds of years ago, but fret not, werewolves, you have caught me in a charitable mood this evening."

"Is that so," Grandmother wondered, doubt dripping off of every word.

"It *is* so," Nikolai began moving around the edge of the table once more, the werewolves now leaning back automatically as he passed by. "Everything I have just finished telling you, this entire horror story, will take place on the next full moon, just over a week from now."

"So, you are giving us time to stop it," Grumpy guessed.

Nikolai was quick to dispute that. "Oh no, there's no stopping it, but I can do even better than warn you of your impending doom. This bad dream never even has to come true. I will agree to call the whole thing off, make sure the humans never find out, and I'll even trade you my trump card, your dear, sweet Kate, freewill and all, as a token of my sincerity." I didn't lean back as he passed in front of me, like everyone else did. I didn't even flinch when he stopped and turned to face me. "All I ask is for one little, tiny thing in return."

"And what's that," I asked him, not daring to move as he crouched in front of me.

His face was just above mine, close enough to reach out and touch, and, with a smirk I knew all too well, he leaned forward and whispered, "Why, it's you, of course."

My surprise lasted long enough to miss how Daimon somehow wormed himself between Nikolai and me, standing protectively in front of me and blocking my shorter view.

Before I could even think to get a word in, the others around the table immediately retaliated.

"What in the world could you possibly need her for?"

"You would ask us to trade you one of our werewolves for another?"

"Like hell you're getting your hands on Maria, you slimy son of a bitch."

"*Wait*," I cut in, moving past Daimon's outstretched arm to stand beside him and face an incredibly amused Nikolai. It was past my turn to play this kid like a fiddle. "You're proposing a trade?"

"I am," he answered confidently.

I had to fight the urge to smile. Play the part, Ria, lead him down the road. "You would call off your plans to tell the humans and give us Kate's freedom in exchange for me?"

"Ria, what the hell–"

"I would."

Now, I could let my smile slip out and enjoy watching his face change from overconfidence to suspicion. By the time I started laughing, all traces of amusement had been wiped clean from his face.

I knew I should start explaining myself sooner rather than later, or at least before the others started thinking I had just lost it, but this was just too damn funny to let go. He was always, *always* one step ahead of us, but now I had the upper hand and the poor guy didn't even know it.

Was this how he felt all the time? No wonder he was so damn cheery.

"Oh, I have to hand it to you Nikolai," I told him in between the laughter that was still slipping out, "you almost had me. An hour earlier and I would have been all yours."

"Is that so," he noted dubiously.

"Mm-hmm, you really didn't think I had any chance of finding it, did you?" As I spoke, I fished out the newly-ripped page from my back pocket and gave it one final look for show before crumpling it into a ball and tossing it to him. "It's not my native tongue, but you shouldn't have a problem with it."

He never took his eyes off of me as he slowly, but surely, unrolled the page. I watched carefully, like everyone else, as he scanned the document over and his eyes narrowed just so.

"Don't feel like reading to the class? How about a summary then?" I looked away from him to address the other werewolves in the room, telling them the truth I had discovered only moments ago. "A monster, a slain werewolf that has been given the vampire curse, only two curses is a little much for one body to take. Thus, the power to overcome the call of its Master is lost, and the creature becomes a slave to the Master's will. It's pretty dark magic, but some of us just don't have the same respect for nature as others. Nikolai has turned Kate into a *pricolici*, am I right?"

I looked back up at Nikolai only to find him staring down at me with an intensity I found downright creepy. "I'll take your silence as an affirmative, and, if that's the case, then your whole friendly deal here? It's shot to shit. A *pricolici* cannot gain back its freewill until its Master has been slain. In other words, the key to Kate's freedom is a stake through your heart."

You could have heard a pin drop in that room. No one dared to move. I barely heard the sound of breathing as all eyes remained peeled on Nikolai, watching to see what he would do next.

His whole countenance was uncharacteristically serious, but, whereas before this seriousness has been fleeting, it now seemed as if I had well and truly stumped the chump.

He took a step to stand on the very edge of the table, as if to approach me, but Daimon once again took his place in front of me. He wasn't alone. The whole of the Elite stood surrounding me, bent on blocking Lunatic's path.

Seeing that he would have to acquire a bulldozer to move this crowd anywhere, Nikolai stopped his advance.

"You have built yourself quite the stronghold here, Maria, but what will happen when you find the need to break free of it, I wonder?"

"That won't ever happen," I assured him. "I don't know what you want with me, or how I fit into this big plan of yours exactly, but it can't possibly be good."

The idea seemed to return him to his old self. "Oh, believe me, it isn't."

"Then, I would come up with a new plan if I were you, Nikolai, because I'm sure as hell not falling for this one."

"Hmm, this is an unfortunate turn of events. I really thought your unwavering loyalty to your beloved friend would blind that reason you cling to, but, alas, you outwitted me at the last minute. I am quite impressed, darling. It has been centuries since anyone has been able to do such."

"Save your congratulations, maybe you can just send a card on your way out of town."

"I'm not quite finished here yet, love."

Yup. I was worried about that.

"I've seen what you've been doing here, arranging your pieces on this side of the board, assembling your little troops, gathering your reconnaissance, and, I must admit, you even made me a little nervous. Why, you almost discovered my ace in the hole." The smirk was back and worse than ever. "But almost is almost, and that's just not quite good enough."

With another snap of his fingers, the doors to the room burst open to reveal two fallen guards and a face I wasn't expecting.

"Malachi?" I asked worriedly, "What are you doing here?"

"Even now you don't see it? I did hide him so well." Malachi strolled into the room as Nikolai spoke, and the doors shut eerily on their own. "You had your little friends looking into those various disappearances, my attempts and failures to get the *pricolici* curse just right."

I didn't even notice Malachi stepping on top of the table until he was standing right next to Nikolai.

Tell me I didn't miss this.

"Kate was not my first success. He was right under your nose the whole time, Maria, and you, out of the goodness of your heart, spilled your deepest, darkest secret to him."

Tell me this wasn't really happening.

I felt my heart stop beating in my chest as Malachi pulled from his pocket a familiar folded photograph and handed it to Nikolai, who reverently opened it.

"Such a charming family, Maria, it's no wonder you miss them so. Why, if you hadn't mentioned it to our friend Malachi here, I wouldn't have ever considered that angle, but this opportunity is just too good to let slip by."

Tell me I can stop him.

Without a thought as to how I could stop him, I launched myself at Nikolai with the intention of ripping his larynx from his neck, only to find myself held back by a fist in the back of my shirt, courtesy of Carter's quick reflexes. The others joined in too, holding my arms and blocking my path, their warnings overshadowed by my malicious growl that promised blood.

But Nikolai wasn't scared in the least. "Just as I thought, you must break free from your fortress, princess, if you wish to save the ones you love. You have until the full moon."

With that being said, the vampires standing in the open windows threw something down into the roaring fire. Within seconds, a thick smoke filled the room, one that had all of the werewolves on the floor gasping for breath.

"Wolfsbane," I vaguely heard the Elder vampire say, "he's using wolfsbane as a cover to escape."

"No," I choked out, struggling to get to my feet. I heard others rush in, opening the windows and putting out the fire, trying to get clean air into the room once more. "Don't let him get away! I won't let him get away!"

It was useless, though. Just as I made it to my feet, I was brought down again, this time by the hands of my friends.

"Ria, you can't go," Cindy tried to talk reason to me, but I wouldn't have it. "Ria, he wants you for something, something terrible, you can't just walk into his trap."

I never expected Bigoty to agree with her. "She is right, Maria. You are obviously a piece of some importance to Nikolai's plan if he went through all of this trouble to get to you. You are simply too valuable to throw yourself away."

"They are more valuable to *me!*" I roared at the top of my lungs. *"That's my family!"*

"I'm so sorry, Ria." It wasn't restraining grips that held me now, but rather the embrace of my packmates. It was Austin speaking to me, his voice just beside my ear. "But we won't give you up."

I raged on, yelling, fighting, struggling, until someone just decided to knock me out cold.

When the blackness slipped over my vision, I noticed the tears streaming down my face.

Tell me it's not too late.

CHAPTER SIXTEEN

The next six days were, quite possibly, the worst of my entire life.

The first time I woke up, a few hours after Nikolai's visit, I was in my room. There were guards posted at the door, and I was ordered not to leave.

Within ten minutes, I had smashed three windows, thrown the bed across the room, and broken four of the guards' bones.

From then on out, it was decided by the powers that be that I should spend the rest of the week in solitary, with one of my packmates guarding the door, knowing that I would be less willing to hurt them than a random guard.

There were certainly plenty of tears, but most of the time I was in a blind rage, screaming to high heaven and demanding that they release me.

I stopped trying to break the room by the third day, and my packmates stopped trying to talk to me through the door by day five.

My thoughts were consumed by all of the terrible things Nikolai could be doing to my family, how it was all my fault, and how they would undoubtedly hate me for this in the end. I swear, on the morning of the last day, I started counting the seconds from sunrise.

My breakfast and a fresh set of clothes were brought in early by Cindy. I was facing the wall with my back turned to her, but I could recognize her light tread anywhere. I heard her set the food and clothes by the door and expected her to leave immediately, but she paused, and I felt the weight of her stare on my back.

"It will be all right, Ria. I'll make this right."

I whipped around to demand an answer, but the door had already slammed shut. I didn't understand what her words could possibly mean.

That is, until the commotion started a few hours later.

It was the sound of a struggle that caught my attention at first, the sounds of punches connecting and bodies impacting against the wall.

By that time of the day, I had resumed my place against the back wall of the cell, facing the door with my folded legs drawn against my chest and my forehead resting on my knees.

I lifted my head as the sound of the lock sliding open reached my ears. I felt my muscles tense as the door swung open, ready to vent some pent up anger and fight if I had to.

But it was not Nikolai on the other side of the doorframe, like I was expecting.

"Well, isn't this just the epitome of irony," I drawled upon seeing the familiar face.

As per usual, Rowan was staring down at me as if I were nothing more than a bug he was contemplating crushing under his boot.

"Get up," he commanded with no preamble.

I felt my eyebrow quirk on my face. "Just so you can giftwrap me for Nikolai? No dice, traitor, I won't trade one prison for another."

All of a sudden, Rowan tossed a bundle at my feet. Keeping a careful, wary eye on him, I reached down to unfold it, only to find my cloak and the arm guards that had been a gift from his parents.

"What's this all about?"

"I'm not bringing you to Nikolai, human," he told me in the imperious tone that I remembered all too well. "You're going to do that yourself."

There were so many questions on the tip of my tongue, but, just then, we both heard the sounds of approaching Kennel dogs.

"If you want to have any chance of saving your family, get moving."

I didn't need any more encouragement than that.

Gathering up the cloak, I slipped the arm guards on as I stalked to the door, following Rowan. Leaving my cell for the first time in six days was incredibly satisfying. However, the first sight of freedom I had was my packmate lying unconscious by the doorway.

"Did you do this," I demanded of him as I knelt by her side, checking to see if she was okay. Surprisingly, there only appeared to be a single blow to her head, which would have been what knocked her out cold.

"She is fine," he answered piteously, his eyes peeled down the hall where the voices were coming from.

I sent him an accusing glare. "Don't you have a single ounce of remorse?"

He didn't even bother looking down. "She questioned whether or not I was going to bring you to your family, and did not put up a fight when I confirmed it." It was like he sensed my skepticism before I voiced it because he followed that up by saying. "Where do you think I got your cloak and other gear from?"

I was astonished until I suddenly found myself recalling our first year together, when I told Cindy all about the little brother I had felt behind.

"Listen, Ria. I'm going to promise you something. If I accomplish anything in my life, it'll be for you to see your brother one more time."

The nostalgia was cut short drastically by a fist in the back of my collar.

"Hey! Let go, dickweed!"

"We don't have time for this, human." He pulled me to my feet.

215

"All right, all right, fine! I have two legs. I can manage this on my own, thank you very much!"

"Then use them. We're going to have company very soon."

Once he released me, I swung the cloak around and let the familiar weight settle over my shoulders. Taking a deep breath, I told myself to forget that I was working with someone who just might have hated me as much as I hated him.

Treat this like any other assignment, I told myself, *and, right now, your job is to get out.*

"There's no way we can get out the front door if they've brought substantial reinforcements."

To my surprise, Rowan turned the opposite way. "We're not going out the front door."

Despite logic screaming that he was leading us to the innermost part of the building where we would be sitting ducks, I followed him. I mean, this *was* the man who busted Nikolai out a year ago.

The Kennel was a place of secrets. As far as anyone knew, there was one way in or out, and that was the heavily-guarded front door. Council Head's grandson or not, the Kennel was its own domain with its own rules. Did he know another way out? To have that information he would have to have been...

"You were a Kennel dog." It wasn't a question.

"For five years," he confirmed without turning around, "when I wasn't working with my own pack."

One moment, there was a blank wall in front of us, and, the next, he had pushed it in and aside to reveal a space I had never even known existed. All I could see past the doorjamb was pure blackness.

My audible gulp was betraying, but, believe me, it was well warranted.

"Not turning back now, are you human?"

That seemed to do the trick. My fear was swept away by a newfound determination to punch him right in his snobby face.

"Why, Rowan? Getting too scared?"

I could've sworn I saw a small smirk adorning his face before he turned around to face the door once more. "They will find us immediately if we use the lift, so we will have to scale the walls. Will you be able to climb in the dark?"

He turned back around just as I used my magic to sharpen my eyesight. Seeing my Transformed eyes, he nodded and walked toward the door.

"It would seem that you are not completely useless, human."

I couldn't help the little victorious smile that rose to my face at his words. That was probably the nicest thing he had ever said to me.

As soon as he disappeared into the darkness, I walked to the edge and was greeted immediately by what looked like the frame of an elevator shaft. Looking up, I saw that the lift was stationed just above the door. Beyond the elevator shaft, I could only see blackness.

"Are you coming or not?"

My head snapped down to find Rowan standing about fifteen feet down on one of the horizontal struts that made up the frame.

"Just waiting for you to get out of my way," I snapped back.

His eyes narrowed. "Do not forget to shut the door behind you."

Did he think I was that stupid? Might as well make some signs for our pursuers complete with lights and big arrows. "Don't want a draft getting in?" I scooted to the very edge. With the door completely shut, there was just enough room for me to balance on my heels.

He had no response as he leapt from his brace to the next one down, and I quickly jumped across the abyss to the spot he had just vacated. It was like a great big terrifying game of "the floor is lava."

Down, down, down we went farther into the pit, until I lost any concept of depth. After a while, I had no idea how far down we'd gone, or how much further we had to go.

How far down does this thing go? I thought as I kept following him. *We've been jumping forever.*

One thing was for sure. I didn't want to know what kind of prisoners they kept down here, because they sure as hell didn't want them getting out any time soon.

Eventually, I heard the sound of Rowan's feet hitting something other than a metal brace.

"One more jump, human, then you will see the walkway."

"I swear, I haven't been called 'human' this often in *years*." I muttered, making my last leap and finding him standing on the walkway he was talking about. "You'd think you'd learn by now."

"Learn what exactly?"

I took the last few steps towards him. Rowan was much taller than me, so I couldn't get in his face. I refused to stand on my tippy-toes to do it, but I had been told more than once that I could be intimidating, my height notwithstanding. I figured having my blackened eyes staring straight into his own would certainly help with that, too.

"I'm not very *human* anymore, am I?"

He looked as if he had something to say to that, but he stopped himself, like there was a secret he was still interested in keeping. Instead, he began making his way further into the dark.

There was barely any light around us, and the only available walkways were creaky metal grates suspended over the gaping black hole that seemed to go on forever. I managed one look over the railing down into its depth. I had no fear of heights, but the ominous drop almost sent me to my knees with fear.

Who was kept down here?

"What the hell is this," I asked breathily, trying to gain back some of my courage.

"This is where Class X prisoners are kept."

"Class X? Are you kidding? There is no such thing as Class X."

Before being detained, each prisoner was given a rating based on how dangerous they were thought to be. This allowed the Kennel dogs to sort them more effectively with Class A being the most dangerous and Class D being the least. Class X wasn't even on the scale.

"Believe it or not, human, but you don't know half of what happens within these walls. The interrogation unit is also stationed down here."

"But there's an interrogation room upstairs. We used it for Nikolai."

"The Kennel dogs knew you would want to interrogate him," he said as if it were the most obvious thing in the world, "but under no circumstances can you come down here unless you are given the highest clearance. They would have had to use the normal interrogation room."

I understood what he was saying, even if I didn't want to. The kind of interrogation that was done down here was not fit for the light of day.

"Where are the cells down here, then?"

He spared one of his hands just long enough to point up to the ceiling we had come down from. "See for yourself."

Convinced he was talking crazy, I lifted my head to look in the direction he pointed to, only to have my confusion traded for horror.

"Oh my God," I whispered, holding a hand to my mouth.

Cages. There were countless, endless, too many cages hanging from a ceiling that was so black I could not see it. I had not noticed them on the way down. To my horror, I could tell that not all of them were empty.

Suddenly, Rowan didn't seem so bad.

This is where Nikolai was kept, I recalled with a shudder.

All of a sudden, he stopped walking so abruptly that I almost crashed right into his back, which probably would have been punishable by death. I heard the whirring and clunking of what sounded like metal from in front of him.

Taking a brave peek around him, I saw that he was fiddling with a series of circular dials that looked like a bank vault, but ten times more complicated. It was composed of several different parts that would change with one another. It was like trying to solve a puzzle that had constantly-changing pieces. However, he moved the pieces of the lock around in a manner that told me he had done this before.

It was then that the sound of the dials sliding into place echoed eerily around us, and, suddenly, it seemed like it was all too much. The fact that I had been imprisoned by my own friends for a week, that Rowan, human-hater extraordinaire, was the one to break me free, that I was now in the underbelly of werewolf society.

Rowan spun around sharply when he heard me take my first step back. He made no move towards me, seeing as I probably looked like some kind of scared animal that would spook at the smallest movement.

"What are you doing, human?" He asked sharply.

"What are *you* doing, Rowan?" I suppose I should have asked this like the moment he broke into my cell, but, there had been no time to question his motives. "You say you're not doing this for Nikolai, and, yet, you literally have nothing to gain from setting me free. Sorry if I seem a little skeptical, but I don't know if I can trust the man who just happens to show up at the perfect moment with a flawless escape route."

He considered me for a moment. It wasn't in that same creepy way Nikolai looked at me, like a predator deciding whether or not it wanted to chase its prey around a little more, or even like how Daimon would sometimes analyze me, as if I was a puzzle he was interested in putting together.

Rowan was all calculation and strategy. When he looked at someone, it was the way our instructors taught us to look at an enemy. Except, in the times I had interacted with him, I noticed that this was how Rowan seemed to look at everyone. It made me wonder what was hiding beneath that impenetrable mask, stonier than even the Council Head's face.

"A little late to be discussing motives, don't you think you should be more worried about being caught by your friends?"

I thought about that and did some calculating of my own. "No," I went out on a limb. "You're much more at ease down here. You said it takes the highest clearance to even know about this place. There won't be many people who know to look for us here."

I took his silence as an affirmative.

"Which begs the question, why would you know about this place? You worked here right out of training. There's no way they would drop this on a new recruit."

His head tilted slightly to the side, something I was beginning to associate more and more with my werewolf peers.

The thing that made Rowan really scary was that you never tell what he was thinking. He could just as soon be contemplating slitting my throat as offering me a plate of cookies hidden behind his back.

As subtly as possible, I tightened the straps on my arm guards, and prepared myself for the worst.

"It's astonishing, really," he said in his scary quiet voice, "how someone so incredibly dull-witted can, in fact, hide such intelligence."

This guy could make me go from terrified to furious in less than a nanosecond. "Dull-witted? I'm sorry what–"

"I approached the Kennel dogs originally, hoping to gain a reprieve from doing work for the Council. They accepted, and brought me in, knowing the information I gained over the years for my grandfather would be invaluable. However, my grandfather was displeased that I resigned from my post working for the Council. You, human, should know better than anyone what happened when someone tried to deviate from my grandfather's set plan."

All at once, he threw open the newly-unlocked door. My eyes were assaulted by the sunlight I'd been kept from for six days. Goosebumps rose on my skin as I heard the sound of hissing from above us. These prisoners probably didn't appreciate sunlight.

The good news was now I had an escape. The bad news was the only thing standing between me and the door was the person I might need to escape from.

Swell.

"My punishment sent me down here, working in what the Kennel dogs fondly refer to as the 'Hellhole.' I was a Hellhound for five years, working in the dark with some of the most twisted and evil minds this world has to offer."

"And I was just starting to forget what a nice guy your grandfather was, too." Sarcasm hid my disbelief. Just when I thought this guy couldn't get any worse. "You know, this does explain the dark and broody thing you got goin' on. You ever thought of just putting it on a business card? I think you'd offend a lot less people that way."

This time, when he smirked, it was hidden by the difference in the lighting on his face. Half of it was illuminated by the sunlight spilling through the open door, the other half was shadowed by the darkness of the Hellhole.

Darn it, I should have brought a camera with me. No one would ever believe that he smiled twice when I got out of this mess.

"Okay, so I have enough faith in your grandfather's terribleness to believe that half of the story, but why help me?"

He was silent for a moment, but it wasn't to study me as he did before; he was pensive. Turning his head towards the door, he stared out into the bit of landscape that was revealed, and his whole face was suddenly clear for me to see.

He looked so much older than the twenty-six year-old I knew he was, I thought with a twinge of sadness, but I had it on good authority that that's how old he really was.

"After Kari was killed, Nikolai drew me in with the promise that he could return her to life. Foolishly, I believed him, but what he has given Kari is not life." He looked me in the eye once more, and, in his gaze, I saw the same conviction that was driving me.

The need to do right by our families.

"What Nikolai is using Kari for…his plans cannot come to pass. It will mean the end for all of us, and, despite the fact you've shown a certain lack of common sense several times over the past few weeks, you're a pinnacle part of Nikolai's plans. Therefore, I think you are one of the only people fully capable of stopping him."

"If we kill him," I found myself whispering, as if he could hear us, "do you think we could get Kate back?"

He shook his head. "I do not know. The kind of magic Nikolai is employing, I've never seen anyone use it. It goes against nature. I am, however, willing to hold on to the hope that Kate is not lost to us."

"Come back, then." I was asking for his parents' sake, really. I had seen their heartbreak upon losing not only one, but both of their children. It would put their hearts at ease to learn that their son wasn't a traitor, not really.

Sadly, though, he shook his head again. "I will be able to accomplish more by Nikolai's side than I will here. I might yet learn more of his plan or a weakness I can exploit. Until then…"

"He's just another evil and twisted mind you have to work with."

Reaching into his cloak, he pulled out what looked like a wallet and handed it to me. Sure enough, when I opened it, it was filled with cold, hard cash.

"There is a driver waiting for you on one of the back roads ten miles southwest from here. He will take you straight to Rochester, but, from there, you are on your own. I do not know what Nikolai plans to do with your family. He has kept me out of it."

This was it. The moment of truth. The big decision, but what was I to choose?

I forced myself to push aside all of the sentimentalities that had driven me to this predicament: the need to protect my family, to avenge Kate, to free my own mind of Nikolai. Feelings and sentiment had already caused me to make some pretty stupid decisions.

If I wanted to save my family AND stay out of Nikolai's dastardly clutches, logic would be my friend here.

Rowan said I could trust him, but could I really? He was freeing me, sure, but the last prisoner he had freed from this place was a royal pain in my behind.

Rowan claimed he only helped Nikolai because he had been promised his sister's return. However, that had turned out less than satisfactory. I could easily see Nikolai as one to make false promises.

But Rowan was the real question here. He said everything he had done revolved around Kate, but this was the man who once told me that he did not want or need sibling affection. Then again, considering who his grandfather was, he had probably been told from the cradle that—

WHY WAS THIS SO HARD.

Rubbing my temples, and the newly forming migraine that had settled there, I looked back up at Rowan and found him patiently waiting for me to sort through my inner turmoil.

"How can I possibly trust you," I whispered.

"Your options are rather limited."

Not the answer I really wanted to hear.

I lifted my hands as if I was physically weighing the possibilities. "Friendly imprisonment, trusting a traitorous asshole. Jail, asshole. What has my life come to?"

"Your time is running out," he firmly intoned.

"All right, kiddo, here's the deal. I trust you just about as far as I can throw you in human form, but I have nothing left, and I'm already here. So, why the hell not, right?" Again, I stepped forward until I was toe to toe with him. "But let me make something abundantly clear to you. If you just used my love of your currently undead sister to get me to crawl into Nikolai's clutches, I swear on every god there ever was, I'll make you wish you were in her shoes."

His stare was impassible as he peered down at me in his usual manner. It was almost as if he was measuring me up.

I'd give him something to measure, all right.

I felt my muscles tense up automatically as he leaned down to my level. I was hardly short, but the gesture was enough to make me feel very, very small.

"Get moving human. There's work to be done." That being said, he made his way through the open door. "And do not let yourself get caught. I don't want to explain to Nikolai how you managed to get out of the unbreachable Kennel."

And he was gone.

I stood for a moment and stared into the passage he had just exited. I realized with a start that I recognized that landscape. Walking out into the light, I looked over my shoulder to see a sheer rock face. At the top there was a solid, flat surface, great for sitting and thinking.

I've been weighing my thoughts for years over a pit where they keep the biggest baddest crirminals this side of the continent has to offer.

Goddammit I'm going to need a new thinking spot now. This really kills the whole mood of the place.

I found myself taking Rowan's words to heart, though, and knew I was just wasting time taking in the view.

Ten miles southwest. A quick little jog through the woods one four hour car ride and I'll be back home.

I just hoped I wouldn't be too late.

Chapter Seventeen

Five hours later, I was exactly where I needed to be. The driver had been instructed to drop me off at a very specific location and had been about as conversational as the car itself, a fact which had certainly not helped my anxiety levels. At. All.

Luckily, I was still familiar enough with this town to figure out which curb he had decided to kick me out on, and realized that it was disturbingly close to what used to be my street.

It was quick work after that to navigate my way unseen through the neighborhood. I was drawn to the house like a magnet, four years of distance seemed more like four days.

An overwhelming sense of nostalgia washed over me the instant I caught sight of my old house. The outside was the same as it had been two years ago when I had hidden from Daimon here. I was willing to bet nothing had changed on the inside either.

I knew that standing on the sidewalk gaping up at the residence would be a little attention-grabbing. So, that's how I found myself crouched within the thickest branches of the apple tree in the backyard, scoping out my surroundings. There were no lights on in the house, and the garage door was shut, all the usual signs that no one was home.

Clearly the neighbors were still home, though, because there was the sound of high-pitched, soul-sucking yapping that I immediately associated with the dachshund that apparently hadn't gone to dog heaven yet. Sparing a glance towards the other side of the tree, I found it on the very edge of what its invisible fence allowed, baring its teeth and growling up at me.

Still a little shit, I see.

Peeking back at the house, I looked for any possible sign of life and wondered in vain where they could possibly be. Had Nikolai gotten to them already? No, the car was gone, they had left on their own. Four years of distance had put me at quite a disadvantage when it came to predicting where they could have possibly gone.

I should have brought Cindy with me, I thought, frustrated. Sharpening my olfactory senses, I took a delicate whiff of the air and grimaced when I found the scent of car and exhaust dulled much of their scent.

This was so much easier in the back woods where there were no people to screw it up.

To make matters worse, I was on a very rapidly decreasing time limit. Once the sun went down and the full moon had its time to shine, I would be stuck human and useless in helping anyone. Seeing as we were closing in on winter in Upstate New York, sunset would be approaching sooner than later.

All I wanted to do was scream my overflowing frustration to the heavens, but that would probably draw attention as well.

Then again, it would probably be drowned out by the infernal yelping of that dog.

Well, couldn't have him blowing my cover, right?

Swinging through the branches until I was on the other side of the tree almost directly over him, I leaned down and let loose a fearsome growl. Just as I predicted, the dog promptly wet itself and ran away crying, which made me prouder than I probably should have been.

However, with that done, I dropped from the branches and started to follow my nose as far as I could.

….which turned out to be not very far. It wasn't long before I found myself at the intersection of three of the busiest streets in Rochester, and the sheer amount of smells crowding my "vision" made it impossible to follow the trail I had picked up from the house.

I felt my frustration boiling over, but knew there was nothing more that I could do for now. I could wait for Nikolai to make the first move, but something told me that could end up disastrous for everyone involved.

The sound of a car honking pulled me out of my thoughts.

"Hey! Are you walking or what?" Someone shouted out their window.

Looking up, I saw that the crosswalk signal was green, and that I was once again drawing attention by just standing around. Jogging across the street, I found myself at a small plaza I used to frequent often.

Seeing no point in standing clueless out in the cold, I decided to step into the local coffee shop, assuming it would be the busiest locale, and, therefore, the easiest place to blend in. However, I found that I was quite wrong. Inside, it was a ghost town; the only soul occupying the place was the barista, who didn't even bother looking up as I entered through the door.

"Yikes," I muttered, "tough night."

"Try a tough week," came the voice from behind the counter. "What can I get ya?"

"Grande hazelnut coffee, please," I told him, fishing out the wallet Rowan had given me and approaching the counter. "How in the world could you ever be having a tough week? Isn't the all-girls' school like five minutes down the road? That's like a guaranteed gold mine."

That got a snort of laughter out of him. "Under normal circumstances it is, but no one's willing to let their kids out of the house anymore. It's just not safe." He put the coffee on the counter, and I forked over the money. "Not very good for business."

"I'm sorry to hear that. I've been looking at colleges around here," I lied easily enough. "Mind filling me in? I doubt I'll hear about it in the guided tour."

"Yeah, that's more than likely. I'm sure they won't want to mention that kids your age are disappearing left and right."

The cup froze halfway up to my mouth. "That's unfortunate."

"Yup." He wasn't even looking at me in this point, which was a relief considering what came out of his mouth next. "Started with a local girl about four, five years ago, she just disappeared from the face of the earth. That was the talk of the town. Now, every once in a while, someone just goes missing and never comes back. No demands, no bodies, no nothing."

"When was the last disappearance?" I asked as calmly as I could.

"Oh, a few months ago. Whatever's drawing these kids away is laying low for the time being, but it's always like this. Just as soon as you think it's over, *bam*, someone else is gone and it's in the news all over again."

He wasn't done, apparently. "That's not the whole story, though." His voice dropped as he rested his elbows on the counter and leaned toward me, assuring that he had my complete and undivided attention. "There's other stuff going on, too, stuff that you can't just put in the news. I'm gonna be honest, this town has its good spots and its bad spots, and, usually, as long as you're not stupid, no one gets hurt. That hasn't been the case lately, though. There's times I don't feel safe making the trip from here to my car."

"Any particular reason for that?" I was doing my best to look properly terrified, but I had seen things in the past four years that would give this guy gray hair.

"Just a feeling everyone has. Although, there was this one night, I was walking across the lot to my car, right? It's pitch black outside, but as soon as I unlock it my lights go off and I can see someone standing right at my back bumper, just standing there. So, naturally, I call out to this person, ask him what his deal is, and I swear, between one blink of my lights and the next he's gone. Just gone."

That would probably be a vampire, kiddo. "Weird."

He stood back up. "I don't know, maybe we've all been watching too many of the crazy horror movies that have been coming out by the dozens. Makin' everybody too damn twitchy."

I opened my mouth to reply when the TV that served as background noise suddenly became interesting.

It was a breaking news report, one that was apparently important enough to interrupt the program that was already on the air. As the rapport between the reporters in the field and the studio rambled on, the single headline at the bottom of the screen caught my attention.

DANGEROUS PERSON INTERRUPTS SECTIONAL VOLLEYBALL GAME.

Well, that would be my cue.

Sighing, I reached back for my coffee and made my way for the door.

"Wait a second," the barista called out, "you aren't thinking of–"

Looking over my shoulder at him, I gave him a small smile. "Lock your doors up. This is about to get real ugly."

Ignoring the way he shouted after me, I pulled up my hood, pushed open the door, and started running as soon as I was outside.

The school was not far from the coffee shop; it was on the same street, actually, a few miles down. Looking to the sky as I ran, my heart dropped in my chest as I realized just how low on time I was running. To make matters worse, the day was a cloudy one, meaning Nikolai and his minions would have no trouble navigating the open streets, whereas my backup would soon be way too conspicuous to be of any help.

The sheer number of lights and sirens surrounding the school would have given me an instant seizure had I not been expecting it. A small, but growing, crowd was held at bay by a police barrier, blocking my line of sight.

I really didn't have time for this shit.

I was all about the throwing elbows, "Excuse me, pardon me, *MOVE*" crowd navigating skills. After all, I was a shameless New York woman by training. It wasn't long before I was first in line, right up against the barrier facing Rochester's finest. I was halfway under the feeble little barricade when one of the officers caught sight of me.

"Excuse me, miss!" Looking up from my limbo position, I saw a displeased officer of the law staring down at me. "No civilians are to pass this barrier."

"Oh good," I chimed in, straightening to stand right in front of him, "you'll find I'm quite excluded from that category."

He, obviously, was not pleased. "I'm afraid I'm going to have to ask you to step back behind the barrier."

"And I'm afraid I'm going to have to say no," I replied, sending my sunniest smile his way, which apparently did nothing to win him over. Seeing as he was about to order me back again, I plundered on, "Look, I can see you're doing your best to protect the commonwealth, keep the peace, and so on, but my family is currently lodging with a lunatic in there and you are by no means equipped to handle him."

He put his hands on his hips and looked as if he was seriously reconsidering his career choice. "And you think you are?"

It only took a moment for my scariest smile to emerge on my face, and, when it did, the cop visibly reeled back a bit. "You could say that."

Out of the corner of my eye, I saw another officer approaching, probably wondering why some rando had been allowed through. By the time he came to stand next to the cop I had been talking to, though, he didn't seem angry as I had expected.

He looked as if he'd seen a ghost.

"I know you," he said, his eyes wide with recognition that made me cautious. "I worked on your missing persons case. You're the girl who disappeared four years ago. Maria."

"Pleased to meet you," I responded as pleasantly as I could, "and congratulations, you found me! Now, if you don't mind, I would really like the first reunion I have tonight to be with my family, and they just happen to be behind your little circus here."

"I don't think so," he refused. "I'm taking you down to the station. You have a lot of questions to answer."

That was when I felt my patience reach its bitter end. Sighing, I peered up at the sky. "I tried so hard to be nice. I really did, but I'm about to stop asking. *Move it or lose it.*"

Sensing things were about to get out of hand, the second cop quickly reached out to apprehend me while the first one continued to block my path.

Well, I could consider this my warm-up before the real game.

Taking hold of the wrist attached to the hand reaching out to me, I twisted him around me and pushed until he came in contact with the barrier and, ultimately, toppled over it. Cop number one was taken out by a quick sweep under his feet. I stepped carefully over him on my way to the gym door.

"Wait!" I heard the first cop call from behind me. Sparing a glance over my shoulder, I saw him still struggling to get to his feet. "The man in there, he's not–"

"I know," I cut him off. "We've met."

And, with that, I turned back and put my foot to the double doors, kicking them open and marching inside the school before anyone else was stupid enough to try and stop me.

CHAPTER EIGHTEEN

The gym was at its maximum capacity. People dressed in school colors were taking up every available inch of space. The instant I entered the room, I felt all eyes on me and saw a fair share of pale, horrified faces, but it was too quiet for this many people. Goosebumps rose on my arms.

I had been through too damn much today to put up with Nikolai's usual dose of theatrical nonsense, and I was certainly in no mood to play hide and seek.

"*Nikolai!*" My shouted greeting echoed around every nook and cranny of the space. "Honey, I'm home!"

Keeping an eye out for possible sneak attacks, I strolled further into the gym. I hated the way the unforgiving wood floor accentuated each of my steps. It made it painfully obvious that, while I could find hide nor hair of my quarry, he knew exactly where I was.

The volleyball net was out of commission, torn down the middle. So, I didn't stop until I stood in the middle of it all, knowing that was exactly where Nikolai would want me, as the center of attention, right in the middle ring of his little circus act.

While continuing my scan of the place, I took a whiff of the air to see if my nose could be any more helpful than my eyes, but, though I could smell the distinct scent of vampire, it seemed to be coming from everywhere at once. I felt the light kiss of a breeze against my heated cheeks and froze as a spark of memory flickered through my mind.

I moved.

Just as it had been last time we met before an audience, his fist met the floor where I had been standing not two seconds prior.

It was about time he made an appearance.

He watched me carefully as I stood up a ways away from him, amusement suffusing all of his features, but there was a darkness to his expression I didn't like. His eyes were the eyes of a hunter staring down its cornered prey.

"Very good, my dear," he praised lightly. "You managed to miss the first hit. Your memory serves you well."

"Old dog, old tricks," I countered.

He didn't even bother denying it. "I must say, I am quite impressed. It takes a special kind of prisoner to escape from the Kennel. I was almost worried you wouldn't make our little party, you, my guest of honor."

"Wouldn't miss it for the world," I bit back.

"However, in your tardiness, I did happen to make the most splendid of acquaintances." His gaze shifted just so, glancing somewhere in the crowd. I flexed the claws on my right hand, ready to make the most of the slightest lapse in attention. "Shall I introduce you, or, should I say, re-introduce you?"

"Maria?"

The voice was so quiet I struggled to hear it, as focused as I was on Nikolai, but the sheer familiarity it carried with it was so powerful that I felt the wind knocked from my lungs. It was a voice that had been relegated to memories and the occasional dream, one that I hadn't heard in years, but one that I couldn't forget, even if I tried.

The sound of my own voice would escape my memory before I forgot that of my mother's.

The world slowed on its axis as I turned and found them immediately, standing just in front of the stands, lined up as if on display. I don't know how I missed them on my way in. My mother stood between my father and brother, and they all shared looks of disbelief and shock. She was the only one with tears in her eyes, but my dad seemed pretty close. Seamus, though....

I hardly recognized him. The barely out of boyhood brother I had left behind had become a man since the last time I saw him. All grown up in his school jersey, it was hard to absorb.

I'd had dreams, both good and bad, about what this moment would be like. In the better dreams, I could feel the warmth of my mother's embrace, see the way my dad's eye crinkled when he laughed, and joke about how Seamus would protest when I ruffled his hair, despite the fact that he was all smiles.

There were other dreams, though, the ones that included tears and screams and rejection, where I saw nothing but their anger and hatred. I didn't know if I could handle it if I was met with that now. I knew for certain I wouldn't be any kind of match against Nikolai if that happened.

My fear was swept away, though, by a single word.

"Sweetheart."

It was my dad who called out to me, the name he had used for me a thousand and one times as a child, but the relief and joy that filled the word was enough to overshadow every nightmare I had ever had. As much as I tried to avoid it, tears came to my eyes and a small, nostalgic smile found its way to my face.

"Isn't this just precious?" My head snapped back to Nikolai as he wiped an imaginary tear from his eye. I couldn't believe I'd let myself so distracted right in front of him. "Honestly, my heart might just explode."

"What's stopping it?"

His laughter filled the space so completely that I almost checked to make sure there wasn't a small army of Nikolais contributing to the sound.

"Oh, my dear," he scolded lightly, "you ought to be a bit nicer. After all, you are here to supplicate to me."

"You called, I came," I told him testily, my temper wearing thin. "What more do you want?"

He spread his arms wide, the picture of the gracious host. "You mistake my intentions. This is all for you. It has been so long since you have seen this wonderful family of yours. Tell them how much you missed them, my dear. Keeping their picture under your pillow was really a nice touch."

I couldn't tell if the tears that were filling my eyes were sad, happy, or angry anymore. "Shut your mouth before I decide to do it for you," I ground out, clenching my hand into a solid fist.

Nikolai took note of this. "So much restraint, usually our conversations have degenerated into needless violence by now. I wonder, is it for their sake, or yours?" His head tilted towards them, and I prepared myself to rush between them if I had to. "I wonder how they would react if they knew just what you have been up to these past four years."

"They don't know, and they don't need to know. I cut them out of my life for a reason, Nikolai. Right now this is about you and me. Leave them out of this."

"A reason I am about to exploit," he said casually enough, taking a single step towards them. The way I jumped forward only proved his next point. "If you wanted to cut yourself off from their world, then you should have made a clean break, but you chose to miss them, remember them, and leave a part of yourself tethered to your childhood, and that was your big mistake. You chose not to come to me on your own, but rather to fight for them, and, thus, you yourself involved them in what I'm planning.

"You really should have known better," he mused, moving to take another step, "but I suppose that's one of your more charming human qualities."

Before his foot even hit the floor, I had sent him flying across the room and into the far wall.

Shaking out my knuckles, I moved between him and my family, where I should have been all along. "I said, leave them out of this."

Still fallen on the ground, Nikolai managed to throw back his head and let out a raucous laugh. "A glimpse? Is that all you're willing to show them? Such a little taste, perhaps I should force the issue…"

"Maria, look out!"

That shout was the only reason I avoided the first strike. I had been poised and ready to rumble, facing Nikolai when the attack was really staged from the rear. A tuck and roll later, I was facing not Nikolai, but Kate.

Judging by the way the crowd seemed to flinch collectively at the sight of her, I knew that Nikolai had already paraded her around for all to see.

He was going to go through with his plan regardless of my presence.

Tapping into my magic reserves, I took note of their weakening state. The sun had almost set, Nikolai had done what he had come here to do, my family was still in danger, and I ran the risk of being captured.

Wasn't this just turning into a great day?

Kate was hardly finished with me, though. Her teeth were bared at me as she growled in a way that gave me the chills. Rushing forward, she hit me hard enough to knock me on my back. I held her back by her shoulders as she snapped and snarled at me. Rolling hard, I got her on her stomach and put a knee in her back.

"Kate, listen to me. Don't do this! You have to fight him, *please!*"

She didn't hear me, though. She evaded my grasp and sent her famous right hook my way; it was enough to knock me to the floor.

The audience was on their feet now, reacting to everything that was happening on the gym floor. I was having some really twisted Trial flashbacks because of it.

"It's no use, Maria," Nikolai called from his place above us. "The only command Kate follows is my own, and, right now, the only instruction she has is to fight you. That is, until you eventually slip up and reveal what you have really become."

Standing on my own two feet once more, I turned to Nikolai. The same smile that had come to my face in the war room when I revealed that I was one step ahead of him was back, and he didn't look happy to see it.

"What a shame," I remarked sarcastically, "it would seem, then, that Kate and I will have to fight all night."

Grimacing lightly, Nikolai lifted his face to the ceiling as if he could see right through it to the sky above. "Ah, I see; the moon is up, and you are powerless for now. I had forgotten about that little detail." He sighed and turned back to me. I stiffened in response; I definitely did not like that look in his eye. "Such a shame, if you had Transformed, I would have been willing to let them walk free, knowing that would have certainly been enough to haunt you."

I heard Kate get up behind me and could almost feel the low sound of her growl.

"Kari, would you be a dear and bring Maria's lovely family to me? We shall have to improvise, it seems."

With a looming sense of horror, I turned on my heel and faced Kate, knowing she was going to be my real opponent for now. Planting myself firmly between her and my family, I spoke loudly and clearly so there was no mistake that some part of her subconscious could hear me.

"Kate, you are going to have to walk over my cold corpse before you deliver my family to that lunatic."

I didn't know if it was because she heard me and cared or because she was devoted to Nikolai's command, but she took a small step forward and snarled warningly.

My only answer was to shake my head. "I'm not moving."

That started the second round of our fight. This time, I felt my reflexes responding much more slowly and felt a little less power in my punches and kicks. I was no match for her like this.

But every time she knocked me down, every time she thought she was getting past me, I put my feet under me and got up again. She may have been stronger, faster, and meaner as a wolf, but I was human, and that overwhelming tenacity that came with it would always give me a little bit of a boost.

It wouldn't, however, give me invincibility. Gasping for breath after her knee had found its way to my ribcage, I went down on one knee and found that the arms that were holding me up were shaking.

"Had enough yet," Nikolai called down to me.

I wanted to say no, I wanted to stand right back up and be able to hold my own, I *really* wanted to remove Nikolai's vocal chords and make a bowtie out of them, but I couldn't do anything but struggle to breathe, it seemed.

I felt a touch on my shoulder and wheeled around, ready to try and fend off what I could of Kate's next attack, but it wasn't Kate who had touched me.

I looked up into blue eyes, eyes that were shade for shade the same as my own.

"What–" A wracking cough gripped me before I could finish. Suddenly, there was a towel next to me.

"There's blood on your face," Seamus said quietly. I started inwardly at how deep his voice had become. He sounded like my dad.

That was when I tasted the blood from my split lip and felt my mouth turn down. "Gross," I croaked, taking the towel from him and wiping it across my face.

"Does this happen to you a lot," he asked casually.

"More than you'd like to know." My attention strayed, though, as I saw Kate begin to move on the edge of my vision. Groaning lightly, I pushed with my weakening arms and found my strength more than failing.

That was when I felt one of my arms being lifted. Pulling it across his shoulders, Seamus stood and lifted me up with him.

"You're heavier than you used to be," he commented in a brotherly fashion that would have been normal literally anywhere but here.

"I've been working out." Once I was fully up, I pulled at my arm, ready to stand on my own and continue protecting the three of them, but Seamus did not budge. "You might want to let go. This is little out of your element."

He just shrugged. "How would I look if I stood back while my not-so-big sister was getting the shit kicked out of her for my sake?"

For the first time in what seemed like forever, I rolled my eyes at him, something I used to do a lot. "Oh, for God's sake, don't pull this super macho shit with me right now. I'm built a little tougher than you."

I felt his gaze as he looked down at me. "Had me fooled."

"Isn't this just adorable," I turned to see Nikolai in the stands observing us. His chin was resting in one of his hands as he gazed fondly down at us. "A little sibling bonding. You know, love, if I didn't know better, I would have thought him your twin."

Kate came forward again. This time, though, I wasn't her target. Bracing myself against Seamus's strong shoulders, I kicked out sideways just as she got a little too close to him for my comfort.

"You know," I froze as I realized that Nikolai's voice came from much closer this time. Whipping around, I found my face only a few inches from his standing on my other side. A second later, I felt Seamus twitch. "I would settle for you just telling him. The full effect would be lost, but it would be well worth it."

Leaning towards him until I could feel his breath on my face, I spoke in my softest, most menacing voice. "Eat shit, Nikolai."

"*Maria!*"

I felt her hand close around my neck just a moment before I was thrown away from the lot of them. Looking up, I saw Nikolai holding Seamus by the scruff of his neck and leapt to get to him, only to be bowled over by Kate again.

Okay, no more Mrs. Nice Lady.

Throwing an unforgiving elbow at her side, I heard the sound of ribs cracking before holding her head between my hands and hitting it with my own. While she was dazed, I lifted my leg and let it come down square on her back, knocking her to the floor.

My attack, however, had taken more out of me than it had out of her. It took all that for me to knock her down, but her single punch in response had me crawling like a bug.

I rolled my back, trying to ease the growing pain in my abdomen, but my comfort was short-lived as both of Kate's hands wrapped mercilessly around my neck and bore down.

"Just until she loses consciousness, Kari," Nikolai said jovially. "Then, we shall wrap her up and be on our way. No need to prolong this any further."

"I wouldn't be so sure about that."

All at once Kate's weight was removed, and I took big, gasping breaths to get the air back into my lungs. There were hands at my shoulders, helping me up and a touch I recognized.

"Daimon?"

He wasn't looking down at me, though. Nikolai and Daimon had locked gazes and were currently having the mother of all stare downs.

It was one of those few times where Nikolai actually looked genuinely pissed off. "Why is it you always show up at the most inconvenient moments?"

"It's a talent of mine," Daimon's voice was just as hard as Nikolai's. No one was joking around here.

Once he was sure I was stable, Daimon rose to his feet.

"Let the boy go, Nikolai. You've lost this round."

Usually, Nikolai's laughter was a loud and boisterous sound that was pleasing enough. However, when Daimon ordered him to let go of Seamus, the sound that came from his mouth was tinged with a little more insanity than usual. It was a small glimpse of what Nikolai kept hidden behind intricate plans and cold smiles, the lunatic I always took him for.

"I haven't lost anything yet," he hissed furiously. "If I can't have her now, I'll just invest in a little insurance."

I will never, as long as I live, forget the horrible sight of Nikolai turning to my little brother, baring his fangs, and sinking them into the side of Seamus's neck.

"*NO!*"

My scream was not the only one that erupted from the crowd. The whole audience was terrified and panic was settling in. Daimon, faster on his feet, rushed towards them. Try as I might, I was stopped before I could get there by Kate.

"You promised," I screamed right in her face. "You *swore* to me that you would let no harm come to them, Kate!"

Impossibly, she paused for a moment, and I felt the hand that was fisted in the front of my shirt shake lightly. One breathless moment later, her fingers released their grip on me. Slowly but surely, she straightened and stood up straight, distancing herself from me.

"Kate," I whispered disbelievingly.

She didn't have the time to surprise me anymore. Once more, she was knocked away from me. This time, though, it was by someone much scarier.

"Are you all right, Maria?" Maximilian held one hand out for me to take, and helped me get to my feet.

"Not even close," I answered, searching for Nikolai and Seamus.

Nikolai was perched at the very top of the stands for all to see, Seamus still held in his grasp. Around ten other people stood around him, members of his coven that had blended into the audience. Others members were still contending with Daimon, who looked more savage than I had ever seen him.

I only took a single step towards Nikolai before I felt Maximillian's heavy hand settle on my shoulder. My focus was reserved for Nikolai, though, and his complete and total attention was fixated on me.

"Heed my words, Maria," he warned, his voice dangerously grave. "If you wish to save your little brother from an eternity of shadows, you will hand yourself over to me before the next full moon."

"*Let him go, Nikolai,*" I roared over the sound of the crowd.

"Not until I have you in exchange," he answered piteously. "Your place in my plans is irreplaceable. I cannot destroy the werewolf species without you. So, do not make me pine too long, darling."

"Wait!" I ashamedly realized that my tone had turned to one of begging. Maximillian held fast, even as I fought his grip to do something, *anything*. "*Stop*!"

"One month, Maria. That is all I'm giving you."

Just then, the windows that lined the side of the gymnasium shattered into a thousand pieces, causing more screams to erupt from the captive audience. In a matter of moments, Nikolai's coven and Kate had gathered around him and, with Seamus in tow, they disappeared into the night.

Seamus and Nikolai were both gone.

I had failed.

Falling to my knees, I screamed with pain that went beyond every injury, physical and emotional, I had ever received in my life, and wondered how I could ever make this right.

CHAPTER NINETEEN

The humans were all evacuated from the gym, but the blaring lights and sirens had not calmed down the slightest bit. Not only that, but camera crews and news reporters were beginning to flock to the scene, bent on getting the first coverage of the story that would change the way the entire world worked.

They wouldn't be getting anything out of us tonight. Authorities were doing their best to keep the media at bay, and Maximillian had told me that discussions were already being held between the leaders of the two sides, trying to decide how to handle Nikolai's mess.

It was a little late for that, though. Thanks to social media and the sheer number of teenagers that had been included in that crowd of hostages, the story had exploded everywhere, complete with video and photographic evidence to back it up.

That cat was officially out of the bag.

Try as I might, though, I could not give a rat's ass at the moment about the whole thing. I was strangely numb now, not caring either way how discussions proceeded.

No amount of discussion would bring back Seamus.

My two scary rescuers had noticed that I required immediate medical attention that wouldn't be available to me if I went back home. Therefore, I had been ushered to the back of an ambulance and was being tended to by a properly terrified first responder.

She had nothing to fear from me. On top of being kicked around six ways to Sunday, I simply did not have the energy to playfully scare her, as I would have normally found some sadistic brand of joy in. After I blatantly refused any mind-mellowing painkillers, I was completely silent. I didn't move or flinch the slightest bit as she cleaned, bandaged, and stitched me back up. Not that I really needed it, at the end of the night Vincent would be able to make it look like none of this happened.

Someone else seemed to think so, too.

"I think that will be enough, thank you."

The EMT did her best to boot, scoot, and boogie away from the simmering supernatural creature she was fixing as quickly as possible.

"You're late," I whispered apathetically.

"I believe you once told me my sense of time was skewed."

Peering up from my slumped position on the back of the ambulance, my gaze, even now, was blurred by tears. "I really messed up, didn't I?"

In a rare moment of physical affection, Grandmother placed her hand on top of my head, and stroked my hair with more gentleness than I ever thought her capable of. "I'm not so sure, little wolf, and, as we cannot go back and change events to see where the fault lies, there is no point in dwelling on it."

"I failed when it mattered most, and now Seamus is the prisoner of his soon-to-be Master." I didn't bother wiping away the tears that fell freely down my cheeks. "How could it not be my fault?"

"Have you ever once thought that this could be the fault of Nikolai's Master? To cure his own ennui, he created a monster, or perhaps Daimon, for not reigning in his blood brother? Maybe it is my fault, little wolf, for not allowing you to kill Nikolai when he was our prisoner, or your pack's for locking you up for a week instead of hunting him down."

Her hand came down from the top of my head to rest on my cheek, where she wiped away the stream of tears that marked it.

"At our lowest points, it is easy to become the target of our own mind, to be the subject of blame because, in the end, the only variable you could have changed was yourself. Perhaps, if you had chosen another path this would have ended differently, but, in a situation like this, there are thousands of variables and an infinite number of outcomes.

"What you have to remind yourself, little wolf, is that you did what you thought was right, the best that you could do given the surrounding circumstances, and that is all that matters."

The tears started afresh, but Grandmother simply brushed them away and kissed me softly on my forehead, a tender reminder that there was no sadness that could truly hurt me, not when she was around.

"Maria?"

Both of our heads snapped up to see my mother and father standing by, obviously waiting for their turn to cut in. However, just the sight of their grieving and haggard expressions was enough for the pain in my heart to return full force.

Despite Grandmother's comforting words, Nikolai's attention had wandered to Seamus because of me, and I wasn't strong enough to protect him. I would always feel guilty for that.

Wiping the rest of the tears away with my hand, I stood up straight, but couldn't find the strength to look them in the eye. "I'm sorry for what happened to Seamus, but I will get him back for you. Then, I'll do what I should have done in the first place and stay out of your lives."

I left without another word.

CHAPTER TWENTY

The next few days, I had a front row seat to the biggest shitshow of all time. This was an unprecedented breach in secrecy. There was no set plan for this eventuality, no procedure to follow.

So, basically, everyone was running around like chickens with their heads cut off, trying to create some semblance of order.

It was acknowledged by both sides that the fault of what happened that fateful night rested entirely on Nikolai's shoulders (that, however, did not stop Grumpy, Bigoty, and Bitchy from giving me particularly nasty looks on their way out the door). In fact, his plan had not merely been contained to Rochester. I only found out later that similar events had happened in various places, not only around the country, but around the world.

In short, humans had officially become aware of the paranormal world that was intermingled with their own. Naturally, this was causing quite a bit of commotion. People were finding themselves at a loss for how to react, much less what to believe, who to trust, or how it should be handled.

I couldn't help but chuckle at that last one. Humans were out of their minds if they thought they were going to "handle" us in any way, shape, or form.

Seeing an opportunity in me, the powers that be had decided, what with my connections to both the human and supernatural worlds, that I was to be the main emissary between the two, which was downright exhausting. It was a mix of televised interviews, top secret political meetings, and rolling my eyes at a lot of stupid ideas.

It didn't take a genius to figure out why Grandmother allowed them to run me ragged between the two groups. It was better than sitting around moping, or going all lone ranger on Nikolai and hunting him down myself. At least, this way, there was always someone keeping an eye on me.

In a rare moment of free time, I found myself hiding, of all places, in the Council's old chamber. Grandmother had wanted the already-destroyed room completely demolished after our little rebellion. I convinced her otherwise, though. It was a good reminder to everyone of the way things used to be, and how much better they had become.

She had made a point to hide the key to the chamber, showing that she would never find the need to use it as they had, but I had pulled that hiding spot out of her ages ago.

Yeah, no one would ever think to look for me here.

That's why I was genuinely surprised when I heard the great wooden doors open behind me. Casting a curious glance over my shoulder, I was even more surprised to find that that person was Desiree.

Gee, just when life was looking so grand, too.

I'm sure my surprise was shared by her. The Great Murderer of the Council Head sitting cross-legged on the runner leading up to his old throne would have certainly thrown anyone for a loop.

"I won't even ask," was the first thing to come out of her mouth.

I snorted at the sheer ridiculousness of the situation and turned my back to her once more. "Come to kick a girl while she's down?"

"I think I've done enough of that over the years," she answered. I heard her footsteps echo as she approached and wasn't as surprised as I should have been when she came to sit next to me. "There are still days I can't believe that he's gone, that their reign is over."

"Some days, I wake up from nightmares," I told her without really thinking better of it, "and I'm almost convinced that it isn't. That he'll show up and do his best to make me his little pawn, just like…" I couldn't make myself say it.

She didn't seem to have trouble with it, though. "Just like Kate?"

"Yeah," I choked out.

"Well, no one can say it was the worst decision you ever made. You would be hard put to find a man more corrupted than him."

I huffed. "How about Nikolai, for one?"

I saw her shake her head slowly and turned to look at her. Her gaze was settled right on the seat in the middle of the table, the place of honor. There was a distant look in her eyes, as if she was looking back rather than at what was there now. "No, you only knew him for a short time. You didn't even see the full extent of what he did. I saw it firsthand."

My mind brought me back to the time I had seen her in the hospital wing visiting her brother, and the startling bit of information he had unwittingly revealed to me.

"She was your friend."

Desiree nodded this time. "My best friend, actually. We were closer in age to each other than we were to our own siblings. We used to be inseparable. I grew up thinking Kate was my sister rather than my cousin. Everything took a turn for the worst, though, when Rowan refused to do the Council's dirty work anymore, and they took her in instead."

"Why didn't anyone stop them," I wondered incredulously. "Why didn't their parents–"

She turned to me sharply, then, and I saw the haunted look in her eyes that answered all of my questions.

"Do you really think the man who had an iron grip on the world would be soft on his family?"

"No, I suppose not." She looked away again, caught in that same spell, seeing without having anything be there. "What changed?"

249

"What do you mean?"

"It's one thing to grow apart from your best friend, but that first day I met you..."

She smirked. "One of my finer moments," she mused. I really didn't know whether to laugh or not. "Yes, Kate and I grew apart. Her business to the Council had her travelling more and more into the human world, the one place I could not follow her. She became different, colder, a loner. That is, until she back with you.

"You see, Council Kari was all about her precious rules; you could never get her to shut up about them. So, how was it that she was able to break the greatest rule of our kind for one stupid human, but wasn't able to stand up to the Council enough to come home?"

I thought about that for a moment, and, finally, after all these years, understood the root of Desiree's hatred towards me. I wasn't saying I appreciated all of the bullying, or that the abuse was justified in any way, but Desiree had been hurt by her best friend, and that was no easy thing to recover from.

The whole matter still didn't make total sense to me. Kate was not one to just throw away her friends, but...

"Maybe, she did it for you. The Council failed to completely brainwash Rowan, did you ever think who might come next in line if Kate wasn't a good girl?"

Desiree was sitting so closely next to me that I felt the way she froze and knew the exact moment when she put the pieces together.

Obviously, it was a lot to take in. Gathering herself, she stiffly stood up and looked down at me.

"This doesn't mean I like you, human."

"Of course not," I joked. "I didn't see any flying pigs when I came in here."

She hid her smile as best as she could, but when she turned to the front of the room for the last time it fell away from her face completely. She spared only one more moment for old memories before turning on her heel and walking out the door, leaving them behind.

"Wonders never cease," I whispered to myself.

I had imagined that, after the whole Desiree thing, I would be done with life-changing conversations for the day, but that certainly wasn't the case.

In retrospect, I should have known he'd show up at my doorstep sooner or later. I just hadn't thought it would be so soon, or that he'd literally end up on my doorstep.

But when I turned down the hallway that led to my room, he was the first thing I saw. Sitting just in front of my door, looking for all the world as if he'd simply misplaced his key, was Daimon.

I didn't ever register that I'd frozen until he turned to look up at me with a pleading look in his eye I'd never seen before. Suddenly, it hit me that he expected me to turn tail and leave just as quickly as I'd come.

Mental Ria was affronted. I wasn't a coward. Realistic Ria, however, very clearly acknowledged the fact that that was one of the first options that occurred to me.

"How long have you been sitting out here," I asked innocently enough.

Understanding that I had no immediate plans to book it out of there, a smile I was more familiar with replaced that pleading look. "Enough that certain parts of my anatomy are permanently numb."

That was enough to make me smile, too. Strolling towards the door, I pulled out my key and unlocked it before looking back down at him. "Are you coming in? Or are you going to wait until you can't feel your legs either?"

He chortled in his usual fashion as he stood up and made a show of stretching before joining me in my newest set of rooms.

Despite our smiles, the room was filled with the tension that existed between us, which was only made worse by his pathetic attempt at small talk.

"This is a lovely room."

And my worse attempt at levity.

"Yeah, the last one had a bit of a draft."

Silence.

Good one, Ria, I thought to myself, *why don't you just joke about shopping for new jewelry or all of the werewolves you find attractive on this campus?*

Backtracking, I blurted out, "I never did properly thank you."

His cautious expression wasn't exactly reassuring. "For what? Destroying your last room?"

"No! No, um…for sort of, kind of, saving my ass. I guess."

"Well, it is quite a fine ass. I happen to be very fond of it."

That was when I lost it.

I didn't know if it was so un-Daimon of him to say, or if I just hadn't been used to having his running commentary lately, but a full on snort-filled, gasping-for-breath, tears in my eyes laugh attack hit me.

It broke down a sort of invisible barrier that had formed between us ever since the fight we'd had, one that I hadn't even recognized before now.

It also brought a beautiful smile to Daimon's face, one that I had missed dearly, and the look of what could only be love and affection in his eyes was enough to stop my laughter and make my heart beat faster.

"I've missed you," he whispered, ever-so-softly.

I bit my lip. There had been too many tears these past few days. "I definitely missed you more."

"Oh, I sincerely doubt that. You, after all, didn't have to live with the awareness that you were the most selfish, misguided fool the world has ever had the misfortune to produce."

"Being a naïve child is bad enough," I joked lightly. "I don't know if I could have handled that too."

"Hope is nothing to be ashamed of," he answered firmly, taking a step towards me, "it speaks of a strength that I lacked. One that took me weeks to find."

"But you've found it?"

He nodded, still approaching me slowly. "I've been going over everything over and over again in my mind, wondering what I could have done differently, wondering what I could do to win you back. It didn't take long for me to figure that the fault was all my own, that I built the wedge that Nikolai forced between us, not him."

Reaching towards me with such care that it made my heart break all over again, Daimon held my face between his hands and stared into my eyes more deeply than he ever had before. "I would have said anything, done anything, to keep you safe from harm, and that was my downfall. You don't need a protector, you need a partner, and I was foolish enough to think that they were one and the same."

Before his hands could fall from my face, I mirrored his position and rested my hands on his cheeks, stroking his cheeks with my thumbs. "I need *you*. I told Malachi that I was safe from Nikolai because I had my loved ones on my side. I should have known he would try to take that advantage away from me. I shouldn't have gotten so angry with you. I should have believed in you. I–"

Not seeing any point in what I *could* have done, Daimon proactively cut off my long list of "What ifs" and "might have been's" by closing the last few inches of space between us and kissing me for the first time in far too long.

I held him close from a long time after that, afraid to let him go. I couldn't have him drifting away from me, I couldn't be that alone ever again, not it a weird, obsessive, needy way, though. I had spoken the truth.

Nikolai was doing his best to isolate me, to take away the thing that made me strongest, the allies and support I had built up since becoming a werewolf. One-on-one with Nikolai would be no contest; he could crush me with one hand behind his back, but with everyone on my side there wasn't an army he could raise that could take me down.

"I'm sorry how things turned out," Daimon whispered softly into my hair.

I had to swallow around the lump that had suddenly formed in my throat. "We'll get him back."

"Before the end of the month." I could have imagined it, but Daimon seemed to hold onto me a little tighter. "You won't have to trade yourself to him, Maria. I won't make you go through whatever he has planned for you."

He let me go then, and reached into his pocket. I almost wept with joy when it was his silver locket that he pulled out.

"Can you find it in yourself to trust me again?" He held the two sides of the necklace out for me, as if it was a peace offering.

My only response was to turn my back and hold up my hair for him.

He deftly clipped the chain around my neck, and, as the familiar weight of the locket settled over my breastbone, I couldn't help but think that, for just a few moments, the world suddenly appeared to be set right.

I didn't ponder the nagging thought that was making itself apparent in my mind. Intuitively, I knew that trading myself to Nikolai was not an impossibility. I would do anything to get my brother back, even hand myself over to a lunatic. It seemed that what Daimon was going to do his hardest to prevent was only an eventuality to me.

He had less than a month to realize it, too.

EPILOGUE

I started out the next day as I had started out all of my other ones since facing Nikolai: by setting out for my spot.

I had thought when I escaped through the underbelly of the Kennel and discovered just what lay under the cliff, that I would have to trade in my thinking spot for one that didn't sit over ruthless criminal masterminds. However, it turned out that high-class super-secret criminals weren't even enough to drive me away.

In fact, it wasn't just for serenity's sake that I found myself sitting on the edge of the cliff watching the sun rise. I was checking, too, checking to make sure that none of those criminals found their way through the door and onto my turf.

This particular morning, though, I found that I wasn't alone.

"You're up early, trouble in paradise already?"

Figures I wouldn't even get to tell her the good news.

"A fixed relationship doesn't just relieve me of all of my work, Grandmother," I admonished, coming to sit next to her. "You're not exactly a morning person either. What are you up to this early in the day?"

"Timezones."

I rolled my eyes. "Elaborate."

Her warm chuckle set me at ease more than anything else. "I have been up all night, contacting the werewolf factions in Europe, Africa, and Asia." When I peered up at her, there was not a single trace of a smile on her face. "They have confirmed the worst. Nikolai's war has gone worldwide."

A deep, world-weary sigh escaped me. "I figured as much. At least we know what his endgame is now, too."

"Yes, the destruction of the werewolf species, I believe he put it, and, somehow, he thinks you are the key."

I turned to look out at the rising sun, knowing that that would, at least, keep the vampires imprisoned under me at bay for now. It was a small comfort.

"He thinks he has us backed into a corner. That, once I hand myself over, he's won."

"Let him think that."

I couldn't help but notice that, unlike Daimon, Grandmother didn't automatically deny the possibility of Nikolai ever getting his hands on me. That was one of the things I loved about her, and that I tried to embody most. She somehow managed to be an optimist and a realist all at the same time.

We stayed in that spot for a while, caught in the spell that the rising sun had over us. Thoughts about the future filled my mind from ear to ear, of what could happen and what my next move should be.

If I had known then the extent of what that future would bring, I might have never left that place, sacrificing the moment of peace that I would be hard-pressed to find in the coming weeks. Maybe I would have even run for the hills to escape it all, but I couldn't have possibly realized just what was coming my way, and, too soon, I found myself on my feet and returning to the real world.

"It's going to be a long month."

ACKNOWLEDGMENTS

And here I thought the second novel would be so much easier than the first. Silly me.

To those who have read the first novel and followed the journey all the way through to the second, I will always be appreciative. Ria also thinks this is pretty solid.

Kellson Davis. This book would not exist without your late night text messages, your top notch editing skills, and, most importantly, your unwavering love and support. Can't live without you, Kell.

And, finally, to my family, who has always supported my writing endeavors, and who brings snacks and tea up to my room when I refuse to leave Ria alone.

ABOUT THE AUTHOR

MACAIRE O'GRADY has, much like her heroine, lived in Rochester, NY for most of her life. *To Be Tried* is her second novel, but many more are soon to follow. When not writing, she is pursuing a degree in bioengineering at Union College

www.ingramcontent.com/pod-product-compliance
Lightning Source LLC
Chambersburg PA
CBHW031938240626
47153CB00003B/783